Finding Cherokee Brown

SIOBHAN CURHAM

Finding Cherokee Brown
Published 2013 by Electric Monkey,
an imprint of Egmont UK Limited
The Yellow Building, 1 Nicholas Road,
London W11 4AN

ISBN 978 1 4052 6038 1

1 3 5 7 9 10 8 6 4 2

www.electricmonkeybooks.co.uk

A CIP catalogue record for this title is available from the British Library

50042/1

Typeset by Avon DataSet Ltd, Bidford on Avon, Warwickshire
Printed and bound in Great Britain by CPI Group

EGMONT

Our story began over a century ago, when seventeen-year-old
Egmont Harald Petersen found a coin in the street. He was on
his way to buy a flyswatter, a small hand-operated printing
machine that he then set up in his tiny apartment.

The coin brought him such good luck that today Egmont has
offices in over 30 countries around the world. And that lucky
coin is still kept at the company's head offices in Denmark.

Praise for **Dear Dylan**, also by Siobhan Curham

'Tender, quirky and cool. Siobhan Curham is a name to watch' *Cathy Cassidy*

'An absorbing, moving novel . . . I'm still thinking about the characters so much that I want to check on them and see how things are going for them now!' *Luisa Plaja, Chicklish*

'A funny, moving, thought-provoking story about a very special friendship' *Tabitha Suzuma*

'Reminds us of the power of true friendships. A wonderful achievement' *Booktrust*

'A great, fast-paced read. All I can say is, "GO, GEORGIE!"' *Bookalicious Ramblings*

'I didn't want to leave these characters behind. A wonderful read full of laughs, tears and heart' *Carrie's YA Bookshelf*

'Truly a diamond of a novel. Touching, funny and full of heart; I just couldn't get enough' *Lauren's Crammed Bookshelf*

'A story to lighten the soul. I laughed and cried and wanted more' *Tales of a Ravenous Reader*

'Fabulous . . . poignant . . . honest' *The Sweet Bonjour*

'Touching and emotional . . . really special' *So Many Books, So Little Time*

'Strong and realistic characters that people of all ages will relate to' *A Life Bound By Books*

'Keeps the reader captivated from start to finish. Intimate and honest . . . I loved it' *I Was a Teenage Book Geek*

'A very beautiful story. You're going to love it' *Darlington Books*

'I really couldn't put it down' *Sarah's Book Reviews*

'A fab story' *The Overflowing Library*

Hi there,

A couple of years ago, a writing magazine that I worked on published a letter from a teenage girl complaining about the lack of interesting, inspirational heroines in Young Adult books. At the time I'd just finished my first YA novel, *Dear Dylan*, and was wondering what and who to write about next, so I decided to use the girl's letter as a challenge. For many years I'd wanted to write about bullying – I know several people who have been affected by bullying and it's something I feel very passionately about – so the seed of an idea took root. What if I created a character who was a victim of bullying but was determined to fight back in her own original way? A character who used her love of books and writing to reinvent herself as a unique and memorable heroine. And so Cherokee Brown was born. I still have the magazine letter that sparked the novel pinned to my noticeboard and I hope I've met the challenge and created a character who's both interesting and inspirational. I have no idea if the girl who wrote the letter will ever read this book, but I'm hoping the fact that I named Cherokee after her will bring it to her attention somehow.

I really hope you enjoy *Finding Cherokee Brown*, and that it inspires you to become the unique and inspirational hero of your own life story – whatever that may be . . .

Siobhan x

For more from Siobhan, please visit her blog:
http://www.dearwriterblog.blogspot.com/

You can also find her on Facebook, or visit www.electricmonkeybooks.co.uk

For Jack Phillips and Katie Bird

— may your souls forever be fearless

Prologue

I've decided to write a novel. If I don't write a novel I will kill somebody. And then I will go to jail and, knowing my lousy luck, end up sharing a cell with a shaven-headed she-he called Jeff who smokes roll-ups and thinks it's cool to keep a fifteen-year-old girl as a slave. But if I write a novel I can kill as many people as I like with my words and never have to be anyone's slave.

It was Agatha Dashwood who first put the idea of writing a book into my head. Last Saturday afternoon I'd gone down to the Southbank – again – and I was browsing through the tables of second-hand books – again – and there it was, stuffed in between a biography of Princess Diana and *A Complete History of Piston Engines*:

So You Want to Write a Novel? by Agatha Dashwood.

There was a photo on the cover of this fierce old lady glaring over her glasses like some kind of psycho librarian. But that didn't put me off, because the first thing I thought when I read the title was, *Yes – I do*. Which was a bit random because I'd never thought of writing a novel before. So I picked the book up and did my usual page 123 test. I do this whenever I'm deciding whether to buy a book. I don't bother reading the blurb on the back, or the first page – the writer's obviously going to be trying their hardest there, aren't they? It's how they're getting on by page 123 that's the real test. If they're rubbish at writing or bored with their story then you can bet they won't be making any effort at all by that point. So I flicked through the yellowing pages, trying not to be put off by the musty smell, and this is what it said at the top of page 123:

> **'The Authentic Novelist Writes About What They Know.**
>
> *Aspiring novelist, if you want your writing to ring true – for your words to echo around your reader's head with passion and clarity, like church bells calling worshippers to mass – then you have to write about what you know.'*

I know the church bells and worshippers stuff sounds a bit nuts, but the rest of it made the hairs on the back of my neck prickle. I snapped the book shut and took it over to pay. With Agatha Dashwood's help I was going to write a novel about my crappy life but, unlike my crappy life, it wouldn't be dictated by my mum or Alan or the brain-deads at school or any of my stupid teachers. It would be my story. Told my way.

Notebook Extract

Character Questionnaire No. 1

'When I started out in my writing career, many years ago, writing short stories and serials for The Respected Lady *magazine, the Character Questionnaire became my most cherished friend. Use the template below before you start your story to get to know your own characters even better than you know yourself.'*

Agatha Dashwood,
So You Want to Write a Novel?

OK, I've got a bit of a problem. I've been trying to do a Character Questionnaire on my main character - namely me. And that's the problem: the 'namely' bit. I mean, who would choose to call their main character Claire Weeks? It's hardly exciting, is it? Hardly the name of a kick-ass literary heroine. I'll just have to invent myself a new name. A heroic name. A name that will sit proudly alongside Anne Frank and Laura Ingalls Wilder on bookshelves and not want to cower in embarrassment.

Possible Kick-Ass Literary Heroine Names:

Roxy Montana – too much like Hannah?

Ruby Fire – naff!

Laura Wild – too similar to one of my real literary heroines.

Anna Franklyn – ditto.

Jet Steele – sounds like a female wrestler!

Hmm, I guess I'll come back to my name later or I'll never get started on the book. I'll just stay as Claire for now. And keep my surname as Weeks, even though it sounds like 'weak'. Just another great thing to thank my stepdad Alan for, I guess. Along with a knowledge of Neil Diamond that borders on child abuse. Why can't he listen to music from *after* 1980? And songs that don't have titles like 'Forever in Blue Jeans'! Is it any wonder I've been driven to seek refuge in the world of literature?

Anyway, back to the questionnaire:

Character's name:
Claire Weeks (soon to be changed to something way more kick-ass).

Character's age:
Fifteen (well, fifteen in one day's time).

Briefly describe your character's appearance:
She is short and thin, with dark brown shoulder-length hair and brown eyes. She needs a radical makeover.

What kind of clothes do they wear?
Black.

How do they get on with their parents?
They don't.

What physical objects do they associate with their parents?
An iPhone permanently attached to her stepdad's hand like some kind of growth.

And a collection of tracksuits in every colour of the rainbow for her mum.

Do they have any brothers or sisters?
No, but they have a couple of alien life forms from the Planet Obnoxious posing as seven-year-old twin brothers.

What was their childhood like?
Grim – and it still is.

Think of one positive and one negative event from their past and how it has shaped them:
Hmm, well, the first thing that springs to mind is the day Helen moved away to Bognor Regis. This was mortally negative on two counts: firstly, I lost my one true friend and secondly, who wants to live in a place that is named after a bog? Seriously! And just because some bright spark added the word Regis (which I think means royal), it doesn't make it any less bog-sounding. Then there was the time last summer when I wanted to go to the Hyde Park Music Festival, but

Alan said I couldn't because Jay-Z was headlining and he felt that listening to too much rap music would be 'bad for my personal development'. Like listening to Neil Diamond droning on about being 'forever in blue jeans' isn't?!! Of course, my mum agreed with him. She always agrees with Alan because he is a life coach and therefore 'an expert at life'. I'm not so sure about that. As far as I can tell, being a life coach basically means that you charge people a load of money to tell them how messed up their lives are and then charge them another load to tell them they need to fix it.

Alan's company is called OH YES YOU CAN! and he likes to do those really annoying mimed speech mark things with his fingers whenever he's talking and wants to emphasise a word. For example, when I told him that I don't even like rap and I actually wanted to go to the music festival to see the rock band Screaming Death, he looked at me and sighed and said, 'I don't really think that subjecting yourself to a day of heavy metal would really be "*helpful*" for your personal development either, Claire.' And he wiggled two fingers on each hand around the word helpful. Personally I think he is a "*complete moron*".

Right, better try and think of a positive event for my character. There was the moment I made friends with Helen, on our first day at Rayners High. I'd been sitting in our classroom, faking smiles like I had a twitch while thinking, *Oh, God, why couldn't I have been born in 1867 to a pioneer family in the American Midwest and only have to worry about making it through the next winter rather than seven long years at high school?* But then, when one of the boys started teasing this Asian girl and everyone else started laughing, I caught sight of Helen. I could see from the way she was frowning that she was thinking the exact same as me - this boy is a total loser. As soon as I managed to make eye contact with her I sort of raised one eyebrow, the way I'd seen this sarcastic cop character do on TV, and she did the same back and then we both started smiling – but proper, mean-it smiles rather than oh-my-god-my-jaw-is-going-to-break-if-I-have-to-prop-this-thing-up-any-longer kind of smiles.

That was a whole four years ago now. It's been six months since Helen moved away. Her leaving is another reason for me writing a book. I don't really have anyone to talk to any more – not anyone who gets me. And the great thing about having an imaginary reader is that you can write exactly what you want, how you want, and you can at least pretend that they'll like and understand you. And won't want to beat you up or call you names.

How does your character speak?
Too fast apparently, at least according to her mum and Miss Davis, her form tutor.

What is their favourite meal?
Fish and chips wrapped in paper, with loads of salt and vinegar, outside on a freezing cold day.

Do they believe in God?
No. Don't know. Maybe. But not a God with a long white beard who sits on a cloud. I gave up on that one the year we went to Florida on holiday and I stared out of the window looking for God for the entire eight-hour flight. No one lives on clouds. At all.

What is their bedroom like?
Full of books. And full of mess according to my mum, but she doesn't get it. I know where everything is and I like having everything close to hand, not shut away in cupboards or filed away on shelves like everything else in our house.

What is your character's motto in life?
Tidying is for wimps. And cleaning is for people with way too much time on their hands, who should be made to move

somewhere deadly dull - like Bognor Regis.

Does your character have any secrets?
Yes. Since Helen left I've skipped school three times to go up to the Southbank to people-watch for the day. And although everyone in my class - including my teacher - knows I'm being bullied, my parents don't. What a great secret!

What makes them jealous?
People who are happy and don't ever get picked on.

Do they have any pets?
No, because a stray dog hair or morsel of cat food might get on to the carpet and cause their parents to have a total freak-out.

Is their glass half full?
She's currently drinking a can - of coke - and it's nearly empty. Bit of a random question!

Have they ever lost anyone dear to them?

Helen when she moved away. And I guess there's my real dad. Although he left when I was just a baby and moved to America, 'because he had commitment issues and was incapable of growing up' according to my mum, and I've never seen him since. Can you lose something if you can't remember ever having it?

Who do they most admire?

Laura Ingalls Wilder and Anne Frank.

Are they popular?

No. But I try not to let this get to me because I wouldn't really want to be popular with most of the people I go to school with anyway. It's kind of like asking Anne Frank if she'd want to be popular with the Nazis.

Do they love themselves?

No, of course not!

What is their motivating force in life?
To get through a day without being beaten
up.

What is their core need in life?
To not feel like the wrong part in a
jigsaw all of the time.

**What is their mindset at the beginning
of your story and what do they want?**
She is totally fed up and she wants to
change everything. Everything.

Chapter One

'Dear writer, imagine if you will that your reader is a trout, swimming merrily downstream. The first paragraph of your novel should be like the maggot on the end of the fisherman's line. Juicy and appealing to the point of irresistible. Hook them with that and then let the rest of your first chapter reel them in.'

Agatha Dashwood,
So You Want to Write a Novel?

If you could pick any date in the calendar to find out that you aren't actually who you thought you were then I suppose your birthday is pretty much perfect. Today, on my fifteenth birthday, I found out that for my entire life I've been living a lie.

I actually got up before my parents this morning as they'd been to this cringey conference called 'Unleash Your Inner Tiger' last night and didn't get home till late. Well, when I say late, I mean late for them. They got back at twelve-thirty. I know this because I was still up re-reading *The Bell Jar* at the time. Normally, my parents go to bed at nine so they can get up mega early and do an hour of Nordic Walking before work. Nordic Walking should be renamed How-to-Totally-Humiliate-Your-Kids Walking. It basically involves striding about in giant steps while holding a pole in each hand – the type of poles you use when you're skiing. This wouldn't look so weird if you were hiking your way through a snow drift, or up a mountain. But when you're walking down a London street in the middle of summer it looks about twenty different kinds of wrong. Anyway, when I got up this morning at seven, there was no sign of them, their walking poles or the twins.

I poured myself a glass of icy water from the fridge and sat down at the breakfast bar, wondering if there was any chance Mum and Alan would let me have the day off as it's my birthday. But getting Alan to agree to me bunking off is like getting the Pope to sell his soul to the Devil – it's never going to happen. So I sat there sipping at my water, hoping it would dilute some of my usual morning sickness. I'm not expecting a baby or anything – just another crap day at school. To be honest, I haven't even been kissed before, let alone anything else. Well, I've been parent-kissed, and too-much-perfume-Grandma-kissed, but not heart-trembling, knee-quivering, boy-kissed. So there's probably more chance of the Pope getting pregnant, but anyway . . .

When the post plopped through the letter box I nearly didn't bother going to see if there were any cards for me. I mean, all of my friends would be giving them to me in person in school, wouldn't they – ha ha! But then I remembered the text I got from Helen last night about the card she'd sent me with a really sick joke on the front and how I wasn't to open it in front of my parents. So I put down my water and trudged along the hall to the door. Fanned out across the doormat were a couple of the insane magazines Alan subscribes to – *Get a Life!* and *Do It Now!* – and some brown, bill-looking envelopes for my mum. Poking out from underneath them I could see two that were obviously cards. I picked them up but only one – the one in Helen's handwriting – was addressed to me. The other one, in a bright blue envelope, was addressed to someone called Cherokee Brown. I double-checked the address, thinking that the postman had delivered it by mistake; there was no way someone with such a cool name could be living in Magnolia Crescent. The most exciting thing to happen around here is when the milkman leaves an extra pint by accident. But the address was definitely ours. I was still turning the envelope over in my hand when Mum came bounding down the stairs in her bright pink tracksuit.

'Happy birthday, pumpkin,' she called, coming over to give me a kiss. Then she saw what I was holding and said, 'Ooh, a birthday card. Is it from Helen?'

I shook my head. 'No. The other one is. This one's for someone called Cherokee Brown.'

Mum stared at me as if I'd said, 'This one's for someone called Adolf Hitler,' before snatching the card from my hand.

'What are you doing?' I asked as she marched off down the hall and into the kitchen. By the time I got there she was stuffing the card into the bin.

'Well, it's not for you so we'd better get rid of it,' she replied, her voice all weirdy high.

'Yes, but aren't we supposed to put it back into the mail or something? Return it to sender like that Elvis song Alan's always singing.'

'Dad,' Mum muttered.

'What?'

'You should call him Dad, not Alan.'

'All right, *Dad*'s always singing.' Now was clearly not the time to get into the whole what-I-should-call-Alan debate. Deciding to play it cool, I sat back down at the breakfast bar and yawned loudly. 'Haven't I even got a card from my own mother then?'

Mum's shoulders softened and she gave me a half smile. 'Of course you have. I'll go and get it. And the boys. Then I'll make us all some breakfast and we can give you your pressies.'

I made my face grin. 'Great.'

As soon as she left the kitchen I darted over to the bin and pulled out the card. The envelope was dotted with grease. I stuffed it inside my dressing gown and ran up the three flights of stairs to my room. Just like Mrs Rochester I live in the attic. (Actually it's a loft conversion but that doesn't sound quite as dramatic, does it?) Flinging the pile of books from my beanbag I sat down, pulled out the card and studied the writing. It was in slightly wonky capitals — like it was from someone who couldn't write very neatly but was trying really hard. I took a deep breath and slid my finger under the seal. I ought to tell you now that if there was a question in Agatha Dashwood's Character Questionnaire saying, 'Do they make a habit of opening other people's mail?' the answer would be a definite no. But something had got my mum rattled and I wanted to know what it was.

I pulled the card from the envelope. The picture on the front was of a country landscape. It was the kind of card you'd buy for an elderly aunt. Or someone who likes cleaning and lives in Bognor. It wasn't really the sort of thing I'd imagine someone called Cherokee going crazy for.

I opened it. There was no printed message or naff rhyme inside; instead the person who'd sent it had written *HAPPY 15TH BIRTHDAY* in large crooked capitals

18

in the middle. At the top, in smaller writing, they had put *To Cherokee* and at the bottom *from Steve*. And at the very bottom, in tiny letters, as if they hadn't been sure whether to say it at all, they had written: *P.S. You can find me most lunchtimes performing in Spitalfields Market. By the record stalls. If you want to find me . . .*

'What are you doing?'

By the time I'd registered that my bedroom door had opened, Mum was standing in the middle of the room, staring at the card in my hand. Then her gaze dropped to the bright blue envelope on the floor.

'I'm just –' I broke off, and I could feel my face flushing. What *was* I doing, opening somebody else's mail?

Mum marched over, holding out her hand. 'I thought I told you to leave it,' she hissed. 'Give it to me.'

I tightened my grip on the card. 'You didn't tell me to leave it, you just threw it in the bin.'

'Exactly. So why would you want to get it out and open it?' Beneath the sheen of her morning moisturiser I could see that her face was flushed too.

'Because –'

But before I could go on Mum made a sudden lurch for the card. I rolled over on the beanbag just out of reach.

'I wanted to read it,' I said. 'I wanted to see what had got you so spooked.'

'I'm not spooked,' Mum spluttered, waving her hands

about like an extremely spooked person. 'But you can't go reading other people's mail. It's not right.'

'Oh, and binning it is?' I stumbled to my feet, clutching the card to my chest. 'It's really weird, because this person, Cherokee Brown, is fifteen today too. Don't you think that's a bit of a coincidence? That we share the same birthday and someone thinks we share the same address.' I didn't have a clue what the coincidence meant, but it was obvious from her flushed face that Mum did.

'What did he say?' she asked, staring at me.

'What did who say?' I watched as her gaze dropped to the card.

'What did he *say*?' This time Mum almost screamed it. I looked at her in shock.

'What's going on, ladies?' We both turned to see Alan poking his head round the door. He never actually sets foot in my room – I think he can sense the anti-life-coaching force field I've erected with my mental powers to keep him out. 'Fiona? Claire? Is everything OK?'

'Yes, yes, everything's fine,' Mum replied sharply over her shoulder. 'Can you go and get the boys up for breakfast? We'll be down in a minute.'

Alan smiled, his teeth all square and straight like the white keys on a piano. 'Okey-dokey. Happy birthday, Claire-Bear.'

I gritted my teeth and smiled back. 'Thanks.'

As soon as we heard his feet padding off down the stairs Mum and I turned back to look at each other.

'What did *who* say, Mum? And how did you know it was from a man?' I waved the card at her. 'You know who sent this, don't you? You recognised the writing and that's why you threw it in the bin. Who is he? Who's Steve? And who is Cherokee Brown? Why won't you just tell me?'

Mum's head slumped. She stuffed her hands inside the pockets of her tracksuit top and scuffed one of her bare feet on the floor. She looked like a little girl who'd just been told she couldn't go out to play.

'You are,' she muttered.

'What?'

'*You* are Cherokee Brown.'

Chapter Two

'It never ceases to amaze me how many writers seem to forget that they have five senses. When you are describing a scene don't just tell the reader what your character is seeing, write about what they can hear, smell, touch and taste as well.'

Agatha Dashwood,
So You Want to Write a Novel?

When most people hear laughter they instantly look around to see where the joke is and whether they can join in. But when you know that you actually *are* the joke, even the slightest snigger makes you want to crawl behind the nearest rock and hide. Unfortunately there aren't any rocks on the way to school. There isn't anything much except house after boring house, all exactly the same with their paved front gardens and green wheelie bins standing guard like giant toads. I've tried loads of things to make the walk more interesting and less like a death-row march. Spying through gaps in net curtains, making up weird titles from the letters on car number plates, only treading on the cracks in the pavement. But today, for the first time in months, I didn't have to do anything to take my mind off the laughter that I knew was coming. My head was rammed to the brim with my mum's revelation. I was Cherokee Brown, or at least that was what I'd been called when I was first born, and the card was from my real dad whose name, apparently, is Steve Brown.

But why had he got in touch now — after fifteen years of nothing? Why had he come back from America? What had happened to his 'commitment issues'? Question after question kept popping into my head, but I still didn't have any answers. Mum had told me we'd have a proper talk about it after school, when Alan took the twins to Beavers, but I wasn't sure I'd be able to make it through the day without going crazy from the shock. Once upon a time I had been called Cherokee Brown.

'Oi, hop-a-long!'

I didn't need to turn round to know that the person shouting at me was David Marsh. And wherever David went, Tricia Donaldson was sure to be swaggering along beside him, pursing her glossy lips and flicking her straw-blonde hair. David and Tricia are the pretend-gangster king and queen of Rayners High, worshipped by their adoring, pretend-gangster followers. I carried on walking and tried to distract myself. What would someone with a name like Cherokee Brown look like, I wondered. She would probably have long dark hair in braids and wear —

'I'm talking to you,' David called out. A load of laughter rang out like machine-gun fire; there were obviously quite a lot of them today. I quickened my pace, still not turning round. Cherokee would wear beads and boots and be really good at horse riding. I felt something hit my back and heard more machine-gun laughter. In my mind I saw Cherokee Brown pull an arrow from a leather sheath on her belt and spin round to face them, her eyes glinting with rage. I took off my blazer. The shattered remains of an egg were sliding down the black nylon, slimy and glistening in the sun.

'Ew, something round here stinks,' I heard Tricia say from right behind me. 'Like blocked drains. Or *rotten eggs*.'

More laughter; this time it was so high-pitched it seemed to drill right into my brain. The sunshine felt like it was getting brighter too, but no matter how hard I blinked I couldn't stop my eyes from burning.

Someone shoved into me as they all jostled past.

'Stupid cripple.'

'Watch out, she might come after you.'

'Nah, she ain't got a leg to stand on.'

This last line got the most laughs, even though it's complete crap. They just can't seem to get over the fact that one of my legs happens to be a few centimetres shorter than the other. I walk with a limp; big deal. But the thing is, in our school you only need to have one freckle out of place and it's enough to have you labelled a freak. When Helen was here it was fine. We didn't really have many other friends but we didn't need them. No one seemed to notice my limp back then; it was as if our friendship was like some kind of cloak of invisibility. But now it feels as if I walk around with a big spotlight on me all the time, under a banner saying CRIPPLE.

David and Tricia and the others walked off, still laughing. I stuffed my blazer into my bag. I'd clean it when I got into school. I looked down the road to where Rayners High loomed like a concrete monster, waiting to swallow me whole. And I thought of yet another crappy day spent drifting round the edges of the corridors, trying to make myself invisible. *Don't let them beat you*, I told myself for about the millionth time. *Anne Frank wouldn't let them beat her. She didn't even let the Nazis beat her. Not where it counted, in her head.* I took a deep breath, pulled myself up straight so my limp wouldn't be so noticeable, and carried on down the road.

After washing my blazer in the sink in the disabled loo – I didn't want to run the risk of bumping into Tricia in the normal toilets – I headed straight for my form room. The bell for registration hadn't gone yet but I like being the first one there; it makes me feel better prepared.

When I got to the classroom I peered through the small pane of glass in the centre of the door. Miss Davis was sat behind her desk with her eyes closed and her chubby hands clasped in front of her. White iPod wires snaked down from her ears, over her huge chest and into her lap. I opened the door and stepped inside. As usual the classroom was baking hot and stank of stale sweat and Miss Davis's floral perfume.

'I am strong.'

I stopped dead and stared at Miss Davis in shock.

'I am strong,' Miss Davis murmured again, her eyes still closed. 'I am strong as a mighty oak rooted in the ground.'

I stood, frozen in horror. She was obviously repeating something she was listening to on her iPod; something she thought she was listening to in private. I started tiptoeing backwards towards the door but just as I reached it the bell for registration rang, making us both jump. As soon as she saw me standing there Miss Davis ripped her iPod from her ears and flushed bright red.

'I was just – it was – it's registration,' I stammered.

'How long have you been here?' Miss Davis asked, her voice all squeaky with embarrassment.

'Oh, I just got here, just this second. Literally.' I felt my own face begin to burn and looked down at the floor.

'OK, well don't just stand there, go and sit down.'

I hurried over to my desk and took my copy of Anne Frank's diary from my bag. I had tucked the birthday card to Cherokee Brown inside it before leaving for school. I opened the book and started re-reading the card. I carried on reading it as my classmates began drifting through the door in giggling, chatting groups. For once I didn't mind that no one wanted to talk and joke with me. I had more important things to think about.

'OK, quieten down everyone,' Miss Davis called out above the noise.

As usual, everyone carried on messing about.

'Please!' Miss Davis cried. 'I need some quiet so I can take the register.'

I peered at her over the top of my book and watched as she took hold of the elastic band she always wears around her wrist and pinged it hard against her pale skin.

'This is your final warning,' Miss Davis yelled. 'If you don't quieten down I'll have to –'

The whole class, including Miss Davis, fell silent as the door crashed open and Tricia and her best friend Clara sauntered in.

'So I told him he couldn't give me a love bite until he had a shave,' Tricia said to Clara.

Jeremy and Gavin, two computer geeks who sit at the desk in front of me, started to giggle.

'Got a problem, virginoids?' Tricia snapped at them.

They immediately went quiet.

As Tricia walked past me, reeking of cigarette smoke, spearmint chewing gum and hairspray, every muscle in my body tensed.

'OK, class, can we please take the register?' Miss Davis called.

'Are you going down the bus station tonight?' Tricia said to Clara as they sat down at the desk behind me.

'John Avery,' Miss Davis called.

'Here, Miss.'

'Helen Buckland.'

'Tony said he's gonna bring some bubblegum-flavoured vodka,' Tricia continued.

'Cool!' Clara replied.

'Tricia Donaldson,' Miss Davis said, looking up from her register.

'And after that we're gonna go round Alfie's Uncle Gary's house,' Tricia went on, totally ignoring Miss Davis. 'He's just got out of prison and Alfie's auntie's throwing him a welcome-home party. She's even had a new tattoo done for him on her boob. It says "Gaz's Forever". It's well romantic.'

'Tricia!' Miss Davis shouted.

'What?'

'I've been calling your name.'

'So?'

'For the register.'

'So?'

'So, can you answer me please?' Miss Davis gave her elastic band another ping and the skin on her wrist flushed red. 'Tony Dunmore.'

'Why?' Tricia asked.

Miss Davis sighed and looked back at her. 'Why what?'

'Why do I have to answer you?'

Miss Davis's face turned as red as her wrist. 'So that I know you are here. Jenny Edwards?'

'Yes, Miss,' Jenny answered, but she, like everyone else in the class apart from me, was looking right at Tricia.

'So, are you blind as well as fat then, Miss?' Tricia asked.

Jeremy started laughing again and I wanted to lean over my desk and shake him.

'James Evans,' Miss Davis said, looking back at the register. I could see beads of sweat erupting on her face like dewdrops on a tomato. I looked down at the picture of Anne Frank on the cover of my book and wondered what she would have done if she'd been trapped inside this classroom instead of the annexe.

'I said, are you blind as well as fat, Miss?' Tricia said.

Miss Davis continued taking the register.

'Ha, she's obviously deaf an' all,' Tricia snorted.

'Wow!' The word burst from my mouth before my brain had time to censor it.

29

I smelt Tricia leaning in right behind me. 'What did you just say, cripple?'

I carried on looking at Anne Frank. If she could deal with the Nazis then surely I could deal with Tricia. 'I said, wow!'

'What did you say that for?'

I took a deep breath and turned round. In my head I could almost hear Anne Frank yelling, *Go on!* 'Because you managed to say a word with four whole syllables.' Inside my ribcage my heart started freaking.

'Theresa Smith,' Miss Davis called in a ridiculously fake cheery voice, as if her class was one big, happy family and she was the greatest teacher ever.

'What?' Tricia growled at me. She was so close I could see the clumps of blue mascara at the ends of her eyelashes.

'You said obviously. Ob – vi – ous – ly. Four syllables. Well done.' I clenched my hands into tight fists.

'No talking please, Claire,' Miss Davis said sharply.

'What?' I turned back and stared at her in disbelief. Why was she telling me to be quiet and not Tricia?

'No talking,' she repeated.

'Yeah, shut your mouth, cripple,' Tricia said, loud enough for the whole class to hear.

Miss Davis looked back down at the register. 'Claire Weeks.'

I stared at her.

'Claire Weeks,' she said again, but she wouldn't look at me.

'Here, Miss,' I eventually replied. But in my head I was yelling, *I'm not Claire Weeks, I'm Cherokee Brown, you pathetic coward.*

NOTEBOOK EXTRACT

Agatha Dashwood says that 'if one is to become a proper writer one must write at every available opportunity'. So I've decided to take her advice and do some writing on the train on the way up to Spitalfields. Well, hopefully I'm on the way up to Spitalfields. I've never been there before so I'm not exactly sure which station it's nearest to, so I'm heading east and hoping for the best!! And at least I'm not in school. I couldn't stay there a minute longer after what happened in registration.

It's so weird to think that I used to love going to school, that I used to be one of those geeky kids who always got their homework done on time and actually enjoyed learning new stuff. I'll never forget the day I discovered there were minus numbers – I was so excited there was something that came before zero! And the English lesson when I read Anne Frank's diary for the first time and realised that books aren't just there to entertain you, they can actually change your whole way of thinking about the world.

Now when the teachers are telling us stuff all I hear is a drone. Kind of like when a radio hasn't been tuned in properly and you only catch the odd word here and there. The only people I hear loud and clear these days are Tricia and her idiot friends. I hate being scared of them (I'm not going to put this bit in my book - no one likes a heroine who's a big old wuss), but it's just that there are loads of them and only one of me. And I'm so short and skinny too. I'm not short and skinny in my daydreams though. In my daydreams I'm a ninja with all the moves. And when Tricia leans forwards and says something like, 'How does it feel knowing you're gonna be a virgin your whole life cos no one wants to sleep with a cripple?' I do a backflip off my chair, land on top of her desk and kick her so hard in the face her head comes flying off.

Don't think I'll put that bit in my book either – I'll sound like a psycho!

Oh no, some freak has just got on the train and sat down opposite me and started talking out loud. I hope he isn't a terrorist bomber. He isn't carrying a rucksack, just a tatty old carrier bag. How big are bombs? Can they fit inside a carrier bag? I saw a programme on Channel 4 once about terrorists in the Middle East and one of them blew up a bus with a suicide bomb clipped to his belt.

This person isn't wearing a belt. I just checked and he saw me looking and now it looks as if I was perving at him. Oh, God – how embarrassing. I'm just going to write in this notebook from now on and not look in his direction at all. Well, maybe I'll take a few sneaky glances, just to make sure he isn't trying to set off his bomb.

I suppose I ought to write a descrip-tion of him, just in case he does turn out to be a terrorist and I need to give evidence. I saw an episode of *Crimewatch* once where this policeman said that in ninety-nine per cent of crimes, witnesses can't even remember the colour of a criminal's hair. Well, I guess the one per cent who do remember must be writers. Agatha Dashwood says that writers have specially heightened observational skills. They have to, to make their stories 'truly come alive'.

NOTES FOR POLICE INVESTIGATION
The potential suspect has greasy, dark brown hair. I'm not sure if it's the grease making it so dark, so it could be a lighter shade of brown when he washes it. He looks pretty old. About thirty, I'd say. And he has a big belly, about the size of one of those green watermelons that are red on the inside, with loads of pips that you end up having to spit out all over your plate. The rest of him isn't fat though, so it kind of looks like he's pregnant. But obviously he isn't pregnant cos he's

definitely a man. Unless he's like one of those women on Jerry Springer who are 'tragically trapped in the wrong body'. I don't think he is though – he has too much stubble.

Oh, crap! He saw me looking at him again.

He has mad, staring eyes. And he likes to mutter a lot. I can't understand what he's saying though.

Oh no, he's reaching into his bag. Should I pull the emergency cord? Do they even have emergency cords on the tube? It's too late, he's taking something out. What if it's a gun, not a bomb? What if he shoots me?

False alarm. It's a book. It's called *One Hundred Ways to Ice a Cake*. He isn't a crazed terrorist at all – he's a crazed cake-maker!

He's stopped muttering now and he's started to read.

I can't believe there are actually one hundred different ways to ice a cake.

I would have done something though – if he had pulled out a gun or a bomb. I wouldn't have just sat here. Because I want to write a book. And I don't want to have to make anything up to make my book exciting. I was thinking about it on the way to the station. The reason I love Anne Frank's diary and the *Little House on the Prairie* so much is because they're true stories. All the cool things the heroines did actually happened in real life. And that's how I want my book to be. I'll still use Agatha Dashwood's book to help me, but I'm going to stick to the facts. And that way I'll have to make my life interesting. And I'll have to become the kind of heroine I like to read about. The kind of person who notices the hair colour of a potential criminal and stands up to bullies and isn't afraid to fight back.

Chapter Three

'For your main character your story has to be a journey. This journey can be physical, but it must always, without fail, be emotional. If your character hasn't grown, learnt and changed by the end of your novel then I am afraid they are destined for the waste-paper bin.'

Agatha Dashwood,
So You Want to Write a Novel?

The minute registration ended I picked up my book and my bag and I started walking. I didn't stop walking until I was on the London-bound platform at Rayners Lane station. I got the train to the very end of the line to a station called Aldgate. I'd never been there before but I knew it was in the East End and I hoped there'd be a map or a signpost for Spitalfields outside the station.

But there were no maps or signposts at all, just loads of cars and buses and taxies all whizzing by at about a million miles an hour. I stood on the pavement in front of the station trying to decide what to do next, and trying not to get trampled on by a herd of commuters with serious anger-management issues. It's funny because for the past few months I've spent hours in lessons dreaming of the day I can leave school and go to work, but judging by the faces of the people who stormed past me today I don't think work can be all that great either.

In the end I decided to go left. Because I'm left-handed. I know that sounds really dumb, and I bet an intrepid explorer like Christopher Columbus would never have done something so stupid. Or maybe he did, and maybe America would still be undiscovered if he'd been right-handed . . . but at least Christopher Columbus would have had charts and a compass to help him. I had nothing. So I turned left, and I walked and walked.

I reached a massive crossroads and waited for the green man to appear. Normally I just cross the road if I see a gap in the traffic, but in this part of London cars and bikes seemed to burst out of nowhere like rockets. The cyclists looked like something out of a horror movie, pedalling furiously and wearing those masks that surgeons wear when they're about to cut somebody open. I clutched my school bag to me, leant against a lamp post and waited. My back was starting to ache from all the walking. I'm supposed to wear specially made shoes to even out the length of my legs, but they look even worse than the limp. The trouble is, when I wear normal shoes it puts loads of pressure on my spine.

I think this is what is known as a lose—lose situation.

Once I'd managed to get across the road I saw a sign that told me I was now in Whitechapel. You know, the crappy brown square on the Monopoly board that only costs about 20p in rent even if you have ten hotels on it. Well, dear reader, I now know why it's so cheap. It smells like a boiled toilet and there's a horrible film of dirt covering everything, like cigarette ash. I would've stopped someone to ask for directions if I hadn't been so worried about stranger danger. Not that I normally worry about that sort of thing, but the people I was passing looked stranger and more dangerous than anyone I've ever seen before. For example, there was a woman with long greasy hair and smeary make-up pushing a supermarket trolley with just an old rusty kettle in it. And a man with two carrier bags tied to his feet, hobbling along, shouting about God. And another man who was drinking beer and singing a Bob Marley song in the doorway of an 'adult entertainment centre' – which we all know is just another name for a sex shop. I wonder what goes on in a sex shop. Do people just walk in off the street and say, 'I'd like to buy some sex, please.'?

I decided that I'd take the next left turn and if it looked just as bad I'd start making my way back to the station. But the next left turn was like finding a black hole in outer space and slipping into another dimension.

Or in this case, slipping into India. As I started walking up the road I realised that nearly every shop was an Indian restaurant, and if it wasn't an Indian restaurant it was an Indian supermarket, or a sari shop, or an Indian sweet shop with trays of rainbow-coloured sweets filling the windows. I got to a small crossroads and looked for a clue to where I was. Somebody had spray-painted PLEASE DON'T BOMB US on the wall and beneath that was a black and white street sign. It said BRICK LANE. I felt a little flutter in my stomach. Brick Lane was near Spitalfields Market. I'd seen a programme once on The History Channel about twentieth-century London migrants (I'd pretended to Alan it was for a history project to get out of going on a family badminton night) and the presenter had talked about Brick Lane being right next door to Spitalfields.

I started walking a bit faster. Up ahead of me two ladies in black burkhas bustled their little children over a tiny zebra crossing. They reminded me of mother penguins. The road was narrower now and cobbled, the complete opposite of Whitechapel High Street. As I walked I peered down each side road looking for any sign of Spitalfields. The names of the roads were really cool – Threadneedle Street, Fashion Street – there wasn't a Magnolia Crescent in sight. And then, as I peered down a side road called Fournier Street, I saw a sign with an arrow saying SPITALFIELDS MARKET. I stopped, as still as a statue. Ever since I'd got on the tube I'd been worried I'd never find Spitalfields, but now I had found it I felt a bit sick. I fumbled around in my bag for my mobile to check the time. Nearly half past eleven. I pulled out the birthday card and opened it again, my fingers trembling.

You can find me most lunchtimes performing in Spitalfields Market. By the record stalls. If you want to find me . . .

I took a deep breath. It wasn't lunchtime yet. I still had time to get to the market and decide what I was going to do. I started walking down Fournier Street. I wondered what my dad looked like. Back when I thought he was all American with commitment issues I pictured him being big and broad and wearing a cowboy hat and boots. And possibly a medallion. But now I knew he had wanted to call his daughter – wanted to call *me* – Cherokee, I wasn't sure what to think. Maybe he was a Native American and Steve Brown was just his English name. Maybe he was really called Growling Bear or Big Stream Running Water. I wondered what he did when he 'performed'. I thought of the men with the long dark plaits who played the pan pipes in Harrow every Saturday. Is that what Steve – my dad – would be doing in Spitalfields? I felt my cheeks start to flush. What would I say to him? How should I act?

'And this is where Jack the Ripper's first victim used to lodge . . .'

I glanced across the street and saw a group of people

gathered in front of a really old house, gazing up at its grimy windows. A man with a clipboard was standing on the steps of the house, giving them some kind of talk. I started walking a little faster. Images of a madman massacring prostitutes were not really what I needed to calm my nerves. At the end of the street a thin white church pointed up into the clear blue sky like a witch's finger. I drew level with it and stopped and stared. There, straight ahead of me on the other side of a busy main road, was a wrought iron gate and a sign that said WELCOME TO OLD SPITALFIELDS MARKET.

Chapter Four

*'When in doubt, place your character in an unusual setting.
Then see your writing come alive!'*

Agatha Dashwood,
So You Want to Write a Novel?

For the first time ever I entered a church without being
forced there in a nasty dress for somebody's christening or
wedding. That's how scary the prospect of seeing my real
dad was. I sat down on a shiny wooden pew about halfway
along the church and took a deep breath. The air was cool
and clean and smelt slightly of Christmas. I looked up
at the huge wooden cross suspended over the altar and
suddenly felt as if I was in a corny movie and this was the
part where the heroine prays to God for guidance. Feeling
slightly desperate, I whispered, 'What should I do?' and
looked at the mosaic of coloured light streaming on to
the cross through the stained-glass window. But nothing
happened. There was no booming God-voice uttering
words of wisdom. Not even a thunderbolt. Nothing but
the hum of the traffic outside.

I sat there for ages in the end, with all kinds of images flashing through my mind. Rayners High, my mum and Alan, the twins, Magnolia Crescent. They all seemed so far away now. It was like I'd been whisked out of my old life into somebody else's. Somebody called Cherokee. It was when I had that thought that I finally plucked up the courage to go. Claire Weeks might have stayed hiding in a church all day, but not Cherokee Brown.

Outside, the sunlight was brighter than ever. I squinted as I made my way to the nearest crossing and waited as a stream of buses, cars, bikes and lorries thundered by. Across the road, on either side of the wrought iron gate, was a row of quaint little shops, totally different to the kind on Brick Lane. These were much posher. The clothes shops had dummies reclining on sofas and eating golden grapes and the restaurants were advertising things that sounded more like medical conditions than food.

Finally the lights changed and I crossed over, trying to ignore my bass drum of a heart. I walked through the gates into the market and down a passageway that was lined with other little shops – one selling antique furniture and another selling twenty-seven different varieties of cheese.

The first thing I noticed about the market wasn't the stalls, it was the people. I'd never seen so many interesting haircuts and amazing clothes. It was even better than the Southbank. I looked down at my school uniform. I'd already taken off my tie and blazer and stuffed them into my bag, but my blue polo shirt and black nylon trousers were hardly what you would call interesting or amazing. In a dreary place like Rayners High, they fit right in, but up in Spitalfields, they looked naff and dull. As I stood there wondering what to do, a girl stopped right in front of me and started texting on her phone. She looked so incredible I couldn't even pretend not to stare. Her hair, which was dyed the colour of vanilla ice-cream, was shaved on one side and hung down like a curtain on the other. On the shaved side her ear had a row of tiny silver hoops running all the way along the edge. She was wearing a flowery sundress and big biker boots and her smooth, tanned skin was as golden as honey. As she texted, a cluster of silver bangles and charm bracelets jingled on her arm. She looked so cool and confident. So different to me.

My heart sank. All this time I'd been worrying about what to expect from my dad, I'd completely forgotten to think about what he might be expecting from me. He'd addressed the birthday card to Cherokee Brown. He didn't know I'd actually ended up as Claire Weeks. Someone who had no friends and who couldn't even walk properly. I was about to turn round and head straight back out when I heard a cheer ring out from the other side of the market. Then there was the strum of a guitar and a man started singing. His voice was deep and gravelly and he was singing the stompy old rock song, 'London Calling'.

The girl with the ice-cream hair finished her text and moved off to look at some jewellery on a nearby stall.

I felt sick and scared and excited all at once. Was that my dad I could hear singing? Was that my dad everyone was cheering and clapping along with?

'London calling,' his voice rang out again. If it was my dad he was really good. His voice had a huskiness that made it stand out from other singers. It was gentle and rough all at once.

With my whole body buzzing like I'd downed ten of those doll-sized-but-deadly espresso coffees, I followed the girl and started looking at the trays of rings and pendants and brooches on the jewellery stall. Looking at them but not really seeing a thing.

What should I do? Maybe if I edged just a bit closer to the music . . .

I started weaving my way through the crowds of people between the stalls, stopping every now and then to pretend to have a browse of some clothes or books or – OMG! – stuffed animal heads, and gather my thoughts. The singing got louder and louder and finally I caught sight of a crowd gathered at the far end of the market. My first feeling was of relief. There were so many people there was no way whoever was singing would be able to see me.

But then I wouldn't be able to see him either. I flicked through a box of records on a nearby stall while I stared over at the crowd. What if it wasn't even my dad? How would I get to find out? I swallowed hard and walked over to join the back of the crowd. Everyone was tapping their feet or nodding their heads in time to the song. When it finished they all started whooping and cheering.

'Cheers. Thanks a lot,' said the singer, slightly breathless.

My heart sank. His accent was from London. East London. He didn't sound American at all. Or Native American. It had to be another performer. He had said in the card that he was at Spitalfields 'most' lunchtimes. Obviously this wasn't one of them. I noticed some long tables over to my right and went and sat down at the end of one. I'd come all this way for nothing. Bunked off school, somehow made my way through Whitechapel without getting mugged or abducted or sold to a sex shop, and all for nothing.

'Oi, Steve, do "Thunder Road".'

I looked up as one of the record stallholders closest to me yelled over the crowd.

'What's that, Tel? "Thunder Road"?' the singer replied over his microphone.

'Yeah,' the stallholder yelled back. 'I could do with a bit of Springsteen.'

But I wasn't listening to what he was saying any more. He'd called the singer Steve. How many Steves could there be performing in Spitalfields at lunchtime? A shaft of sunlight spilled through the glass roof of the market and fell hot on my face. From the centre of the crowd I heard the sound of a harmonica and then that husky voice again. This time he was singing a lot more softly, and strumming gently on an acoustic guitar. The whole crowd fell silent and stood motionless as they listened. It was a beautiful song all about a man trying to persuade a woman called Mary to come for a drive with him to this place called Thunder Road. He wanted her to just climb into the car and see where they ended up. It reminded me of the first time I bunked off school and ended up at the Southbank. On the day Tricia had changed the words to a Britney Spears song to be all about me and my limp, and Miss Davis had laughed along with the rest of the class. Just like today, I'd been so desperate to get out of school I'd walked out of the nearest fire exit and gone straight to the tube, not caring where I ended up, just as long as it was miles away from Rayners High.

I stood up, as if I was in a trance; as if the beautiful words of the song were drawing me forwards like a spell. I started edging through the crowd, past the men in their tight jeans and pointy boots and the girls in their summer dresses and flip-flops.

'Excuse me, excuse me,' I muttered as I went.

And then there was just one row of people in front of me. I stopped behind a couple of women wearing business suits and trainers and I tried to swallow but my mouth was too dry. Through a gap between the women I could just make out a pair of tanned hands playing a guitar. The singer was wearing a faded black T-shirt and torn jeans but I still couldn't see his face. All I had to do was move slightly to my left and stand on tiptoe, but I was scared he would see me. Even though he didn't know me and wouldn't recognise me I was worried I'd do something to give myself away. My heart was thumping and the palms of my hands were sticky with sweat.

A massive cheer rang out as the man in the song begged Mary again to come with him so they could escape from their town full of losers and go somewhere they'd be able to win. I thought of Rayners High and Magnolia Crescent and my eyes went glassy with tears. Then suddenly the women in front of me turned to leave and one of them swung her huge shoulder bag right into me, catching me in the face. I stumbled sideways and on to the ground.

'Are you all right, darlin'?' I heard the singer ask over the mic as I scrambled to my feet.

I had to get out of there. I didn't want him seeing me like this, like everyone else always saw me: clumsy and awkward and embarrassed. I grabbed my bag from the floor but then, just for a split second, I looked in his direction.

He was staring straight at me, holding his microphone in one hand and his guitar in the other. He was short and thin and had shoulder-length dark brown hair, held back by a red and white bandana. His face was tanned and his eyes dark brown. He looked like a rock star from the eighties. The kind who would have gone out with one of the original supermodels and thrown televisions and toasters and stuff from hotel room windows. And had the vanilla-ice-cream-haired girl for a daughter, instead of me. The tears that had been building in my eyes spilled on to my cheeks. I turned round and started pushing my way back through the crowd. It had all been a massive mistake. I should've stayed in school. I should've realised it would never work out. My life isn't worthy of being a stupid novel – not unless they bring out a new genre called Disaster Lit. Nothing ever goes the way I want it to.

I finally made it through the crowd to the edge of the market. I took a deep breath and started marching towards the gate. I didn't care that this made my limp look even worse – I had to get out of there. I had to get back to my boring, crappy life in Rayners Lane and forget any of this had ever happened.

But then there was a loud squeal of feedback over the speakers. I stood still for a second.

'Cherokee!' His voice rang out over the microphone, full of concern. 'Cherokee, come back.'

Chapter Five

'One of the crassest mistakes a new novelist can make is to waste acres of paper telling their reader all about their characters and their motivations. You must SHOW us this information, dear writer, through the character's actions, rather than tediously tell.'

Agatha Dashwood,
So You Want to Write a Novel?

'How did you know it was me?'

Steve – Dad – *Steve* looked at me. Then down at his pint. Then all around the beer garden.

After he'd called to me on the microphone I'd stood rooted to the spot. Then I'd heard footsteps running up behind me and felt a hand on my shoulder. I turned round and there he was. 'Cherokee?' he'd said, as if he was asking a question. I just nodded and stared. What happened next was all a bit of a blur. I followed him back to where he'd been performing, watched him pack up his things and apologise to everybody for finishing so soon. And then we'd come here. To a pub called the Water Poet at the back of the market.

'Well, there's the fact that you're the spit of me,' he finally replied, looking back at me with a nervous grin.

'The what?'

'The spit. You look just like me.'

'Do I?' I tried to study him without looking obvious. When he smiled crescents of small lines formed around his dark brown eyes like fans.

'Yeah, course you do. And then there was the stake-out.'

'The what?'

'The stake-out. At your house. Last week.'

'You staked out my house?' I took a sip of my lemonade to try and stop myself from giggling. Nerves were bubbling up inside of me like gas.

He shook his head and sighed. 'Yeah, man. They wouldn't tell me where you lived so I had to follow your mum home. And then I waited outside, till I saw you.' He took a cigarette paper from the packet on the table in front of him and a pinch of tobacco from a plastic pouch.

'Are you serious?' I was so shocked at what he was telling me that for a second I forgot to be nervous.

He placed the tobacco on the paper and began rolling it with his finger and thumb. ''Fraid so.' He licked the edge of the paper. 'I didn't want to, but I had no choice. I wanted to see you.' He looked away, obviously embarrassed.

I replayed what he'd just said in my mind. 'Who wouldn't tell you where I lived?'

'Your nan and granddad.'

I looked at him blankly. He was staring at some fat men on the next table who were stuffing their sweaty faces with burgers.

'Cheryl and Paul. Your mum's folks. I went round to their house. Wasn't even sure they'd still be living there to be honest but I thought I'd give it a go. I was made up when Cheryl answered the door. But as soon as she realised who I was she went all moody and told me to do one.' He lit his roll-up and a wisp of smoke ribboned around his face. 'So I left, but only as far as the end of their road. Then I waited for Fi – your mum – to turn up.'

'But how did you know she would turn up?'

'I didn't. And she didn't.' He sighed and more smoke streamed from his mouth. 'Not for days.'

'Days?'

He nodded. 'Yep. Well, nearly two days, stuck in deepest darkest Surrey with only my guitar for company. Good job I've got a camper van, eh?'

'You waited for two days outside my grandparents' house just to see if my mum would turn up?'

He nodded again. 'Yep. Nearly didn't recognise her at first, she looked so – well, anyway, once I'd worked out

55

it was her I waited for her to leave and then I followed her back home. To your place.'

'Oh my God.'

He frowned. 'Sorry, I know it sounds a bit radio rental.'

'A bit what?'

'Radio rental – mental. It was just that I really wanted to see you and I didn't want any more arguments. There's been too much bad karma as it is. I thought tailing her would be the best option. The quietest option.'

I nodded, but not really understanding at all. 'So when did you – ?'

'When did I what?'

'See me.'

'Oh. Last Monday morning. On your way to school.'

My heart sank. 'On my way to school?'

'Yeah.' He frowned and looked away.

'Did you follow me?'

'What?'

'To school. Did you follow me to school?'

He shook his head. 'Nah, course not. I just wanted to see you and then I thought I'd send you the card. See if you wanted to see me too.' He began to smile. 'I was made up when I saw you there in the market, on the floor.'

My face burned as the whole tragic falling-over scene very kindly replayed itself in slow motion in my mind.

'I wasn't made up that you was on the floor,' he added

quickly. 'I was made up you'd come. I'd been crappin' it all morning, wondering whether you'd show.'

I glanced across the table at this person, this stranger, who I was technically biologically half of. He looked down at his hands and began fiddling with a silver skull ring on one of his thin brown fingers.

'I mean, I wouldn't have blamed you if you never wanted to see me at all. I ain't exactly been Dad of the Year, have I?'

'No.' My reply popped out before I could stop it. There were so many things I wanted to ask him but I felt way too shy.

'I've always thought about you though,' he went on, still looking down. 'Always wondered what you were doing and what you were like.'

My face started to burn again. I wondered how different I was to what he had been expecting. 'So why didn't you . . . ?' I couldn't finish the question.

He looked straight at me. 'I was an idiot – when I was younger. I suppose your mum's told you all about it?'

I didn't say anything; I wanted to hear his version of things.

'I suppose I just wasn't ready,' he shrugged slightly and tilted his head, 'for the responsibility – of a family and that.'

Whenever my mum goes on one of her rants about

my real dad and his commitment issues I always end up feeling angry and hurt, but now he was sat in front of me saying it to me himself I felt weirdly numb.

He took a drag on his cigarette. 'I was a twat. My band had the chance to tour America — to take part in this music festival in Austin and —' he took another drag, 'your mum told me if I went that would be it for me and her. And us.' He stopped again and shifted sideways on his seat. 'Bloody hell, this is hard. When I practised last night on Harrison it came out all right, I sounded like Winston Churchill going on about fighting on the beaches, but now —'

'Harrison?' My heart sank. He had a son, another family. One he wanted to live with.

He nodded. 'Yeah, my lodger. He's not much older than you actually. Eighteen. He thinks I'm a twat too, for leaving you.'

I breathed a sigh of relief. 'Do you have any kids? Any other kids?'

He shook his head. 'Nah. That's why —' he broke off, looked around, then back at me and I saw that his eyes were all shiny. 'That's why I want to get to know you. I mean, I know it's too late for me to be your dad and all that.' He picked up his lighter and began flicking it on and off. 'I saw your stepdad during my — er — stake-out. He looks . . . nice.' He put the lighter back down and stared at me. 'He is, isn't he? Nice? I mean, you like him, yeah? He treats you all right?'

I nodded numbly. Alan is the king of nice – that's the problem, he uses his 'niceness' to get everything his own way the whole time.

'Cool. Cos when I got back from America your mum told me she'd met him and that you were all settled and happy. She said it would only confuse things if . . .'

'If what?'

'If I tried to be a part of your life.' He wiped his eyes with the back of his hand and looked away.

'Oh.'

I started doing some calculations in my head. My mum had met Alan when I was one. She had last told me my real dad was in America last Christmas when I'd got all emotional after watching *It's a Wonderful Life* and *The Champ* back to back. But if Steve had spoken to her since then why had he needed to stake out Gran and Granddad's to find out where I lived?

'When was that?' I asked, for some reason suddenly finding it really hard to swallow.

'When was what?'

'The conversation you had with my mum. When did you get back from America?'

'Oh – about thirteen years ago. Yeah, you would've been about two.'

'Thirteen years?' I whispered.

He nodded, obviously embarrassed. 'I know. I'm sorry. She was right though. I probably would've been a crap dad.'

Yes, I wanted to yell at him, *but couldn't I have been allowed to decide that for myself?* I sat on my hands and stared down into my lap. For all this time Mum had been lying to me. All these years I'd been imagining my dad in his Stetson and medallion, having commitment issues along with his pancakes and syrup and he'd been – well, where had he been?

'So where have you lived since you got back from America?' I muttered, not daring to look up.

He coughed and I heard the clunk of his glass being put down on the table.

'Here, mainly.'

'Here, as in the UK?'

'Here, as in east London.'

My world began to shrink in on itself. I'd been thinking there was an entire ocean between us and it had been a tiny little underground line.

'But you could have –' I broke off, suddenly remembering that really he was a total stranger and I probably shouldn't shout at him.

'I'm sorry.' He coughed and shifted in his seat again.

We sat in silence for a while. Only it wasn't silence

for me because the voice in my head now seemed to have acquired a loudhailer. *HOW COULD SHE HAVE LIED TO ME ALL THIS TIME? WHY DID SHE TELL HIM WE WERE BETTER OFF WITHOUT HIM? HOW COULD SHE THINK I WAS BETTER OFF WITH ALAN WHEN ALAN ISN'T MY REAL DAD? WHY DIDN'T I HAVE ANY SAY IN IT?*

On the other side of the beer garden a girl started laughing. Her hair was short and spiky and dyed jet black with electric-blue tips. She looked so happy and relaxed – despite the metal bolt through her nose and her unbelievably tight leather trousers. I wanted to scream at my mum till I had no voice left.

'Happy birthday, Cherokee,' Steve said gruffly. I looked at him and he smiled and a dimple popped up in his right cheek. I smiled back, knowing that an identical dimple would have popped up in exactly the same place on my own face. I felt a weird tug inside of me, like there was some kind of invisible cord linking us.

'So, what do you want?' he asked.

'Oh, er –' I picked up my glass of lemonade. It was still half full. 'It's OK, I've got loads left thanks.'

He shook his head and laughed. 'Nah, I don't mean to drink. I mean for your birthday. What do you want for your birthday?'

'Oh!' In all the drama I'd completely forgotten what day it was. I gave an embarrassed laugh and some lemonade sloshed over the top of my glass. Across the beer garden the girl with the nose-bolt leant back on her seat and ran her hand through her electric-blue hair.

'A haircut.' Oh, God! Where had that come from? Now he was going to think I was crazy for sure.

'A haircut?' Steve looked at my stupid stringy hair and frowned.

'Yes, but not just any old haircut . . .' I stopped mid-sentence, mortified. It was like some idiot game-show host had seized control of my mouth!

'Oh yeah?' Steve's dimple sprang into life again as he grinned across the table at me.

I nodded, figuring I had nothing left to lose. 'I want a cool haircut. Like hers.' I pointed to the girl with the blue hair who just at that moment let out a loud belch.

Steve started to laugh and I wanted to crawl under the table and dig myself deep into the dry ground. Now he'd be thinking I was some stupid wannabe kid. He probably wished he'd never sent me the card, that he'd been right to leave it for thirteen years. I may as well just tell him I wasn't Cherokee Brown at all – that my name was Claire Weeks-as-in-weak and I had no friends and actually people preferred to call me names and throw eggs at me and –

'Come on then.' Steve got to his feet and picked up his guitar.

'Where are we going?' I felt sick. He'd had enough of

me and wanted me to go. He was probably going to march me to the station and put me on the first train back home.

'Your wish is my command, madam.' He held out his hand to me, then stuffed it into his jeans pocket. 'If a haircut's what you want, then a haircut's what you're gonna get.'

'Really?'

'Really. But don't worry – I ain't gonna do it. Not unless you want a skinhead? I'm a dab hand with a set of clippers.'

'No!'

He threw his head back and let out a raucous laugh. 'I'm joking, man. Come on, I know just the place. And don't worry, it's so cool you'll come out of there with frostbite.'

Chapter Six

'The gifted writer won't need pages and pages of description. Often they will be able to sum up what they need to say in just one word.'

Agatha Dashwood,
So You Want to Write a Novel?

I followed Steve out of the beer garden and along the side of the market back to the busy main road. As we waited for the traffic lights to change I saw two women on the other side of the road staring at him. I recognised the look they were giving him immediately – it was the kind Helen and I used to give the hot skater boys at the Southbank when we were checking them out. I glanced at Steve out of the corner of my eye. He was standing chewing gum, his head gently rocking to some silent beat, a small smile playing on his lips. His guitar case was hitched over one shoulder and both of his hands were stuffed into his jeans pockets. I was so used to being seen in public with Alan and people shooting him mocking stares as he talked really loudly on his phone, it was totally weird to be with my real dad and have women checking him out. Weird, but kind of nice. I felt my must-text-Helen reflex start to twinge – she was not going to believe the birthday I was having.

'Right then,' Steve said as the lights changed and he guided me across the road and past the drooling women. 'Let's get that barnet sorted.'

As I walked along beside him, trying my hardest to disguise my limp, I felt all of the following in one go: excited, terrified, sick, giggly, angry, tearful and in a state of shock. Steve, on the other hand, seemed totally laid-back – as if being reunited with your long-lost daughter and taking her for a haircut within an hour of meeting her was the most normal thing in the world.

'We'll try the Truman Brewery,' he said, leading me down a side street.

'Brewery?'

He let out a laugh. 'Don't worry, it ain't a brewery any more.'

I followed him into a large courtyard. To our left, clusters of people sat around wooden tables, drinking wine and eating pizza in the sun. To our right, a group of Japanese tourists were traipsing into some kind of art gallery, huge black cameras dangling from their necks. And straight ahead of us, grey-brick, factory-style buildings loomed high into the sky, dwarfing the row of food stalls beneath them. Across from the stalls a queue of people snaked out from an old graffiti-covered trailer. The graffiti spelled out the words DANCING CHOPSTICKS and it shone like a metallic rainbow in the sun. It seemed to be some kind of crazy Chinese takeaway on wheels. The courtyard buzzed with the same kind of people I'd seen in Spitalfields. People with wedged, spiked and dyed hair and every clothing combination you could possibly imagine. Suits and Converse high-tops. Prom dresses and cowboy boots. Jeans and pork-pie hats. It was like an industrial estate had mated with an art college and we were standing slap bang in the middle of their freakish offspring. I instantly fell in love with it.

'The hairdressers is round here, by the Chill Bar,' Steve said. He stopped and looked at me. 'You sure you still want to do this?'

I nodded. I felt as if I was sleepwalking my way through some crazy, psychedelic dream, and I definitely didn't want to wake up yet.

'And you're OK hanging out with me for a bit longer?' He suddenly looked really nervous.

I nodded again. 'Yes. Definitely.'

His face broke into a grin. 'Sweet! OK, follow me.' He led me past one of those old-fashioned double-decker buses with the open back — only this one had been converted into an organic wine bar. I wondered how much randomness a human brain could take before it actually exploded! We turned right at the end of the courtyard and into a section of the brewery where the ground floor had been converted into shops. This time the clothes store mannequins were skeletons on skateboards, playing guitars, and the coffee shop was also a record label. The text to Helen I'd been composing in my head started filling with OMGs and WTFs.

'Here we go.' Steve came to a halt and I gazed up at the shop in front of us. It was called PUNKED and it took me a moment to realise it was actually a hairdressers, not a nightclub. If I had to choose just one word to describe it then that word would be BLACK. From the sign above the door, to the door itself and the walls and the floor. Walking in was like entering a cool, dark cave.

'Can I help you?' A woman emerged from the darkness to greet us. She was wearing so much black she looked as if she'd been drawn in charcoal.

'Yeah, man. We'd like a haircut please. *She'd* like a haircut,' Steve said, gesturing to me.

As I felt my face start to burn I was kind of grateful for the surrounding gloom.

'Cool,' the woman replied. 'Take a seat.' She waved me over to one of the black leather chairs facing jagged-edged mirrors on the wall. Steve sat down on a black leather sofa by the door, propping his guitar case next to him.

'Hello.' A male hairdresser appeared from the back

of the shop. Like the woman he was dressed from head to toe in skin-tight black leather. He was also wearing some kind of cowboy holster slung across his narrow hips – but instead of a gun it held a pair of scissors and lots of different combs. He held out his thin, pale hand to shake Steve's. 'I'm Wayne. Can I help you?'

Steve shook his head. 'No thanks, man, I'm just here to watch,' and he nodded over in my direction.

'I'm Raven,' the woman said to my reflection in the mirror.

'I'm Cl– Cherokee,' I replied, and the thermostat in my face cranked up a couple more notches.

'Wow, what a cool name,' Raven said, starting to play with my hair the way hairdressers always do at the start of an appointment. 'How come you're called that?'

I felt a surge of panic. I didn't have a clue.

'Cos her great-grandmother was a Cherokee Indian,' Steve called over. 'From the Great Smoky Mountains in North Carolina.'

'Wow!' Raven replied and I thought in unison. 'That's so cool!' Raven looked back at my hair. 'So what kind of style are you after, Cherokee?'

I looked back at her in the mirror and it felt as if my heart was singing. I could practically see little crotchets and quavers floating up my throat and out of my mouth. I had a great-grandmother who was a Cherokee Indian.

From an awesome-sounding place called the Great Smoky Mountains. In North Carolina.

Suddenly anything seemed possible.

'Could you cut it so that one side is long and kind of hangs down over my face and the other side is really short?'

Raven went and got a magazine from a rack over by Steve. Then she flicked through it until she got to a picture of a model with exactly the same hairstyle as the vanilla-ice-cream-hair girl from the market.

'Like that?' she asked.

I nodded and smiled. 'Yes, please.'

While Raven washed my hair, Wayne started talking to Steve about music and by the time she'd finished Steve had got his guitar out and was strumming it absently.

'Do you know any Rolling Stones?' Wayne asked.

Steve let out a snort of laughter. 'Is the Pope a Catholic?'

I felt another tug inside of me. Could making puns about the Pope be another thing we had in common, like our dimples? Maybe my Cherokee great-grandmother had made them too, while sitting around the totem pole beneath the Great Smoky Mountains. I pictured an Indian chief in full headdress sitting cross-legged next to a beautiful squaw and asking her, 'Would you like a tote on this peace pipe, Cherokee's great-grandma?' And the beautiful woman smiling back at him before grabbing

69

the pipe and saying, 'Is the Pope a Catholic, Big Chief White Bear?'

The glint of Raven's scissors snapped me from my daydream and I felt a sudden wave of panic.

'Would it be OK if –' I broke off.

'If what?' Raven asked.

'If I turned round, so I'm not facing the mirror.' I could barely look at her I felt so embarrassed.

Raven stared at me blankly for a moment, then her face broke into a smile. 'Oh, I get it,' she exclaimed. 'So it'll be like one of those makeover shows on the telly and you'll only see the before and after. Cool!'

I nodded and breathed a sigh of relief. As long as she didn't realise I was too much of a chicken to watch what she was doing, it didn't matter what she thought.

Over on the sofa Steve started singing softly.

'Oh, I love this one!' Wayne exclaimed.

'Me too,' Raven said, swivelling my chair round so I was facing into the shop.

As she started snipping away at my hair I decided to try and lose myself in the song to stop myself from panicking, which wasn't difficult as it was really beautiful. I didn't want to embarrass myself by asking what it was called, but I figured out from the chorus that it must have been 'Wild Horses'. As I watched Steve playing, the voice in my head went all serious and newsreader-ish. *He is your dad. That man is your dad. Your name is Cherokee. Your great-grandmother was a Cherokee Indian. That is why you look nothing like the rest of your family. But you do look like your dad. And you probably look like your great-grandmother too. And that is your dad. That man playing the guitar and singing so amazingly. Oh my fricking God!*

The song came to an end and Wayne burst into applause. I couldn't help clapping too and even Raven stopped snipping for a few seconds to join in. Then I looked down at the floor by my chair. It was covered in dark hair. *My* dark hair – and judging from the amount, pretty much all of it. Holy crap! Mum's face popped into my head, the two lines between her eyebrows that always remind me of a claw-print, deep with rage. What was she going to say when I got back home? But then I remembered all the lies she'd been telling me all these years. She'd have no right to be angry at me. Not after what she had done.

'You got any requests, Cherokee?' Steve asked, tightening the strings on his guitar.

'Oh – er –' I wondered if he knew any Screaming Death. Everything he'd played so far had been pretty old-school.

'No, wait up, I know.' Steve strummed a few chords and then began to sing. 'Happy birthday to you, Happy birthday to you –'

'Oh my God! Is it your birthday?' Raven exclaimed.

71

I nodded, trying really hard to stop a stupid grin splitting my face in two.

'Wow! That's so cool!' She and Wayne joined in the singing and I felt like my heart might burst with embarrassed joy.

Afterwards Steve and Wayne started talking about Stevie Wonder and Raven bent forwards so close I could smell her minty breath. 'Your dad is so cool!' she whispered.

'But how –' I was going to ask how she knew Steve was my dad, but I stopped myself just in time. She had automatically assumed it, which meant that I must look as if I belonged with him. But before I had time for that fact to sink in Raven had turned on a set of clippers. I sat, frozen rigid as she worked away, the clippers buzzing at the side of my head like a swarm of angry wasps. After what seemed like ten years she turned them off and picked up a hairdryer. I felt a surge of relief – at least there was still some hair left to dry! And then it was done.

Raven put the hairdryer in its holder and stood back, looking at me as if I were an exhibit in an art gallery. 'Wow!' she said. 'Cool!'

Steve put his guitar down and he and Wayne walked over to join her.

'Awesome!' Wayne said.

'Rock and roll!' Steve murmured. 'Rock. And. Roll.'

'Are you ready?' Raven asked.

'Yes,' I lied, my stomach attempting some kind of backflip.

She swivelled my chair round and I stared into the jagged-edged mirror. Only it wasn't like looking into a mirror, it was like staring through a window at another girl. A girl with big brown eyes and hair that looked as if it had been carved into her neck on one side while it hung down in a silky dark curtain on the other. Even my face looked totally different – more heart-shaped, less long.

'Oh my God!' was all I could say.

'Oh my God!' the girl said back.

'Good job, man,' Steve said to Raven with a wink. Then he looked at me in the mirror and smiled. 'Happy birthday, Cherokee.'

'Thank you,' Cherokee replied.

Chapter Seven

'There has never been a bestselling novel about a blade of grass growing, or a drop of paint drying. The reason for this is simple, my dear. Readers crave drama and if you don't create conflict for your characters you cannot create drama.'

Agatha Dashwood,
So You Want to Write a Novel?

The first time Helen and I got a train up to London by ourselves we invented the 'Which Station Am I?' game. Basically, one person has to come up with a cryptic clue for the name of an underground station and the other person has to try and guess what it is. We'd supposedly invented it to help pass the time, but I think we both knew it was also a way of calming our nerves. We'd only just turned fourteen and although we'd dreamt of going up to London on our own for absolutely ever, like all the big things you dream of, it turned out to be pretty scary too.

The game had worked really well that first day I played it with Helen. We'd arrived in Oxford Circus laughing our heads off and not thinking about terrorist bombers or knife-wielding muggers at all. But now, as I sat on the train home, trying to make up cryptic clues for myself, it just wasn't the same. *'Place where you find loads of cakes – Baker Street. Angry monarch – King's Cross,'* one voice muttered in my head. But another, much louder voice yelled, *'You're going back home with half of your hair missing. Mum and Alan are going to kill you!'* I gave up on the game and sent Helen an epic text about my day instead.

When I got to Rayners Lane station I had to go through the whole oh-crap-what-if-someone-from-school-sees-me panic. I kept my head down, hunched my shoulders over and tried to shrink myself, Mrs Pepperpot-style. It's weird because when I was walking back to Aldgate with Steve I hadn't felt self-conscious at all. In fact I'd felt about six feet tall. But now everywhere I looked I saw sensible haircuts and outfits straight from BHS. I couldn't have felt any more out of place. To try and distract myself I thought some more about Steve and the amazing few hours I'd just had.

When we'd got to Aldgate station he'd suddenly gone all awkward and shy.

'So,' he said, looking down at the dirty floor. 'Do you want to meet up again?'

'Yes!' My reply came flying from my mouth like a bullet.

'Get in!' he exclaimed, grinning broadly and raising

his hand. It took me a moment to realise he wanted to high five. Then he fumbled in his pocket and brought out an ancient-looking mobile phone. 'Can I give you the number for this thing?' he asked, nodding at it.

Inside my head there was a chorus of whoops. 'Sure.'

'Cool!' He looked down at his phone and frowned. 'I don't suppose you know how I can find out what my number is, do you? I'm a bit crap when it comes to all this modern technology stuff.'

I took the phone from him, called my own phone from it and then sent him a text back, saying:

thank you from Cherokee

'Bloody hell, you're even quicker than Harrison,' he said, shaking his head. 'I have to warn you, I ain't the best at texting, the words don't always come out the way I want them to. It's been a bleedin' nightmare at times.'

'What do you mean?'

He sighed. 'Well, I've got this actress friend and one night she was meant to be coming around mine to rehearse her lines, so I texted her to say don't forget to bring the script. But for some reason when she got the text it said don't forget to bring the rapist!'

I looked at him blankly for a second and then I realised what must have happened. 'You must have your predictive text switched on.'

He frowned. 'My predictive what?'

76

I laughed. 'Never mind.'

'You will call, won't you?' he asked anxiously.

I nodded. 'Of course I will – if you want me to?'

He blushed and looked at the floor. 'Course I do, you doughnut.'

We both fell silent. Then he slapped me on the back.

'See you later, Cherokee.'

'See you later – Steve.'

'Oh my God, Claire! What the hell have you done?' Mum stood rooted to the spot in the middle of the kitchen, a large wooden salad spoon in her hand. She looked like a really angry Statue of Liberty. 'Your hair!' she screeched.

The twins came flying into the room, their eyes wide with excitement.

'Claire's had her hair cut. Claire's had her hair cut!' Tom began chanting.

'You look like a boy,' David added.

'Why did they only cut one side off?' Tom asked. 'It looks stupid. It looks like you only had half a haircut.'

'Shut up,' I muttered. My cheeks were hot, but from frustration this time not embarrassment.

'And where have you been?' Mum demanded. 'The school just rang. They said you haven't been in today and apparently you've been absent at least one day a week for the past six weeks. They want us to go to a meeting tomorrow with your form tutor and Mr Richardson. What's going on, Claire?'

'My name isn't Claire.'

'Yes it is,' the twins chorused.

'No it's not,' I snapped.

'Where have you been?' Mum repeated, staring hard into my eyes. I forced myself to stare back just as hard. The atmosphere in the kitchen was a bit like that weird time right before a thunder storm, when the light goes kind of yellow and the air feels as if it could burst into flames at any moment.

'I want you to go to your room.' Mum's voice was robotic with anger. At first I thought she was talking to the twins, but she was still looking straight at me.

'What?'

'Go to your room.'

Angry tears started burning my eyes. 'But why?'

Mum took a deep breath. 'Claire.'

'I told you – that's not my name!' I looked away so she wouldn't see the tears spill on to my face.

'Go to your room!' This time she shrieked it and there was a clatter as she flung the salad spoon on to the counter.

I had never seen her so angry. My heart thumping, I turned and started making my way out of the kitchen. But then I remembered how she'd lied to me for years about Steve being in America.

'My name is *Cherokee*,' I yelled back over my shoulder. 'And I was going to my room anyway. Why would I want to stay down here with a liar?'

For once the twins stayed completely silent.

'What did you say?' I heard my mum call after me, but this time she didn't sound angry, she sounded shocked. I ignored her and stormed upstairs. When I got to my room I went straight over to my CD rack and looked for something to play – something that would sum up how I was feeling. Something loud and angry that would blast through the floorboards and into the kitchen and spin my mum up in a tornado of noise. How dare she send me to my room after all the lies she'd told me? I should be the one sending *her* to her room. I was about to march back down and tell her that when my bedroom door burst open. Mum stood in the doorway, her eyes weird and starey. I couldn't tell if she was angry, shocked or upset.

'What did you call me?'

I turned back to my CD rack. 'A liar.'

A second passed. Then another. I waited for the yells and the lecture. But when she did finally speak her voice was soft and calm.

'So where did you go today? Where did you get that haircut? And where have you been going all those days when you should have been in school?'

'I went to see my dad.' I turned to face her, my hands

clenched into tight fists. She let out a little gasp and stepped into the room. 'What?'

'My dad. My real dad. You know, the one you said was living in America but was actually living in London. The one you made me hate but who is actually really nice.'

Mum looked as if I'd just slapped her round the face. 'But how? Where?'

I went and sat down on my bed so I wouldn't have to look at her. 'He told me where I could find him in my birthday card. The one you tried to throw away.'

'Oh my God!'

I glanced up. Mum was clinging to my bedroom door as if it was the only thing keeping her standing.

'Why are you so shocked? He's really nice, Mum. Why shouldn't he want to see me? Why shouldn't I want to see him?'

Mum closed the door and came over to the bed. 'But what about Alan?' she whispered.

'What about Alan?' I sighed. Why did everything always have to come back to Alan?

'He's the one who's brought you up your whole life, the one who's been here for you through thick and thin, not swanning off around America and –'

'But my dad hasn't been swanning off around America,' I interrupted. 'He's been in London for the past thirteen years – and you've known that all along.'

Mum's face flushed and she began scuffing her foot on the carpet. 'No, I haven't.'

'All right – when was the last time you saw him?'

Scuff. Scuff. 'I can't remember.'

I shifted right to the edge of the bed to make her look at me. 'Thirteen years ago. When I was two. He'd come back from America and he came to see you and you told him to go away. You told him we didn't need him. You told him we had Alan and we were better off without him.'

Mum started twisting her wedding ring round and round her finger. 'Well, we did. And we were.'

My heart started to pound. She wasn't even going to deny it. Or apologise. 'Says who? What about me and what I wanted?'

'You were only a baby.'

I shook my head in disbelief. 'But he was my dad. Why should you make that decision for me?'

She finally met my gaze and I saw that her eyes were full of tears. 'I'm your mum, Claire. I'd been in a relationship with him. You don't know what that man put me through.'

'Oh, yes I do, you've told me enough times. Left you all by yourself with a brand-new baby, never paid a penny in maintenance, couldn't have cared less about his own daughter. Only cared about himself. But they were all lies, weren't they, because he did come back, and you told him to . . . you told him to go away.' My voice started to wobble. I clasped my hands together and swallowed hard.

'But he would have hurt us again,' she whispered. 'I couldn't put myself – put *us* – through that a second time. And by then I'd met Alan and we were so happy. I didn't want him ruining that.'

'But what if he hadn't ruined it? What if he'd stuck around and got to know me? Then I could've had a real dad.'

'And what if he'd stuck around and you'd got to know him, got to love him, and then he'd buggered off again?'

I stared at her in shock. There's more chance of the Pope saying, 'Free condoms for all,' than hearing a swear word come from Mum's mouth.

'What if you'd had to go through the pain I did?' A tear started running down her face, making a shiny trail through her foundation. Normally that would be enough to get me to fling my arms round her, but not this time. I stayed frozen to the bed.

Downstairs the front door slammed shut and the twins cried, 'Daddy!'

'Hi, honey, I'm home!' Alan called out.

'Just a moment,' Mum called back to him, her voice all fake-happy. 'You mustn't tell Alan what's happened,' she whispered. 'You mustn't tell him Steve's been in touch.'

'Why not?'

'Because it wouldn't be fair. Not after he's done so much for you . . . for us.'

'But Steve's my dad. You can't stop me from seeing him.'

Mum frowned. 'Oh, yes I can. I don't want him coming anywhere near you.'

I looked at her in shock. 'But why not?'

'Why not? Look at you. He's back in your life for just one day and you're skipping school and wrecking your beautiful hair. He's a bad influence, Claire. He hurts people and lets them down, he —'

'Stop it!' I don't think I'd ever shouted so loud at anyone in my life. I sprang to my feet and stood right in front of her. 'Stop it, stop it, stop it!' I shouted until I felt dizzy. 'I'm sick of you bad-mouthing him. Don't you understand? I want to be able to make up my own mind — not have it poisoned by you. I'm fifteen, I'm not a little kid.'

'But I know him, Claire. I know what he's like.'

'Yes, and I *don't* know him. And I should. He's my dad.'

'And I'm your mum. And I know what's best for you.'

'You know nothing about what's best for me.' I turned away from her and sat back down on the bed. 'How can you? You're always too busy looking after your perfect twins and your perfect husband and your perfect house and your perfect lives. I'm just the freak who lives up in the attic room –' I took a pause for breath – 'the spare part who messes up family photos and – and – badminton doubles. You have no idea about what's best for me – if you did you'd know why I've been skipping school and you'd have done something about it. And I started skipping school way before Steve got in touch.' I started to cry and I didn't even bother trying to hide it.

'Is everything OK up there?' Alan called from the landing below.

'Yes, yes, we're fine,' Mum replied in a sing-song voice. I felt the end of the bed dip as she sat down. 'What are you talking about? What's been going on?'

All the stuff I'd been keeping bottled up – the months of loneliness and feeling like a freak, the insults and the whispers and Miss Cowardly Davis – all came boiling up inside of me and spilled down my face in hot, angry tears.

'Everything's gone horrible since –'

But before I could say any more the bedroom door burst open and Alan poked his head in.

'What's going on up here?' he asked. 'The twins told me you've been shouting at each other. Tom says Claire's not been in school today and she's had her hair cut. Oh my God, Claire, what have you done to your hair?'

My heart sank. I grabbed my pillow and hugged it to me.

'I need to talk to you,' Mum said. But when I wiped

my eyes and looked up I saw that she had got to her feet and was talking to Alan. 'I'll be back in a minute, Claire, I just want to fill Alan in on what's been happening.'

What, lie to him too? was what I wanted to say. But all the fight had drained out of me. I hugged my pillow tighter and muttered, 'OK.'

As soon as the door closed behind them I heard my phone bleep. I took it out of my bag. It was a text from Helen.

cool - wot a bday surprise! Can't chat now got a date wit boy from library I was telling u about. Will call tomo. Hope u liked my card lol xxx

Helen had a date. Since she'd moved to Bognor-Crappy-Regis she'd had no problem making new friends and now it looked as if she'd even bagged herself a boyfriend. How had she found it so easy fitting in somewhere brand new, when I couldn't even fit in somewhere I'd lived my whole life? It wasn't fair. I lay back on my bed and stared up at the ceiling. Who wanted to fit into a place full of losers anyway?

Then I remembered the song Steve had been singing when I first saw him. The one about the man and woman leaving their town full of losers so they could go somewhere they could win. Maybe that was the answer? Maybe sometimes, when you just can't change things for the better, you have to admit defeat and go somewhere new and start all over again? My phone bleeped and I picked it up. I thought it might have been Helen again, with more info about her date. But when I looked at the screen I saw it was from Steve. My heart did a little leap.

made up 2 have met u. let me no when u want 2 meet chain

I frowned at the screen. Who was Chain? But then I remembered what he'd said about texting and I started to smile. He hadn't meant to say chain, he'd meant to say *again*:

let me no when u want 2 meet again

NOTEBOOK EXTRACT

Character Questionnaire No. 2

Character's name:
Cherokee Brown.

Character's age:
Fifteen.

Briefly describe your character's appearance:
She is short and wiry, with dark brown hair – shaved on one side and shoulder-length on the other. She has big brown eyes and a heart-shaped face.

What kind of clothes do they wear?
Black and alternative, bought mainly from Spitalfields Market.

How do they get on with their parents?
She gets on really well with her dad: an awesome rock musician. She really

looks like him too and everywhere they go people comment on the resemblance. Unfortunately her relationship with her mum is not so good but this is because her mum has been brainwashed into a life of perfection by a life-coaching maniac.

What physical objects do they associate with their parents?

A really cool guitar and a silver skull ring with her dad. And a collection of tracksuits in every colour of the rainbow with her mum.

Do they have any brothers and sisters?

No, but they have a couple of alien life forms from the Planet Obnoxious posing as seven-year-old twin brothers.

What was their childhood like?

Grim for the first fifteen years but then it started getting amazingly better.

Think of one positive and one negative event from their past and how it has shaped them:

All of the negative events happened before she found out she was Cherokee. Stuff like her best friend moving away and getting bullied and having to put up with her mum's husband. The major positive event to have happened to her was her real dad coming back into her life and her finding out who she really is.

How does your character speak?

She is fast-talking and wisecracking and her words are full of imagination and spark. Only dumb-arsed idiots think she talks too fast.

What is their favourite meal?

Fish and chips wrapped in paper, with loads of salt and vinegar, outside on a freezing cold day. And traditional Native American fare like – well – roast bear or something.

Do they believe in God?

Like the rest of her people she believes in the Great Spirit Chief who rules above the sky.

What is their bedroom like?

Her bedroom is full of books and some day there will be a whole shelf of stuff that she has written. Starting with the bestselling book about her own life that will inspire victims of bullying and life-coaching step-parents everywhere. There will be a Native American dreamcatcher hanging in the window and she will have posters of her favourite rock stars all over the walls. No one will ever tell her to tidy up or what she can and can't have on display. She will burn incense to her heart's content because she knows it isn't a 'fire hazard' and it doesn't make the house 'smell like a hippy convention'. It will be full of brightly coloured throws, cushions and rugs and none of them will match. At all.

What is your character's motto in life?
A quote from the Cherokee Indian, Methoataske: 'Your feet shall be as swift as forked lightning, your arm shall be as the thunderbolt, and your soul fearless.'

Do they have any secrets?
Yes. She has decided it is time to fight back. To take control of her life. And to be fearless.

What makes them jealous?
Nothing. Jealousy is a complete waste of energy. Anger and courage are far more constructive.

Do they have any pets?
Not yet. But one day she will have a dog. Or a horse.

Is their glass half full?
It depends on how thirsty she is.

Have they ever lost anyone dear to them?

Her best friend Helen when she moved away. And her real dad when she was a tiny baby. But she got him back in the end.

Who do they most admire?

Laura Ingalls Wilder and Anne Frank. And the Cherokee Indians for their bravery in the face of extreme hardship.

Are they popular?

Yes, with the few people who really count.

Do they love themselves?

Yes. Not in an arrogant way, but for having the courage to stand up to her bullies and for not being afraid to be herself.

What is their motivating force in life?

To get away from the people who don't understand her.

What is their core need in life?
To be free.

What is their mindset at the beginning of your story and what do they want?
She is nervous but excited. She knows things are about to change for good.

Chapter Eight

'I am a great fan of the perfectly placed quotation. Sometimes another person's words can add great depth and meaning to your own.'

Agatha Dashwood,
So You Want to Write a Novel?

On the wall behind my Year Head Mr Richardson's desk there's a poster of the ocean above a quote by someone called Johann Wolfgang von Goethe. It says: 'Whatever you can do or dream you can, begin it. Boldness has genius, power and magic in it!'

As I sat sandwiched between Mum and Alan, opposite Mr Richardson and Miss Davis, I wished I was bold enough to take a running jump out of the window. Mr Richardson liked to use that quote at every possible opportunity: in his talk on the first day of each school year, printed on the inside flap of our school planners, at random assemblies. He was always going on at us about the magic of boldness. But it's very hard to be bold when people are out to get you all the time, and even your teacher won't stick up for you.

'I can assure you, Mr Richardson, Fiona and I are just as shocked as you are to learn of Claire's attendance shortfall,' Alan said in his best I-am-a-life-coach-and-therefore-one-of-life's-good-guys voice.

I glanced at him. Attendance shortfall? Why did he always have to come up with such dumb names for things? Why couldn't he just say skiving off?

'We really are at a loss as to why it's been happening,' he continued as if I wasn't even there. 'All we can think is that it's connected in some way to her friend Helen leaving at the start of the year.'

Mr Richardson nodded and looked at me. 'Hmm. Hmm. You and Helen were very close, weren't you, Claire? It's not surprising you'd feel a bit lost after her going. But it's been six months now; there are plenty of other lovely students in your form. I'm sure that if you tried a bit harder to – er – integrate, you'd have no problem making new friends. Isn't that right, Miss Davis, hmm?'

'Yes, absolutely, Mr Richardson.'

I watched Miss Davis nodding smugly at Mum and Alan and it made my skin crawl. *What about what happened in registration yesterday?* I wanted to say. *What about all the times my lovely classmates hop up and down making fun of my limp and you do nothing to stop them? And what about the times you actually laugh along? Even that time when you saw I had tears in my eyes.* I kept staring at her until she dropped her gaze and her shiny cheeks began to flush.

'Well, Claire, don't you think you could try and make some new friends?' Mum said, turning to face me.

I sighed. This was why I hadn't bothered telling her the truth in the end last night. After she'd come back from seeing Alan I told her I was too tired and didn't want to talk any more. I was still so angry at her for lying to me about Steve and, anyway, she wouldn't understand if I told her about the bullying. Mum made friends the way sickly people catch colds. She just had to pop down to the corner shop and, whoops, she'd found another person to invite around for coffee or exchange beauty tips with. So I ended up spending my birthday night looking up stuff on the Internet about Cherokee Indians and re-writing my Character Questionnaire for the novel.

I realised that all of them were staring at me, waiting for me to say something.

'We only want to help, Claire,' Mr Richardson said with one of his lopsided smiles.

I glanced up at the giant quote on the wall behind him. One word kept jumping out, like it was taunting me: BOLDNESS.

'Maybe you could go and see Mrs Butcher next week, hmm?' he continued. 'Mrs Butcher is our student welfare counsellor,' he explained to Mum and Alan. 'She really is rather fabulous.'

My head began to fizz and pop with anger. *But there's nothing wrong with me*, I wanted to yell at him. *I'm not the one who's making another person's life a misery. Why should I have to go and see the school shrink?*

'That sounds like an excellent idea,' Alan chimed. 'Maybe she could give Claire a bit of help with her social skills.'

My social skills? What about David Marsh and Tricia Donaldson? Since when has throwing eggs at people been the height of social etiquette? Or telling a person they're going to kick their teeth in? Or slamming a swing door in someone's face so hard they get a nosebleed? Why weren't *they* being hauled off for counselling?

'Well, Claire, what do you say?' Mr Richardson asked.

'I don't want any counselling. I don't *need* any counselling,' I muttered, slumping back in my seat and tipping my head forwards so that the long half of my hair fell over my eyes.

'Maybe you ought to give it a go, darling,' Mum said gently. 'What do you think, Miss Davis? You see Claire every day in her form group. Do you think she could benefit from some help making new friends?'

I sat bolt upright and pushed my hair back so I could look Miss Davis in the eyes.

'Y-yes, yes, maybe,' she stammered, 'maybe Mrs Butcher could teach her some – some confidence-building exercises.'

What, after you've sat back and watched my confidence get trampled on for the past six months?

'Hmm, well, maybe we ought to ask Claire what she would like,' Mr Richardson said.

Hallelujah! We'd been in his office for nearly half an hour and finally he thought to ask what I wanted.

All eyes turned to me again. I could practically read the comic-style thought bubble above Mum's head: *Please don't say anything to jeopardise our subscription to Perfect Family Dot Com.*

'I don't want to see Mrs Butcher,' I repeated. 'I don't need counselling,' I looked directly at Miss Davis, 'and I don't need confidence-building. I'm not the one with the problem.'

Mr Richardson cocked his head to one side and frowned. 'That's an interesting thing to say, Claire. It would seem to imply that someone else might have a problem.'

I was still staring at Miss Davis. She looked away, out of the window, as if something really fascinating had just raced by – like her sense of shame.

'Are you having difficulties with any of the other students, Claire?' Mr Richardson asked.

For a split second I thought about telling him . . . but what was the point? Things would only get a million times worse if Tricia and David could add 'snitch' to their list of insults. 'No, sir,' I replied automatically, still looking at Miss Davis. She continued to gaze out of the window.

'Right. Good. Good,' he replied, looking thoughtful. 'Well, maybe you could join an after-school club then, hmm? It's a very good way of meeting students with similar interests.'

I couldn't take any more. I had to say whatever it took to get me out of there.

'Yes, OK, sir.'

'You will?' He seemed genuinely surprised.

'Yes, sir.'

Mum turned and gave me one of her X-ray stares but Alan seemed to have fallen for it.

'Excellent,' he said, with a beaming smile. 'Maybe you could try out for one of the sports teams? Do you have a badminton club, Mr Richardson? Claire loves her badminton, don't you, honey?'

I squirmed. If Alan had ever taken the time to talk *to* me rather than at me he would have known that sports are torture central when you have one leg shorter than the other. I'm always last to be picked for a team, and everyone laughs at me when I crash into the hurdles or fall off the beam. He'd also know that I hate badminton. But in Alan's life no one is allowed to be their own person. It's like we're all extensions of him. So if Alan loves badminton, we all love badminton. End of story.

'Yes!' Mr Richardson exclaimed, as if his number had just come up on the lottery. 'We have a badminton club. What afternoon do they meet, Miss Davis?'

'I'm not entirely sure, Mr Richardson. I think it's a Monday.'

'Fabulous,' he replied. 'You can start next week.'

'Fabulous,' Alan echoed. And that was that. The Claire Weeks Attendance Shortfall Crisis averted.

'Excellent,' I added to the chorus, just wanting to end the agony as soon as possible.

Mr Richardson gave one of his deranged grins and I had a sudden, horrific vision of him leaping on to his desk and bellowing about the magical boldness of going to badminton. Thankfully he stayed put. 'OK, Claire, why don't you run along and grab some lunch before afternoon lessons start, hmm? Miss Davis and I will finish up here with your parents.'

'Right.' I got to my feet. 'See you later,' I said to Mum, without looking at her.

'See you later, darling,' she replied.

'See you back at the ranch,' Alan called.

I made my way out of the room and as I closed the door I heard my mum thanking Mr Richardson. What a joke. I forced myself along the corridor, feeling sicker with every step. The meeting hadn't solved a thing – in fact, it had made it worse because now I had to find a way out of going to the mortally tragic badminton club.

I made my way to my favourite lunchtime haunt – the library. David, Tricia and the gang were way too cool to spend their lunchtime surrounded by books. They preferred to stand chewing gum and swearing down by the bike racks. The only problem was that I wasn't able to eat my sandwiches in the library, but I'd got used to going hungry by now.

I sat down at one of the PCs and logged on to my email account so I could print off my English homework. I saw the email from Tricia straight away. The title kind of made it stand out:

U might have a new haircut but ur still a cripple

I clicked the email open – it was blank. I sat there staring at the words in the title until the tears in my eyes made them swim across the screen. So now she was going to get at me online too. Even when I came to the library I wouldn't be able to escape her. I pictured Mum and Alan and Mr Richardson and Miss Davis, all high-fiving each other and thanking heaven for the badminton club. Even though I hadn't eaten since breakfast I felt sick to my stomach. Three of them didn't have a clue what was going on and the one who did was so scared of the bullies she sat back and did nothing.

I looked at the outline of my head reflected in the computer screen and the sharp contours of my new haircut. My Cherokee Brown haircut. If I really wanted to be a kick-ass literary heroine with a life worth reading about then I couldn't be scared of Tricia. I couldn't. I wiped the tears from my eyes and looked back at the email.

U might have a new haircut but ur still a cripple

My heart pounding, I pressed reply and began to type:

And u might have a heart but ur still a bitch

Chapter Nine

'Now, as an artiste, I tend to avoid scientific language like the plague, but if your novel were a graph you should expect to see three dramatic peaks. The first is known as Plot Point One – a mini climax that propels the protagonist into the second act.'

Agatha Dashwood,
So You Want to Write a Novel?

The first lesson after lunch was PSHE – Physical and Sexual Health Education or, as I prefer to call it, Please-make-it-Stop Health Education. As always, I timed my journey back to the classroom to arrive first and avoid any corridor ambushes from Tricia and David. When I got there Miss Davis was already sitting behind her desk.

'Oh, hi, Claire,' she muttered as I sat down. 'Mr Richardson asked me to talk to you about making an appointment with Mrs Butcher.'

I stared at her. She stared at her computer screen. 'But I thought we'd agreed I didn't need to see her,' I said. 'I thought I was going to badminton instead.'

Miss Davis continued looking at her computer screen, as if she was reading a script from it. 'Yes, well, after you left we had another little chat with your parents and we all thought that it might be best if you do see Mrs Butcher for a while, you know, to help you cope with the pressures you're under at the moment.'

I stared at her. 'What pressures?'

She looked up at me, then immediately looked away. 'Well, your mum told us that your dad, your real dad, had got in touch with you recently and that it had caused quite a bit of upset at home.'

'What?' I was so shocked I had to make a conscious effort to stop my mouth from hanging open. The only person Steve's reappearance had upset was Mum, not me. I couldn't believe she'd told my teachers and risked ruining our image as the perfect happy family. But before I could say anything else the door opened and the rest of the class started clattering in. As I waited for Tricia and Clara to arrive I remembered what I'd read about the Cherokee Indians on the Internet the night before and how fearless they'd been, even when they were forced to give up their land and face death and destruction. I had that same fearless blood in my veins, even if it had been diluted a bit through the generations since my great-grandma.

But before I could think any more something slammed

into my head and I was knocked sideways.

'Whoops,' Tricia exclaimed, as she swung her bag on to her desk behind me.

I looked up at Miss Davis. She was staring straight at both of us and must have seen what happened.

'Careful, Tricia, you nearly had Claire's head off,' she said, her face flushing.

Tricia stood rooted to the spot. Then she looked down at me. 'Good point, Miss. We don't want her looking even more deformed.'

Laughter rippled around the classroom. The side of my head was throbbing and I felt sick. I watched Miss Davis to see what she'd do next.

'That's enough, Tricia,' she said. 'Everyone, settle down please.'

Tricia sat down at her desk. I heard her whisper something to Clara. I heard Clara snigger.

I thought of my favourite bit in 'The Long Winter' when Pa tells Laura Ingalls Wilder that the blizzard wasn't going to beat them because it *had* to give up at some point but they didn't. Well, I didn't either.

'Right, can you all turn to page twenty-seven of your PSHE books please,' Miss Davis called out, turning to write something on the whiteboard.

The minute her back was turned, Tricia leant across her desk and whispered in my ear.

'You get my email?' she hissed.

'Yes. You get mine?' I replied calmly, turning to face her.

She frowned. I knew she wouldn't have had a chance to go online since I'd sent my message but she clearly hadn't been expecting me to reply at all.

'No. Why? What did it say?'

'You'll see.'

Looking confused, Tricia sat back and whispered something to Clara.

'Tricia, do you have something to say?' Miss Davis asked, turning to face the class.

'No, Miss,' Tricia replied sulkily.

I felt a tiny pinprick of hope – maybe the meeting from hell had worked after all? Maybe it had made Miss Davis realise she couldn't just ignore the bullying any more.

'Well then, can everybody read the section on safe sex beginning on page twenty-seven please.'

The classroom filled with the sounds of sniggering and pages turning. I flicked through my book and started to skim read the words. But none of them registered. My mind was buzzing from what had just happened. Maybe today would be a turning point.

'Can I ask a question please?' Tricia asked.

'Yes, Tricia?'

'Have you ever had sex, Miss?'

Snorts of laughter erupted around the classroom.

Miss Davis's face flushed again.

'I don't think that's any of your business, Tricia, do you?'

'Well, yes, actually I do. Cos if you haven't had sex then how are you supposed to teach us about it?'

Miss Davis started shuffling folders on her desk. Her face was bright crimson and patches of red were spreading down her neck like stains. She couldn't crumple now – I had to help her.

'Yeah, just like all history teachers have to be five hundred years old,' I muttered over my shoulder at Tricia.

'What did you say?' Tricia snarled.

'You heard.'

'You think you're so clever, don't you? Yeah, well, you won't be feeling so clever when I've finished with you later.'

I turned right round in my chair. 'Why? What are you going to do?'

Tricia's eyes widened. 'What?'

'What are you going to do?' Something weird seemed to be happening to my blood; it felt like it was swelling inside of me. I could hear it roaring through my ears like an ocean.

Tricia stared at me, her cold eyes made even harder by their rings of dark blue eyeliner. Then she started to shake her head slowly. 'After school,' she whispered under her breath before looking back at her book.

'After school what?' I was practically shouting now.

'After school you die,' she hissed, still looking at her book.

'Oh, really?' I leant over and pushed the book from her desk, sending it clattering on to the floor.

'Hey, what's wrong with you?' she yelled.

I jumped to my feet and leant over her. 'How am I going to die?' I yelled back. 'Who's going to kill me?'

'Claire, please, what's got into you?' Miss Davis asked, hoisting herself to her feet.

Tricia was on her feet now too. 'She threw my book on the floor, Miss. She's mental.'

'*I'm* mental? What about you? You want to kill me? Well, go on then. Do it.'

'Miss?' was all Tricia could say.

'Claire,' Miss Davis said. 'Please sit down or I'll have to send you to Mr Richardson's office.'

I don't think I've ever hated anyone as much as I hated her in that moment. 'Sit down, Claire.'

I bent down and picked up my bag from the floor. Then I pushed my chair back so hard it went crashing over.

'Claire.'

I looked at Miss Davis, clinging on to her desk with trembling hands.

'I'm not called Claire,' I said through gritted teeth, before turning and marching towards the door.

'See, I told you she was mental,' I heard Tricia say as I left.

But for once nobody laughed.

Chapter Ten

'One sure-fire way to start a new chapter with a bang is to plunge straight in with some dramatic dialogue. Try it and see . . .'

Agatha Dashwood,
So You Want to Write a Novel?

'Claire, wait. Please, Claire, come back!'

I turned and saw Miss Davis huffing and puffing up the corridor behind me and for a moment I wanted to slide down on to the floor and laugh and laugh. We must have looked like the naffest chase scene in history, what with her waddle and my limp.

I stood still and waited until she reached me.

'I'm going home,' I said.

'But you can't just walk out of class like that.' Huff. Puff. 'And after our meeting at lunchtime.' Puff. Gasp. She leant against the wall to steady herself. 'Think of what your parents will say. And Mr Richardson.'

I had no idea what Mr Richardson would say but would have been willing to bet it would begin with 'hmm'. And possibly end in 'fabulous'.

'They won't find out,' I replied through gritted teeth.

'But if you leave the building I'll have to report you.' Long lines of sweat started trickling down the sides of her face.

'Well, if you report me, I'll have to report you,' I replied.

We stood there for a moment in silence and I think I was as shocked as she was by what I'd said. But I couldn't hang around to get the crap beaten out of me on the way home at four o'clock.

Miss Davis shifted herself away from the wall. 'What do you mean? Why would you report me?'

But the panic in her voice told me she knew exactly what I was talking about. I felt sorry for her, but I had no choice – I had to get out of there.

'Say that you had to send me home sick.' My heart was pounding. I couldn't believe I was telling a teacher to let me bunk off. There was no way she would agree to it.

'OK,' she mumbled.

I stared at her in shock.

Miss Davis dropped her head and for a moment I thought she was going to cry. I had to fight the urge to grab hold of one of her hands and tell her I was sorry. She turned and trundled back along the corridor. I stared after her for a moment, wondering if I ought to call her back. But then I thought of Tricia and her mates waiting for me at the school gates, and I turned and ran in the opposite direction.

It was just gone two o'clock when I got out of school. As I couldn't go home yet I decided to hide out in the local library for a couple of hours. I skulked along the high street, my heart still racing. I had just told a teacher that I was walking out of school. I had just threatened to *report* a teacher. And I had stood up to Tricia again. In front of the whole class.

I was officially dead.

The back of my throat tightened. How was I ever going to be able to go back to school now? Tricia and her mates would kill me for sure. At least it was Friday. At least I had two whole days to try and plan my survival.

I limped up the wheelchair ramp into the library. I needed a distraction, so I went to the main desk to book a computer. The librarian behind the counter peered at me over her glasses and gave me a quick up and down glare, as if to say, 'Why aren't you in school?' She reminded me of the photo of Agatha Dashwood on the cover of her book. I waited for her to start questioning me but she just pursed her lips and squinted at her computer screen.

'Number five is free,' she said.

I muttered thanks, then turned and made my way through the library cafe.

As I breathed in the smell, I remembered how coffee shops had always made me think of my real dad in the past: picturing him sitting in a squishy armchair drinking an Americano like a character from *Friends*. But all the time he'd been smoking roll-ups and drinking beer in east London.

Once I got to my computer I did another Internet search for Cherokee Indians. This time I found a site that talked all about their settlement in the Great Smoky Mountains. I felt a weird tingling in my stomach as I looked at a grainy photo of a group of Cherokees gathered round a fire. With their prominent cheekbones and oval-shaped eyes they looked so proud and wise. I wondered what my great-grandma had looked like.

I took my phone out of my pocket and texted Steve.

I'd really like to know more about my great gran

To my surprise he texted straight back.

Ape zou in skool

It took me a few seconds to work out what he meant. My heart quickened. Should I tell him I'd walked out? Somehow he didn't seem like the kind of parent who'd be flying up to see Mr Richardson and frogmarching me to badminton club if he found out I was skiving, but still.

I didn't want him thinking I was some kind of juvenile delinquent. But I didn't want to lie to him either.

No — I texted back — in library, got afternoon off.

I waited for what felt like forever for my phone to bleep. When it did a librarian immediately gave a loud tut from the shelf she was stacking and put her finger to her lips. I switched my phone to silent and clicked open the text.

Wicked in picking us Harrison from a job near you could swing by and take you for a drink. Could be these in twentieth minutes

As soon as I decoded his text I panicked. He could be here in twenty minutes! What if Mum or one of her friends saw us together? What if I was caught skiving off with the Devil-dad — for the second day in a row? Was it possible to be grounded for life? Or forced to play badminton for life? But at least if I saw Steve it would take my mind off what had just happened. And seeing him yesterday had made me feel so confident and strong — so like the kind of person who would be called Cherokee Brown. I pressed reply.

Ok - am in rayners lane library on a road called alexander avenue - by the traffic lights. Will wait outside for you

*

I heard Steve before I saw him. At first I thought the massive bang was a gunshot but, as soon as I'd got over the fright, I turned and saw the battered blue camper van pulling up beside me and I realised it must have been the exhaust backfiring. The cloud of white smoke behind it was a bit of a giveaway.

'All right, Cherokee,' Steve yelled over the tinny rock music blasting from the stereo. 'Climb aboard.'

My face burning, I opened the door and clambered in. The floor by the passenger seat was covered in old newspapers and crumpled wrappers.

''Scuse the mess,' Steve said, nodding to the floor. 'Still ain't cleared it out from the stake-out.'

I laughed a bit too loudly and tried to put my seatbelt on, but it wouldn't budge.

'You need to pull it up towards the roof,' Steve said.

'Oh. Right.' I pulled the seat belt upwards and it came shooting out. 'Thanks.'

I sneaked a quick sideways glance at Steve as he drove out into the traffic. He was wearing a blue bandana and a checked shirt over faded blue jeans that had rips in both knees. There was a black leather friendship bracelet round his wrist and the same silver skull ring on his finger as the day before. He was my dad. The realisation hit me like a lightning bolt all over again.

'Nah, nah, nah, nah, nah,' he sang along to the track

that was playing before turning the volume down. 'This is a result, isn't it? You getting the afternoon off when I'm in the area. You'll like Harrison. He's a bit quiet, but he's sound. Sound as a pound.'

'What? Are you picking him up now?' I couldn't even begin to hide my alarm.

Steve nodded as he focused on the road. 'Yeah, he finished at two – you know what it's like in the building trade.'

I nodded, even though I didn't have the first clue.

'They prefer to work from the pub on a Friday afternoon,' he went on with a chuckle. 'He's been doing a job over in South Harrow. Putting up a wall for someone. He's a brickie. A brickie by day anyway, but by night –' he paused to lean across the dashboard to pick up a pair of sunglasses – 'Well, I'll let him tell you what he gets up to at night.' He turned to me quickly and smiled. 'It's good to see you again, Cherokee.'

'Yeah, you too,' I tried to smile back but I felt a bit like a toddler who'd been thrown in the deep end of a swimming pool. It was weird enough being with my real dad and not knowing what to do or say. How was I supposed to act if his brick-wall-building lodger was with us too?

'So, you want to know more about your great-gran, do you?' Steve asked, before hurtling the van round a roundabout.

I clung on to the handle on my door, while trying to look cool and laid-back. I don't think I succeeded. 'Yes. Yes please.'

'Well, she was a bit of a legend, old Rose Cloud.'

'She was called Rose Cloud?!' My nerves vanished.

Steve nodded. 'Yeah. Apparently she was born during a proper mental sunset. The sky was so red they actually thought it was on fire, which was kind of apt because she had a real fiery temper on her when she got going. She was a right stunner too – even when she was older. I've got a picture of her in my wallet if you want to see what she looked like.'

'Cool. Yes please.' My face broke into a grin. 'So was she your mum's mum or your dad's?'

'Mum's. Mum was a real looker as well – obviously runs in the family.' He looked at himself in the rear-view mirror and ruffled his hair before letting out a laugh.

I felt a weird pang of disappointment. 'Was?'

His face clouded over. 'Yeah. Mum died when I was a kid. Breast cancer. I've got a picture of her too – if you're interested?'

'Of course!' I sat back in my seat and stared out of the open window. For a split second I had thought I had a new grandma to go with my new dad. It was strange feeling a pang of loss for someone you never even knew, someone who'd died before you were even born. I turned back to look at Steve. 'What about your dad?'

'He's dead too. Died earlier this year.' Steve turned to look at me. 'You'd have loved him. Everyone loved him. He was a top bloke.'

We sat in silence for a minute as I tried to take it all in.

'Do you have any brothers or sisters?'

He shook his head. 'Nah. Or uncles or aunts. I'm afraid this is all that's left of the Brown family now. Yours truly. And, well . . .' There was another silence and then he turned to glance at me. 'Does your mum know we've met up?'

I stared straight ahead through the scratched windscreen. 'Yes.'

'Cool. And what does she think about it? I mean, is she all right with it?'

'Yes, yes she's fine.' I immediately felt a stab of guilt. 'Well, she's OK. She got a bit upset at first, but I'm sure she'll come around.'

Steve nodded. 'Maybe I ought to have a word with her.'

I thought of Steve standing in our immaculate living room in his torn jeans and scuffed boots and I squirmed. But what if he did have a chat with Mum and made her realise that he was actually a nice guy and me seeing him wouldn't do any harm at all?

'Maybe,' I replied, turning to look at him.

'Cool.'

A new song came on the stereo. Steve reached for the volume and cranked it up.

'This song's blinding. Do you know it?' he asked.

I shook my head – it sounded pretty retro.

'It's "Won't Get Fooled Again" by The Who,' he said. 'One of the best driving songs known to man.' He started tapping the steering wheel in time with the beat. 'This is my *Greatest Driving Songs Ever* tape,' he added. 'Well, Volume Six anyway.'

'Tape?' I asked, looking at the stereo, which, like the rest of the van, looked pretty museum-worthy.

'Yeah, can't be doing with all that downloading shite,' he replied. 'I'm a strictly tape and vinyl man. You know where you are with a cassette or an LP.'

Just then the music started grinding down into some kind of weird audio slow motion. At first I thought it might have been a trippy special effect they had back in the sixties or whenever the song had been made, but Steve immediately leant across and hit the stop button.

'Bollocks!' he exclaimed. 'Tape's been chewed. Never mind, here we are – Acacia Drive.'

We pulled into a residential road and Steve started scanning the houses. 'We're looking for number twenty-seven,' he said.

A bit further down the street I saw an older teenage boy sitting on a garden wall. He was holding some kind of metal ruler in his hand and flicking it up and down really fast, obviously deep in thought.

'Oi, Harrison!' Steve yelled, leaning out of his window. 'Your lift's here.'

The boy sprang up from the wall and put his ruler into a battered old rucksack on the floor, which he then slung over his shoulder. His cropped hair was almost exactly the same shade of golden brown as his skin and he had a really elaborate tattoo on his forearm. He started walking round to the passenger side of the van, then stopped dead when he saw me. I let my hair fall forwards to try and hide my embarrassment.

'Shall I get into the back?' I muttered to Steve.

He grimaced. 'Nah, let him get in the back, he's been working all day. Don't want him stinking out the front – I've got to drive.' He looked across me through the window at Harrison. 'All right, H, this is my, er, daughter, Cherokee.'

'Oh.' Harrison looked at me and kind of half smiled. 'All right?' He spoke with a soft Northern accent.

I nodded back but for some reason my mouth seemed to have become paralysed and was finding it completely impossible to smile or utter a single word.

'You'll have to get out to let him in,' Steve said to me. 'Only got two doors, I'm afraid.'

'Oh, right,' I said, struggling with my seat belt. If

embarrassment had a calorific content, right then I would have been chronically obese. I finally got the seat belt undone and clambered out of the van. Harrison threw his bag into the back and climbed in after it. As he passed me I noticed that he actually smelt really nice. Like freshly lathered soap.

'So, anyone hungry?' Steve asked as I got back into the front seat and started wrestling with the seat belt again.

'Mmm, a bit,' Harrison mumbled behind me.

'How about you, Cherokee? You had any lunch?'

I shook my head.

'Fancy some fish and chips?'

I nodded, even though I was way too nervous to be hungry.

'What about you, H? Fancy some chips?'

'Yeah, sound,' Harrison replied softly.

'Sweet. Let's go to that one off the A40,' Steve said. 'The one with the wicked sauce bottles.'

The van fell silent apart from the chug of the engine and the occasional bang of the exhaust. And the nervous chatter in my mind, which I *really* hoped no one else could hear.

The wicked sauce bottles turned out to be shaped like giant tomatoes, complete with bright green plastic leaves and stems. It was one of those fish and chip shops that's pretending to be a restaurant. It had two Formica-topped tables for people to eat at and a huge fish tank along the back wall – right opposite the fish fryer, which was pretty sick and twisted when you stopped to think about it.

Practically as soon as we'd sat down and the sour-faced waitress had taken our order, Steve disappeared off to the toilet – leaving me sitting opposite Harrison. Complete-and-utter-stranger Harrison. I pretended to be really fascinated with my paper napkin. Harrison picked up a knife and started flicking it up and down the same way he'd been doing with the ruler earlier. I wondered if his mysterious night-time job that Steve had mentioned was as the drummer in a band. The silence ticked by in long, drawn-out seconds – like time itself was being tortured on a rack. I imagined writing this scene up for my novel and heard Agatha Dashwood screaming for some dialogue.

Still studying my napkin, I opened my mouth to speak. 'Steve – my dad – told me you do something at night.'

OH MY GOD COULD THAT HAVE SOUNDED ANY MORE STUPID? AGATHA WOULD BE MORTIFIED! I couldn't bring myself to look at Harrison so I started ripping my napkin to shreds.

'Oh yeah?' he muttered.

I glanced up quickly, not quite making eye contact, staring instead at the tattoo on his tanned arm. It was of a pair of red hearts, but when I looked closer I saw that the hearts weren't hearts at all – they were actually skulls, with hollow gaping mouths and eyes.

'Yeah. I mean, he said you have another job you do at night.'

'Oh.'

I risked peering at him through my hair. He was still flicking the knife up and down, so fast now it was actually blurring. Another few seconds of silence stretched by.

'So what do you think of him then?' he finally asked.

I looked at Harrison properly and I noticed that his eyes were a really startling shade of green. 'What?'

'Your dad? What do you think of him?'

'I like him.'

Harrison nodded and put the knife back down on the table. 'He's a top bloke.'

'Yeah, I know.' My reply came out more abruptly than I meant it to. The truth was, I was actually quite relieved to hear Harrison say he liked Steve. But as well as being reassuring it also made me feel a bit jealous. This stranger with the bright green eyes knew my own dad better than I did.

'He's helped me a lot, since I've been down in London,' Harrison said.

I wasn't sure how to reply to that but thankfully just then Steve came back to the table, bringing with him a suspicious waft of cigarette smoke. 'All right?'

We both nodded.

'You two been getting to know each other?'

We both nodded again, although we hadn't exactly got to know a lot.

'Nice one!' Steve picked up the tomato sauce bottle and started to laugh. 'Cracks me up every time,' he said, giving it a massive squeeze. A jet of bright red sauce shot out of the green stem into the air and splattered on to the ceiling.

'Shit!' Steve and Harrison said in unison before turning round to see if the waitress had noticed. She hadn't. She was too busy nagging a spotty-faced man who was working the fryer.

I bit down hard on my lip to stop myself from giggling.

Steve stood up and pulled his wallet from his back pocket. Then he sat back down and took a battered black and white photo from it. 'Here you go,' he said, passing the photo across the table to me. 'Meet your great-gran.'

I picked up the picture and turned it over. What I saw made me gasp out loud. A beautiful woman of about twenty stared straight into the camera like she was looking down the long tunnel of time to this very table in this very fish and chip shop in Harrow. Her hair was tied in a long, shiny braid and hung down in front of her shoulder. Her high cheekbones tapered perfectly to her ears, and her jawline led to a tiny chin, making her face an almost perfect heart shape. And there, on her right cheek, in exactly the same place as mine and Steve's, was a dimple.

Chapter Eleven

'My dears, it's all fine and dandy knowing your characters inside out, but what do they think of each other, and how do you let the reader know?'

Agatha Dashwood,
So You Want to Write a Novel?

A couple of weeks after the twins were born Alan's mum and dad came to visit. Alan's mum and dad are like a game-show host and his glamorous assistant – everything he says is mega loud, as if he speaks in capital letters, while she just gazes at him adoringly from underneath a fog of perfume. Anyway, when they came to see the twins for the very first time they brought a Harrods bag crammed full of beautifully wrapped presents. I remember sitting on the floor in the living room while the adults talked about boring things like birth weights and christenings and looking at that bag longingly and wondering which present was for me. It turned out that none of them were. They had bought the twins a pair of silky-soft teddy bears. They'd bought Mum a beautiful basket of bath stuff. And they'd bought Alan a T-shirt with NEW DAD printed on it. But nothing for me. It was as if I didn't exist any more.

When Steve gave me the photo of my great-gran and I saw that exact same dimple on her cheek, I finally felt part of a family again. Then he gave me a photo of his mum, Rose Cloud's daughter and my grandma. This probably sounds really weird, but looking at their photos and hearing all about their lives was like finding out about myself too. Apparently Rose Cloud's grandparents were among the few Cherokees who'd managed to avoid being banished from their land by hiding out in the Great Smoky Mountains. Seventy years later Rose Cloud was born in North Carolina, just south of the mountains. She met my great-grandfather Jimmy when he emigrated to America from Scotland as a child. They got married when they were just teenagers and she came back to Scotland with him soon after. Steve said she was a 'proper legend' because she refused to give up any of her Cherokee traditions when she arrived in Scotland, and there's still a village somewhere in Aberdeenshire that makes cornbread and celebrates the harvest by dancing around a huge fire. How cool is that? Rose Cloud and Jimmy moved to east London when World War Two broke out, and my grandma, Steve's mum, was born shortly after the war ended. She stayed true to her Cherokee roots too – Steve said she was a 'wicked' archer and she even got married in a brown, tasselled suede dress!

'I called you Cherokee as a tribute to both of them,' Steve said, smiling down at the photos on the table.

I knew then that there was no going back. Cherokee was my real name and I didn't care what my mum or Alan or the school might say – I was never going to answer to Claire again. But the minute I thought of school I started to frown.

'You OK?' Steve asked.

I nodded, but I couldn't bring myself to speak. In two days' time I would have to go back and face them all again. What was I going to do?

'It's a lot to take in,' Steve said, still looking at the photos.

'Yes.'

He looked up at me, his brown eyes clouded with concern. 'I hope it's not too much. I mean, I know you've already got your mum and your stepdad and the rest of your family. I'm not trying to muscle in or anything, it's just that –'

He stopped as the scowling waitress arrived at our table and started slamming down our meals.

I stared at the fish and chips in front of me. It was all very well feeling like I finally belonged, but what was going to happen on Monday? No amount of photos would see off Tricia and her mates.

'No, it's fine,' I replied, forcing myself to smile. 'I want to know all about them. They're just as much my family too.'

I looked up at Steve and suddenly my eyes filled with tears.

'Hey,' Steve said, putting down his knife and fork.

I could feel Harrison staring at me and I wanted to die of shame.

'Do you want me to leave you two alone for a bit?' he asked. 'I could take my chips outside or summat?'

'No, honestly. I'm fine,' I replied, the words catching in the back of my throat. 'It's just –'

Steve nodded. 'It's all a bit nuts, isn't it?'

I nodded back and gave him a weak smile. 'Yeah.'

I wished I could tell him the truth. But how could I? I hadn't even told Helen how crap things had got at school. It was way too embarrassing.

We all looked down at our food, silent for a second, as if none of us knew what to do. Then, one by one, we picked up our knives and forks. But I still had no appetite.

'So – how are you getting on at school?' Steve asked. I put my knife and fork back down. How had he done that? Did real dads have some kind of spooky ability to read their daughters' minds or something?

'What?'

'School? You doing all right in your studies, like?'

I looked across the table and saw Harrison raising his eyebrows at me.

'Yes. Well, OK, you know,' I replied lamely.

'Nice one,' Steve said. He stuffed a forkful of fish into his mouth. 'What's your favourite subject?'

'English,' I said automatically.

'Yeah? You a big reader then?'

I nodded. 'I like to write too.'

Steve put down his knife and fork and looked at me. 'Oh yeah? What kind of stuff?'

I stared down at my chips and tried to ignore the flames of embarrassment leaping through my body. 'Well, I used to write poems but they're all a bit depressing to be honest – you know, about death and dying and stuff.' *Don't tell him about the death poems!* Agatha Dashwood screamed in my head. *You are supposed to be a fun-loving, feisty heroine. And there's a teenage boy present. Do you want him to think you're a psycho?* I sighed and tried again. 'I've just started writing a book.' But as soon as I said it I regretted it. It sounded pompous and stupid – a fifteen-year-old girl writing a book. But I could hardly tell them the real reason behind it, could I? That I was writing a book to try and force myself to be a better, braver person.

'Bloody hell – that's awesome,' Steve replied.

He nudged Harrison. 'See, I've got a genius for a daughter.'

'Hmm,' Harrison replied. 'So what's the book about?'

'Oh, er, just life and stuff,' I muttered.

'What, *your* life?'

I was starting to hate him. 'Kind of.'

'Wicked!' Steve looked ecstatic. 'Am I going to be in it?'

I couldn't help laughing. He looked so happy and so, well, proud. 'Maybe,' I answered, pushing a chip around my plate with my fork.

'There you go,' he said to Harrison. 'Writing obviously runs in the family.'

Harrison nodded and half smiled.

'What do you mean?' I asked.

'You're writing a book, and I've been known to write a few songs in my time, and your gran was a bit of a poet on the sly.' Steve grinned. 'She wrote a lot of poems about death, too – I think it must be part of the job description for being a poet: must be able to rhyme and write about dying.'

As we all laughed, happiness started tap-dancing inside of me, and the feeling of belonging that had started with the photos grew a bit stronger.

We carried on eating and talking about our favourite writers. To my surprise, Harrison had not only heard of Sylvia Plath but had actually read *The Bell Jar,* and Steve had read another of my favourites, *The Catcher in the Rye,* twenty-seven times (once a year since he had first read it at thirteen).

When we'd all finished eating Steve went up to the counter to pay.

'I've never seen him so happy,' Harrison said, picking up a teaspoon and starting to flick it between his finger and thumb. 'He's been pretty down since losing his dad, like.' Harrison looked so genuine I forgave him for asking about my book.

'Right then, I suppose we ought to be getting you home,' Steve said when he came back to the table. 'And maybe I could have a word with your mum when I drop you off. Just to try and clear the air, if we're going to be seeing each other regularly.'

Panic must have flashed across my face because straight away Steve frowned.

'Are you sure everything's OK?'

I looked over at the fish in the tank, shimmering away under the lights. I couldn't let Steve meet Mum today. It would be a complete and utter nuclear-style disaster.

'Well, it's just that –'

'What?'

'There's sort of been a bit of trouble.' I kept staring at the fish tank, thinking how nice it must be to swim around all day and not have to answer any awkward questions – even if you do have to witness your fellow fish being battered and fried a couple of metres away.

'What do you mean?' Steve asked.

'Well, at school . . .' I glanced at him and saw that his face was etched with concern. 'Don't worry, it's nothing major. It's just that I had this friend called Helen and she moved away at the start of the year and ever since then things have been a bit difficult.'

I sat back in my seat and took a deep breath.

Steve was still frowning. 'What do you mean, difficult?'

I sighed. This was going to be really painful, but I had no choice. I had to tell him something to convince him not to speak to Mum. But I couldn't tell him the *whole* truth. Steve was part of my new life. My book life. The one where I wasn't a victim of bullying. I wasn't a victim of anything.

'Making new friends,' I muttered. God, I wished Harrison wasn't there. I must have sounded like a total loser. I couldn't look anywhere near him, but I just knew those bright green eyes were boring into me.

'You're joking?' Steve looked genuinely shocked.

I shook my head. 'Mum and Alan had to come up to the school this morning to see my teachers about it. So maybe it would be better if you wait a bit before you see Mum – she's a bit stressed right now.'

'What's the name of your school?' Steve asked.

'Rayners High. Why?'

'Must be full of plonkers.'

'What do you mean?'

'Well, if they don't want to be mates with you. Bloody idiots.' He looked genuinely angry. Which, despite everything, made me feel weirdly happy.

'So what happened in the meeting then?' he said. 'If you don't mind me asking?'

'Well, er, they told me I've got to go to badminton club.'

'What?' Steve's reply was so loud even the moody waitress stopped nagging the chip-fryer man to turn and stare.

'I've got to join the after-school badminton club – to try and make new friends.'

Steve looked bewildered. 'Do you like badminton?'

'No.'

'So why are they making you join it then?'

I paused, not really sure how to answer. 'It – it was Alan's idea. He loves badminton.'

'Oh. Right. But you don't?'

'No.'

'Bloody hell! What's the point of that then? Haven't they got a writing club or something?'

I shook my head.

'Badminton!' Steve shook his head again. 'I need a fag. Come on, let's go outside and get some fresh air.'

We all stood up and I managed to get all the way out

of the restaurant without once making eye contact with Harrison.

We followed Steve back to the van where he lit a roll-up. Then we all sat down on the kerb.

I took a deep breath. 'There's something else you should know.'

'Don't tell me – they've got you taking up knitting too?' Steve said, smoke puffing from his mouth. Harrison let out a laugh. I went back to hating him.

'No. It's to do with my name.' I had to tell him. If he was going to meet Mum one day then he had to know. 'My mum – well, she changed it. After you – after she met Alan. She renamed me.'

Steve nodded. 'Yeah, I figured you might not be called Brown any more. So what's your surname now?'

'Weeks.' For some reason I expected Harrison to laugh again, but he didn't – he just started rummaging in his rucksack for something.

'Cherokee Weeks,' Steve said. 'Yeah, that's OK. Got a certain ring to it.'

I shook my head, my face burning. 'They changed my first name as well.'

'What?'

I started picking at the hem on my shirt. 'To – to – Claire.'

'But –'

'I didn't want to tell you cos I didn't want to hurt your feelings. I didn't even know I'd ever been called Cherokee till I got your card. And I love Cherokee and I want to be called Cherokee. That's why I didn't tell you before because what was the point in telling you I was called Claire when I was going to change it back to Cherokee anyway?'

Steve ran his hand through his hair. 'Bloody hell!'

'I'm sorry.'

He shook his head. 'What are *you* sorry for? I'm the one who should be sorry. I had no idea.' He looked down at his scuffed boots. 'Didn't even know my own daughter's name.'

Gloom weighed down on me like a heavy coat. It was all going so wrong.

'I'm sorry,' he said again.

Harrison stood up. 'I'm just going down the road to get some chewing gum,' he muttered.

'All right,' Steve said, nodding absently.

As Harrison slouched off Steve turned to me.

'I'm so sorry,' he said again. 'I feel like I've let you down big time and I –' He broke off and looked along the road after Harrison. 'I don't know how I can even start to make it up to you.'

I took a deep breath. It was all so confusing. Maybe I should have felt angry at him but I didn't. The truth was

I was so unhappy I didn't care how long he'd been away, just as long as he was there for me now.

'One thing I'll say is this,' Steve went on. 'If you do want me to be a part of your life, I promise I'll never walk out on you again.' His voice started to waver. 'I mean it. I'm here for good now – if that's what you want?'

Hot, fat tears started spilling down my face. 'Yes,' was all I could say as I shut my eyes and began to sob. I felt his arm go around my shoulders, then he pulled me towards him and I could feel that he was crying too.

'Sorry,' he kept saying, over and over again. 'I'm so sorry.'

Chapter Twelve

'There is always so much focus on the dialogue between characters when it comes to writing. But what about the silences between them? What could they mean?'

Agatha Dashwood,
So You Want to Write a Novel?

By the time Harrison got back we were in the van and Steve was showing me one of his all-time favourite albums, *Born to Run* by Bruce Springsteen. On cassette of course. As I scanned the list of songs on the back I saw that one of them was 'Thunder Road' – the song he'd been playing when I'd first seen him the day before.

'I love this one!' I exclaimed, as if I'd heard it hundreds of times before. 'Especially the bit where he talks about leaving the town full of losers.'

Steve put his hand up for a high five. 'Nice one, Cherokee – Claire.'

'Cherokee,' I said firmly.

'Bet you she's got it on CD though,' Harrison said, rolling his eyes at the cassette case.

'I'll have you know, my vinyl copy of *Born to Run* is worth thirty-five quid and rising,' Steve replied. 'It's a limited edition, white vinyl,' he added to me.

I nodded as if I knew what he was talking about. 'I don't actually have a copy,' I confessed. 'But it's a great song.'

'You don't have a copy of *Born to Run*?' Steve practically shrieked. 'Right, we'll have to do something about that. Come on.' He turned the key in the ignition.

'Where are we going?' Harrison asked, putting on his seat belt.

'To get Cherokee here a copy of the greatest album on earth. Where's the nearest CD shop?' he asked me.

'Bloody hell, don't tell me you're actually going to buy a CD?' Harrison said.

'Yeah, well, I don't suppose you've got a record player?' Steve looked at me hopefully.

I shook my head.

'Well, then I'm prepared to forgo my principles for the sake of your musical education. I hope you appreciate it,' he added with a wink.

I grinned at him and nodded. 'Absolutely.'

I directed him to the closest CD shop. It wasn't a very big one but I knew it was getting dangerously close to half past four, the time when I would normally be getting home from school.

Steve pulled into the first empty parking space past the shop.

'You two wait here. I might get you a couple of extras while I'm in there,' he said, grabbing his wallet from the dashboard. 'For a surprise, like.' He gave me a wink, jumped out of the van and slammed the door.

I peered into the wing mirror and watched him race off down the road.

'I hated high school,' Harrison said suddenly from the back.

I shifted in my seat to face him. The way he looked I'd have thought high school would've been a breeze – full of football matches, parties and girls.

'Really? Why?' I asked.

But he just shook his head and stared out of the window. Conversation over.

I turned back and looked out of the windscreen, and to my horror saw Tricia's friend Clara and her mum getting out of a car in front of us. I slid down in my seat and put my hand over my face. Waves of panic washed over me. When I was sure they must have gone I sat back up again.

'Who was that?' Harrison asked.

'What?' I turned back round to face him.

'The lass who just walked past looking like she was chewing on a wasp.'

I couldn't help laughing. 'Her name's Clara. She goes to my school.'

Harrison started tapping his fingers on his knee. 'Is your school near here then?' He tapped faster and faster.

I nodded. 'Yeah. About ten minutes away.'

Silence. He was frowning slightly as if he was trying to work something out.

'And it's called Rayners High?'

'Yeah. Why?' Now I was frowning too. Why would he want to know where I went to school?

Silence.

I turned back to look in the wing mirror and willed Steve to appear. After about five minutes – which felt more like five hours in the silence of the van – he did, clutching a carrier bag. He got back into the driver's seat and plonked the bag on my lap.

'There you are. Should keep you going for a while.' There was obviously more than one CD in it. I took them out and looked at them. As well as *Born to Run* there was *London Calling* by The Clash and *Automatic for the People* by a band called REM. I felt a shiver of excitement run down my spine as I looked at the covers. They were cool and edgy – in a retro kind of way – the kind of albums Mum and Alan would hate.

'Make sure you play track four on the REM album when you get home,' Steve said as he revved up the van and pulled out into the road. 'I want you to listen to the words.'

I nodded and put the CDs back into the bag. Then I directed Steve to the road that leads into Magnolia Crescent. 'Can you drop me off here, please . . . so my mum doesn't see?' I asked, feeling horrible.

But Steve just nodded. 'No worries. I hope it all gets sorted at school.'

It was bizarre being with an adult who was so laid-back and who just seemed to get things. 'Thanks,' I said, picking my school bag up from the floor of the van.

'Otherwise I'll be up there to sort *them* out.' He gave me a quick look. 'Just kidding,' he added with a nervous laugh.

'It'll be fine,' I said, breezily, hoping my worry wasn't showing this time. 'Thanks for the CDs. I can't wait to play them.'

Steve grinned. 'Let me know what you think. And don't forget – track four on the REM one. Listen to the lyrics.'

I looked at him and wished he'd put his arm round me again, like he had on the kerb when we'd started to cry. 'Track four,' I echoed. 'OK.' I turned to half look at Harrison. 'Bye.'

'Yeah, see ya,' he replied, still tapping his knee and looking out of his window.

'Let me know when you want to meet up again,' Steve said as I got out of the van. He flashed me another of his dimply grins.

'Sure,' I said, smiling back.

I shut the door and started walking along the street, pulling my back up as straight as possible. Behind me I heard a bang from the exhaust and then the van chugged past me, followed by a cloud of smoke. As I watched it fading into the distance I felt my hope start to fade too. Now it was just me again, with two days at home to get through and then who-knew-what to deal with on Monday at school. I shoved the CDs into my bag so that Mum wouldn't see them and trudged on up the road.

When I reached our driveway I could hear the hum of the hoover from inside the house. I breathed a sigh of relief. Not that I get some kind of freaky kick out of hearing household appliances or anything, but it meant that Mum was home and there was no danger she'd have spotted me with Steve. Now I just had to hope and pray Miss Davis had kept her word and hadn't reported me.

As soon as I opened the front door I was hit by a sickly cloud of air freshener and polish. There had obviously been a major cleaning operation going on, which usually meant that Mum was majorly stressed. Whereas some people turn to drink or drugs when they get stressed, my mum turns to cleaning. Don't ask me why. Maybe the aerosol in the polish makes her high or something. All I know is that cleaning is the only thing that can calm her nerves.

'Hello!' I called from the hallway. All of the gold-framed family photos on the hall table had been lined up like soldiers on parade. I went through to the kitchen. Alan was sitting at the table, tapping away on his laptop. He was wearing his smart-casual-working-from-home uniform of ironed jeans and pastel-coloured polo shirt. Tucked in. Today he'd gone for the candy-floss pink one.

'Claire!' he exclaimed as if I were some long-lost relative he hadn't seen for years. Still, at least he was in a good mood, which meant they definitely hadn't heard from the school. 'How was your afternoon?'

'OK,' I said, going over to the fridge and helping myself to a can of diet coke.

'Fiona,' Alan called, 'Claire's home.'

I wondered whether I ought to push my luck and tell him I was no longer answering to Claire, but decided against it for the moment and went to sit at the other end of the table.

'We were thinking that maybe it would be nice if we all went out for a meal this evening – to make up for not doing anything last night on your birthday,' Alan said, still tapping away.

I frowned. He was being mega friendly given what had

happened in the morning. 'Oh – er . . .' was all I could think of to say. I felt like I might be walking into some kind of trap.

The hoover went silent and I heard Mum running down the stairs.

'Claire!' she exclaimed as she entered the kitchen. 'How was your afternoon?'

'Fine.'

Mum brushed her hair from her face. Her cheeks were flushed from the hoovering. 'We were thinking –'

'It's all right, I already told her,' Alan cut in. He peered over the top of his laptop at me. 'We thought we could go for pizza.'

'Pizza?' The fish and chip boulder in my stomach lurched.

'Yes,' Mum went on. 'You love pizza. We wanted to treat you.'

'So, what did Mr Richardson say after I left?' I asked, with a growing sense of foreboding. Mum and Alan usually *hate* us having pizza – 'deep-pan heart attacks', Alan calls them.

Mum went over to the fruit bowl by the window and took out an apple. Then she rearranged the rest of the fruit into a perfectly symmetrical pattern.

'Well –' she began.

'He was a great guy, very insightful about this whole

attendance business,' Alan interrupted. 'Gave us some excellent advice.'

I wrapped my hands round the icy coke can to try and stop them from sweating. 'What do you mean?'

'Well, he said that you've actually been displaying some of the classic signs of school phobia.'

'School phobia?' I stared at him, my hands tightening round the can.

Alan nodded but didn't look up from his laptop. 'Uh-huh. But don't worry, I had a spare window this afternoon so I went online and looked it up and your mother and I know just what to do.'

I looked at Mum. She walked over to the sink and rinsed her apple under the tap. Upstairs I heard one of the twins yelling. Inside I heard myself scream.

'So what – what do you have to do?'

'Well, we – along with Mr Richardson and Miss Davis – decided that maybe you ought to see Mrs Butcher after all,' Mum said, coming over to join us at the table. Her apple was so red and shiny I wondered if she'd actually polished it during her cleaning fit.

I nodded and looked down at my coke. 'Yes, I know, Miss Davis told me, but I don't think –'

'It's for the best, Claire,' Mum continued. 'Mr Richardson says you've become really withdrawn since Helen left.'

'I know some great neurolinguistic-programming techniques in confidence boosting,' Alan chipped in. 'I thought we could have a session tomorrow, before badminton. Get you feeling good about yourself again.'

I looked around the kitchen. Sunlight was bouncing off every centimetre of shiny work surface. How could the weather be so lovely when everything else was so rubbish? I wished I could tell Mum and Alan the truth – that the problem wasn't me. It wasn't that I didn't feel good about myself. I wasn't phobic of school, I was phobic of people who tried to make my life a misery. But what if they didn't believe me? In Alan's world people aren't allowed to be weak or scared. His world is all about success and 'OH YES YOU CAN!' He would never understand. But maybe . . . I looked at Mum . . . maybe she would?

'I'm going to go upstairs for a bit,' I said, getting to my feet. 'Mum, can we have a chat?'

'Can't we have it down here?' she asked.

'It's fine, honey, maybe Claire needs a little "girl talk",' Alan said, taking his hands off his laptop to do the speech mark gesture.

I forced myself to smile at him and then headed upstairs. Mum followed behind.

'What is it?' she asked as soon as we got to my room.

I stood with my back to her, pretending to tidy the pen

holder on my desk. 'This school phobia stuff. I'm not sure if it's . . . if I'm . . .'

I heard Mum sigh. 'Come on, Claire, I think your teachers know what they're talking about. They must have seen enough cases by now. And, anyway, I think they're right. When Alan looked it up online earlier it said that school phobia can often be triggered by a close friend moving away. And why else would a grade-A student like you start missing school? It makes perfect sense.'

I sat down on the edge of my bed and started fiddling with the trim on my duvet. There was an urgency to Mum's voice, as if she needed to put a label on what had been going on so that she could file it away in her 'taken care of' box. The trouble was, she'd got the label all wrong.

I took a deep breath. 'But what if there was more to it than that?'

She instantly looked panicked. 'How do you mean?'

I thought of Tricia and her mates all waiting for me on the way to school on Monday with something far worse than egg-throwing planned. I had to tell her. 'What if some people at school were making things difficult for me.'

'Difficult? In what way?'

I stared at my duvet until the patterns all started to merge. 'Well, you know, picking on me. Since Helen left.' The minute I said it I felt a little bit lighter. I still couldn't bear to look at Mum though.

'People have been picking on you?'

I nodded, head down, feeling about six years old.

'Who? Why?' Her sudden concern made me want to burst into tears.

'Just some people in my class.'

'But why didn't you say anything about this earlier, in the meeting?'

'Because I didn't want to make it any worse,' I whispered.

Mum came and sat down on the bed next to me. I turned to face her.

'You can't say anything to my teachers, Mum. Please.'

'But if you're being bullied I'll have to tell them.'

'No you don't. You could just take me out of Rayners High and send me to a different school.'

Mum shook her head and smiled at me gently. 'I don't think it works like that, honey. We have to report it so that the teachers can do something to stop it.' A vision of Miss Davis leaning on the corridor wall, sweat trickling down her face, loomed into my head. I felt sick. I should never have said anything. Now it was only going to get a million times worse.

Down below us the twins started yelling and the claw-print crease between Mum's eyes deepened. She sighed and turned to the door. 'Boys, keep the noise down,' she yelled before turning to face me again. 'How long has this been going on?'

'It's fine. It's nothing. Just a bit of teasing.' I pictured Mr Richardson ordering Tricia and David to his office. And them whispering, 'You're dead,' to me on the way past.

'But —'

'Honestly, Mum, it's fine. I'm being silly. I'll go and see Mrs Butcher. I'll do that national linguini programming thing with Alan.'

'Neurolinguistic programming.'

'Yeah, that. I'll sort it out. You don't need to tell my teachers.' I forced my mouth into a smile and hoped that she couldn't see the fear in my eyes.

She frowned. 'Are you sure?'

'Yes!' It came out too desperate, too high-pitched. I forced another smile. Took another deep breath. 'It's fine, honest.'

She stood up. 'OK, well, let's go and tell Alan.'

'Tell Alan what?'

'That people have been bullying you. I'm sure he'll know what to do.'

I grabbed her hand to try and stop her. 'No, Mum, please. I don't want him to know.'

She looked at me like I was nuts. 'Why on earth not?'

'Because it's embarrassing.'

'But why would you feel embarrassed in front of Alan?'

'Because —' I broke off, not knowing what to say. Why had I thought for one moment that I could actually tell her something private without her wanting to run straight to him?

I sank down on my bed. The panic had subsided a bit, but it had been replaced by a dull ache in my head. I would never get her to understand. 'OK, you tell him then.' My voice came out in barely a whisper.

'Don't you think you ought to?'

I shook my head. *Don't cry. Don't cry.* 'I've got a bit of a headache actually. I think I might have a lie down.' Now I knew how Sylvia Plath must have felt when she stuck her head in that oven.

'But we were going to go for pizza.'

'It's OK, we can always go another night.'

Mum hovered by the door for a moment, obviously not sure what to do.

'I'm fine,' I said. 'I promise. I just need to get some rest.'

Mum smiled at me but I could tell she was faking it — I'd become an expert on faked smiles. 'OK then. If you're sure?'

Part of me wanted to grab her hand and beg her not to leave. But another part of me knew there was no point — she'd only want to send for Alan.

She turned and left and I listened to the thud of her

feet going down the stairs. Then there was silence. I pictured her in the kitchen, telling Alan the latest development from the freak in the attic, and I squirmed with embarrassment. Maybe they were right. Maybe there *was* something wrong with me and I needed professional help. But all I wanted to do was live my life without being hassled.

I lay there for a bit thinking gloomy thoughts and wondering if maybe I should write a poem about how bad I was feeling. Then I remembered Steve telling me about his mum's poems and I couldn't help smiling.

I got off the bed and pulled the CDs he'd bought me from my school bag. I took the REM album from its case, placed it into the CD player and skipped to track four. It was a song called 'Everybody Hurts'. I recognised the melody as soon as it started but this was the first time I'd really listened to the words. They were all about feeling lonely and having had enough of life. Almost exactly how I'd been feeling. The singer's voice was haunting. I lay back on my bed and hugged my pillow to me. It was like listening to the world's saddest lullaby. But then, as I listened some more, I realised that it wasn't sad at all. Knowing that everybody hurts at some point was sort of reassuring. I thought of how Steve had chosen this song specially. I closed my eyes and imagined that he was singing it to me. That he was the one telling me I wasn't alone and that I shouldn't give up. And I thought of how we'd sat on the kerb earlier and how he'd hugged me and told me he'd never leave me again and I felt that weird tugging feeling inside of me.

I got up from the bed and went and pulled the photo of my great-grandma from my bag. I placed it on my pillow and looked at it for a while. I thought of how scary it must have been for her, coming to a new country on the other side of the world at the age of nineteen. How lonely and afraid must she have felt? And yet she got through it. I looked at the way she was staring straight into the camera lens, so fearless and proud. The song was right. Everyone goes through hard times. You just have to remember that you're not alone.

The song came to an end. I looked down at the floor and saw the Agatha Dashwood book lying there – her face glaring up at me. I picked it up and opened it on a random page and started reading.

It is up to you to decide upon the theme of your novel. It doesn't matter what the theme is, but by jingo your story should have one.

NOTEBOOK EXTRACT

Character Questionnaire No. 3

Character's name:

Harrison.

Character's age:

Eighteen.

Briefly describe your character's appearance:

Average height and slim but arms are very muscly. Has a really cool tattoo that is more like a work of art on his left forearm. Cropped, golden brown hair. Tanned skin. Eyes as green as jade.

What kind of clothes do they wear?

Scruffy, paint-splattered jeans and T-shirt to work. Not sure what he wears outside of work – probably the same kind of stuff. Scruffy but cool.

How do they get on with their parents?

Well, his parents must be northerners like him so I suppose he calls his mum 'mam' and she probably calls him 'ducks' or 'choock'. His dad is probably quite gruff and manly but he really loves him. In a northern, gruff way.

What physical objects do they associate with their parents?

Maybe a teapot with his mum? Or some hair curlers? And maybe his dad also works as a builder so he'd associate some kind of builder's tool with him. Like a hammer, or one of those silver ruler things that he was flicking earlier. Actually it would be really cool if his dad was a builder cos then he'd be really proud that Harrison had followed him into the same job, but he would never tell him so because he is northern and gruff.

Do they have any brothers and sisters?

I can imagine him having a sister who still lives up north and is a hairdresser. Yes, she's a hairdresser and her name is Sandra or Sharon and she never wears tights – even in the winter.

What was their childhood like?
Northern and fun – with loads of time spent in the local pub and the corner shop, like on Coronation Street.

Think of one positive and one negative event from their past and how it has shaped them:
Maybe the positive event could be getting his tattoo? Or playing drums in a rock band. Although he loves his dad and is happy to follow him into the building trade, his first love is playing the drums and he is constantly tapping out a beat with anything he can lay his hands on, like rulers or knives and forks. Becoming a drummer has given him the joy of seeing a dream come true.

And the negative event could be the reason why he doesn't talk very much. No – it's the reason he hated high school. But what could that be? He can't have been picked on. Maybe his best friend moved away and left him on his own and for some weird reason he couldn't make any new friends. No, that's too much like me. And anyway there's no way someone who looks like him could have had a problem making friends. Maybe it was a girlfriend? Maybe a girl broke his heart and that's why he finds it really hard to talk now. His first true love ran off with his best friend.

How does your character speak?
Hardly ever!

What is their favourite meal?
Fish and chips, judging by the way he wolfed it down today!

Do they believe in God?
I doubt it – not with a tattoo like that.

What is their bedroom like?
Probably quite dark cos he never opens his curtains. Maybe a drum kit in the corner? Rucksack slung on the floor with his work stuff in. Pants on the floor

because apparently all boys keep their pants on the floor!

What is your character's motto in life?
He has something written around the bottom of his tattoo but I wasn't able to see what it was. Maybe it's his motto and it's 'silence is golden'!

Do they have any secrets?
Yes. I bet he has loads. All crammed like precious jewels behind those bright green eyes.

What makes them jealous?
Nothing. He seems too in control to get jealous. Maybe the drummer in a famous rock band? Or maybe he got jealous when his first true love ran off with his best friend. If that actually happened.

What is their favourite swear word?
Probably 'tits' as that seems to be most builders' fave word!

Do they have any pets?
Don't think so, but if he did it would
be a dog.

Is their glass half full?
He drinks from a can.

**Have they ever lost anyone dear to
them?**
His girlfriend and his best friend.

Who do they most admire?
Probably some drummer in a rock band.

Are they popular?
They would be if they talked a bit more.

Do they love themselves?
Not sure – is he quiet because he's shy?
Or is it because he's arrogant?

What is their motivating force in life?
To be the drummer in a famous rock band.

What is their core need in life?
To drum!

What is their mindset at the beginning of your story and what do they want?

He seems pent up - like he wants to break free from something. Or like he's keeping something hidden from the world.

Chapter Thirteen

'The theme for my first novel, The Proud Maiden, was the sanctity of virginity and for my most well-known novel, The Eternal Volcano, it was the abiding power of love. Decide today upon the message you want your own novel to convey.'

Agatha Dashwood,
So You Want to Write a Novel?

I spent most of Friday night working on my book. Inspired by REM and Agatha Dashwood I decided that I most definitely did not want the theme of my life story to be *how to be a complete loser*. I'm not sure I wanted it to be the sanctity of virginity either, but I hoped that if I at least started writing I might find some kind of inspiration.

First of all I tried to do a Character Questionnaire for Steve, but had to give up after the second question as it was depressing realising how little I still knew about my real dad. So I did one for Harrison instead, which ended up being a complete work of fiction because he'd hardly told me a lot about himself. Then I wrote up everything that's happened over the past couple of days.

I've discovered that something truly magical happens when I sit down to write – it's even more of an escape than when I read. My fingers flew over the keyboard as all of the events poured out of my head and on to the screen. Agatha Dashwood says that it's important to let your first draft flow. She says that trying to edit while you write is like trying to 'drive a motor car with the handbrake on'. The speed I was going it was like I had my foot pressed flat on the accelerator. I only came screeching to a halt when I got up to the present moment. I put a new chapter heading at the top of a fresh page and then I stared at the glowing white screen in panic. What would be in the next chapter? Would I even be alive to tell the tale? One thing I knew for sure though, after I turned off my laptop and snuggled down into bed, was that I was going to do everything in my power to make it something I would want to read about. Something that would make me want to cheer not cry. As I clung to that thought like a life raft, I eventually drifted off to sleep.

On Saturday morning I made my usual phone call to Helen. When she first moved away we used to call each other every day, but lately, as she's has got more and more busy with her new life, the daily calls have turned to texts and we only really speak at the weekend.

Although at first it was a relief to hear her voice, after

just a couple of minutes I realised she sounded different. Distracted.

'Have you got someone with you?' I asked.

'What? Oh, no, I'm just lying on my bed,' she replied dreamily.

I could hear some kind of soppy love song playing in the background.

'What are you listening to?'

'Mariah Carey.'

'What?' Helen and I had always made fun of love songs before. We called them 'songs to watch paint dry to'.

'Sophie lent me her greatest hits on CD.'

'Oh.' Sophie was Helen's BFIB (Best Friend in Bognor). It had been my mission for the past six months not to hate her too much. After all, she was actually *from* Bognor. She deserved pity, not hatred. But this latest development was too much.

'But I thought you couldn't stand that kind of music?'

There was a moment's silence, filled by a strangulated wail from Mariah. Then a tight little laugh from Helen. 'Yeah, when I was a kid.'

A horrible, fearful feeling started creeping through me like an icy fog. 'What do you mean?'

'Well, it's different now I'm going out with someone.'

'You're *going out* with him?'

'Mmm hmm.' I could almost hear the smile in her

voice as she spoke. 'Josh asked me out officially last night. Behind the bus station in town. It was so romantic.'

'Oh.' I took a moment to let it sink in. 'That's great news. I'm so happy for you.'

'Thanks. He's absolutely gorge, Claire, he –'

'Cherokee.'

'What?'

'I've changed my name to Cherokee, remember? I told you in my text yesterday.'

'What? Oh. Right. Were you actually being serious about that then?'

I frowned. 'Yes, of course I was. It's my proper name.'

'Yeah, but it's a bit –' she broke off.

'A bit what?'

'A bit weird. Don't you think? I mean I know it was what your mum and dad named you when you were a baby, but your dad hasn't been around all this time and you've been called Claire most of your life. Don't you think you should keep that as your name? It seems a bit strange changing it now. And how are you going to get people to remember to call you Cherokee?'

I sighed. 'I'll just keep reminding them until they do.'

Helen gave another of her Bognor-style laughs. 'It all seems like a lot of hassle to me. What does it matter what you're called anyhow?'

Sometimes it takes another person's doubt to make

you really certain about something. It mattered a lot what I was called. Why couldn't she see that?

'Anyway, what are you up to this weekend? Doing anything nice for your birthday?'

I squirmed. 'Oh, I don't know, I think I'm doing something with my real dad.' The lie popped out before I could stop it, but I could feel my one-and-only friend slipping from my grasp and I desperately needed some way to reel her back in. 'And Harrison,' I added.

'Harrison?' For the first time in our conversation she actually sounded interested.

'Yes, he's this drummer I know. A friend of my dad's.'

'Oh.' She sounded bored again and I realised she probably assumed he was Steve's age too.

'He's eighteen.'

'Oh!' Now I really had her attention, but it felt all crap and wrong. Instead of feeling pleased, I felt sad and desperate.

'So – give me the goss,' Helen said.

'Well, I might be hanging out with him again tonight.' My face started to burn with shame.

'Again?'

'Yeah, I saw him yesterday. We went for something to eat.'

'OMG, Claire. Why didn't you text me?'

'Cherokee. Well, I didn't really –'

'Sorry, Cherokee. Oh my God, this is so cool – both of us getting boyfriends at the same time. We'll be able to compare notes and stuff.'

'Well, he's not exactly my –'

'So what does he look like? Is he lush?'

'Er, yeah, I guess. He's really tanned and he's got a really cool tattoo.'

'Oh my God. You must feel amazing when you're out with him. Can you text me a picture?'

'Well, I don't have any of him yet, but as soon as I get one I will.' It was awful. I felt torn between feeling guilty about my lies and happy at having my friend back again.

'OK, well I've got to go food shopping with Mum now but promise me you'll text me with any goss. I can't believe you didn't tell me about him yesterday!'

'Sorry – I –'

'Don't worry. Look, we'll speak later, OK?'

'Yeah, OK.'

'Bye.' The line clicked dead.

'Bye.' I collapsed down on to my bed and groaned. What had I done? And why had I done it? How had someone I'd only met once and who had barely even spoken to me suddenly become my boyfriend? It wasn't as if I liked him either. He was unfriendly and rude. And what if Helen decided she was going to come back to London for a visit and she wanted to meet him? How would I get out of that one? I'd have to invent a break-up the next time she called. But then she might go back to being bored with me. Arrrgh! My phone bleeped and I jumped as if a bomb had gone off. I picked it up nervously. I thought it would be Helen saying, OH MY GOD! But it was actually from Steve.

all sight Chernobyl - I no ur prob sick of sight of me but I am playing in a gig tonight and wondered if u would like 2 bond along? I could pick u up at about 6. queue x

Bond along? I stared at the message trying to decode it. Then my phone bleeped again.

sorry - feel like we have so much time 2 catch us no

I felt a rush of happiness as I realised what he had meant to say: we have so much time to catch up on. It was exactly how I felt too.

Before I could reply there was a knock on my door.

'Yeah?' I called.

'Can I come in?' Mum asked from outside.

Clearly, being diagnosed as a school phobic had some bonuses. Mum and Alan had never been so polite. 'Yeah,' I called back. The door opened and Mum came in.

'What are you doing?' she asked, slightly nervously.

I put my phone down on my bed. 'Nothing much. I just called Helen.'

'That's great!' Mum said like I'd just told her I'd got a place at Oxford. 'Alan says he's ready whenever you are, you know, for some NLP?'

I forced myself to smile. 'OK.'

'And you're sure you don't want me to talk to your teachers?'

I shook my head. 'No, really, it'll be fine. I was just feeling a bit stressed yesterday, after the meeting and everything. It's not as bad as I made out at all. Actually . . .' I paused.

'Yes?'

'I just got a text from a girl in my class. Clara. She's having a party tonight and she wondered if I'd like to come.' I held my breath and waited.

Mum's face broke into a smile. 'That's fantastic.'

I nodded. 'Would it be OK? It might be a good way for me to make some new friends.'

'Absolutely,' Mum said. 'Where does she live?'

'South Harrow,' I replied instantly. 'Acacia Drive.'

Mum nodded. 'OK.' She came over and gave me a hug and for the first time in ages I properly hugged her back. I felt terrible lying to her but I had no choice. There was no way I was going to miss the chance of going to Steve's gig.

'Right,' I said, pulling myself together. 'Time for some NLP.'

*

NLP might stand for neurolinguistic programming but it's basically just a form of brainwashing.

'What we're going to do is shut down your negative thought patterns and replace them with positive ones,' Alan explained, smiling at me from behind his desk.

We were in his study and I was sitting on a leather chair facing him. In the living room next door I could hear the twins whooping and giggling as they played on their Wii. Is wishing you could be playing with your brothers a 'positive thought pattern'? Maybe I should tell Alan, and try and end this torture before it even began.

'We need to forge some new neural pathways, get you out of your old ways of thinking,' Alan said, turning off his iPhone.

I nodded numbly, reminding myself that if I didn't agree with him Mum would call the school and tell them I was being bullied, and then I'd be dead for sure. Brainwashing seemed like the lesser of two evils.

'So, how about you give me an example of the kind of negative thoughts you have about school?' Alan made his hands into a tent shape and rested his chin on his fingertips.

School is crap. It's full of morons. The teachers suck. I can't wait to get out of there. Every day is a living hell. It's like a survival course, not an education. I hate it.

I looked at Alan and wondered which one to pick.

'School makes me feel lonely,' I said eventually, wishing that the leather chair I was sitting on would turn itself back into a cow and swallow me whole.

'That's good,' Alan replied.

Yeah, great, I thought, but I made myself smile.

'OK, "school makes me feel lonely",' Alan repeated. 'What we need to do now is take that thought and work out its opposite.'

I sat there and waited.

'Well?' he said.

'Oh, you want *me* to do it?'

He nodded.

'School doesn't make me feel lonely?'

He shook his head. 'You still have the word *"lonely"* in there. You need to replace it with a positive, affirming word.' He stood up and puffed out his chest before continuing. 'At school I am surrounded by friends. I feel happy and loved.'

I wanted to laugh out loud.

'Go on. You try it.'

This had to be a joke. But he was still staring at me expectantly.

'At school I am surrounded by friends,' I began.

'Come on, more feeling!' he exclaimed.

'At school I am surrounded by friends. What was the next bit?'

'I feel happy and loved,' he replied.

'I feel happy and loved,' I repeated, in a voice that I'm sure was the least happy and loved he had probably ever heard.

'OK.' Alan sat back down and tapped something into his laptop. 'I want you to tell me about your ideal vision of how school should be.'

'What do you mean?'

'Well, if you could picture your perfect school life what would it include? Most people find it helps if they close their eyes for this bit.'

I closed my eyes. I had to do whatever he said to get out of there. 'Well, I guess I'd have lots of friends . . .'

'Yes?'

'Helen would still be there.'

'But Helen isn't there any more so who would you be friends with instead?'

I thought of everyone in my class and how they were all so settled in their groups and pairs. How I'd tried smiling and making conversation but was always frozen out or talked over. This NLP thing was like torture – all it was doing was reminding me of how rubbish everything was. I felt myself getting wobbly but then thought back to the previous night in my room, listening to the REM song and looking at the photo of my great-grandma and how, as my fingers had flown over the keyboard, I'd had the magical feeling I was writing my way into a better life.

'I'd be friends with Clara, a girl in my class,' I said. 'And we'd sit together all the time and go for sleepovers at each other's houses.' I hoped he couldn't detect the sarcasm in my voice.

'That's good. And how would that make you feel, having Clara as your best friend.'

Totally crap, I wanted to reply. 'Great,' I said through gritted teeth. 'Really great.'

It went on and on: Alan prompting and me lying, until I'd concocted a complete fantasy picture of an idyllic life at Rayners High, complete with best friends and fantastic teachers and places on various school sports teams.

'I think you did really well,' Alan said as he typed something into his laptop. Then he went over to the shelves and pulled out a CD. 'I want you to listen to this every night.'

'What is it?' I asked.

'It's a meditation CD designed to help improve confidence.'

He pressed a button on his computer and the printer sprang into life. 'I've written you some affirmations too. You need to repeat them out loud every morning and every evening. And any time in between when you catch yourself thinking negative thoughts about school. It's all about reprogramming those neural pathways!'

'Right.'

He took the paper from the printer and handed it to me with a flourish.

'Thanks.' I glanced down at it and saw the first one: SCHOOL IS A HAPPY AND NURTURING PLACE. I folded it up and got to my feet.

'Er, Claire?'

'Mmm hmm.'

'Your mum tells me that your real dad has been in touch.'

I looked at him defensively. 'Yes.'

'And you met with him?'

'Yes.'

'Was he –? Well, did he –?'

I waited. It was weird seeing Alan lost for words.

'He hurt your mum very badly, you know.'

I felt a ball of anger well up inside me.

'I don't want to see her getting hurt again. Or you for that matter.'

'I'm not going to.'

He nodded. 'Good. Good. I just think it's for the best if you don't see him again.'

I was so shocked I had to grab on to the back of the chair to steady myself. 'Best for who?'

'Well, for all of us.'

'But he's *my* dad.'

Alan winced. 'That's as maybe, but he's hardly acted like it, has he?' Then he gave me one of his biggest, brightest smiles. 'Anyway, let's not argue about it. Are you coming to badminton? It's a lovely day out there.'

Let's not argue about it?! He was telling me I couldn't see my own dad and I wasn't even allowed to argue about it! My fury must have shown because he actually looked slightly sheepish.

'I don't think I will actually.' *Don't look angry. Give him a proper reason.* 'I've got a ton of science homework. And maybe I should listen to the meditation CD.'

Alan smiled again. 'That sounds like a great plan. Your mum tells me you're going to a party tonight.'

I nodded.

'I'm sure it won't be long before you make some new friends.'

I nodded again.

'You'll look back on this time one day soon and laugh.'

'Yeah,' I said, walking out of the room. Ha ha ha ha ha.

Chapter Fourteen

'I firmly believe that there is no place in literature for the common swear word. Others might argue that it is somehow 'authentic' or 'realistic' to use such language. To which I say, poppycock!'

Agatha Dashwood,
So You Want to Write a Novel?

'Are you sure your mum is OK about this?' Steve said, the minute I got into the van. I'd asked him to pick me up where he'd dropped me off the day before, and told Mum and Alan I was meeting a couple of girls from my class and getting the bus to the party with them. It was scary how easily I was adapting to my new life as a master liar, but I guess when you know your days are numbered – and that number is currently one and a half – little things like honesty don't really mean as much any more.

'Yeah, fine,' I said as I pulled my seat belt upwards and clicked it into place. Steve was dressed all in black this time – black bandana, black waistcoat over black T-shirt and black jeans. I glanced over my shoulder as casually as I could. The back of the van was empty and I didn't know whether to feel disappointed or relieved. The night would certainly be more relaxed without Harrison, but then what would I tell Helen when she rang?

'I thought she might get a bit funny,' Steve said. 'With us seeing each other every day since your birthday.'

I shook my head, wondering if maybe a lie wasn't quite as bad when you didn't actually say it out loud.

Steve turned the key in the ignition and the van juddered forwards and out on to the road. 'The thing is, I'm going away on Monday so I wanted to see you again before I go and I thought —'

'You're going away?' I'm not sure how I managed to keep from screaming it. All I could think was, Mum was right, he's leaving me all over again.

'Yeah. But only for a few days,' he added, obviously sensing my alarm.

'Oh.' I felt some relief, but not a lot. What if he forgot all about me while he was away? What if he didn't come back?

'Where are you going?'

'To Paris.'

'Oh.' My entire vocabulary seemed to have shrunk to that one little two-letter word.

He cleared his throat. 'I'm actually going there to perform.'

For the first time since he'd said he was going away, I was able to look at him. 'Really?'

'Yeah. I've qualified for the finals of the European Street Musicians' Contest.' He gave an embarrassed laugh. 'Not quite the MTV Awards but . . .'

'So you're just going for the contest? Then you're coming back?'

He looked across at me and smiled. 'Yeah. Then I'm coming straight back.'

I smiled back at him. 'Good. I mean, it's good you're in the finals.'

He nodded. 'Yeah. I s'pose. Probably be out first round though.'

'No you won't. You're brilliant.' I felt my cheeks instantly flare up.

But Steve's smile was so broad it looked as if it might split his face in two. 'Thanks, man. Mind you, I'm not sure how much you're basing that on. I seem to remember you passing out at my feet the only time you saw me play.'

'I didn't pass out, I got hit in the face with a bag!'

Steve chuckled. 'I was winding you up, you doughnut!'

'Oh.' I laughed and shook my head. 'So where is this gig tonight then?'

Steve pulled out on to a dual carriageway and I could feel the van's engine shuddering from the change of pace. 'Ealing Rock Festival. A mate of mine is headlining and he's put together a ten-piece band for the grand finale. He's asked me to be lead guitarist. Should be mental.'

I nodded and mentally pinched myself. Could I really be sitting in a van on my way to Ealing Rock Festival, to watch my dad, my *real* dad, perform? And in the headline act?

We carried on for a while in silence, a stream of cars overtaking us on the right. I wracked my brains for something to say. The trouble was I had so many thoughts going crazy in my head it was hard to focus. Finally Steve spoke.

'So, what have you been up to today?'

I thought of my disastrous NLP session with Alan. 'Nothing much. Did some homework and listened to the CDs you gave me.'

'Yeah?' He grinned. 'What did you think?'

'I loved them. Especially that REM song.'

He nodded. 'Nice one. I hoped you'd like it. It always makes me feel better when I'm a bit down.'

I couldn't help looking at him curiously. It was hard to imagine Steve feeling down; he always seemed so cheery and full of life.

'So where's Harrison tonight?' I asked, casually gazing out of my side window in case I happened to blush – I was learning that it's better to be prepared.

'Oh, he's at the gig already, helping set up. He's my unofficial roadie.'

I felt a surge of relief. I'd have something to tell Helen after all.

'Listen, I was thinking,' Steve said, 'about what you said about your school and that.'

I looked down into my lap. 'Mmm.'

'Well, is there anything I can do? You know, to help. You can tell me to butt out if you like but –' Steve took a roll-up from behind his ear and reached for his lighter on the dashboard. 'Do you mind?'

I shook my head. He rolled his window all the way down and lit up.

'This is weird, innit?' He looked at me and smiled kind of shyly.

'What do you mean?'

'Well, when I sent you that card, part of me was worried that if we met there wouldn't be anything. We wouldn't feel anything. It would be like being with a stranger. But it's not. You're my daughter.' He shook his head and laughed and plumes of smoke streamed from his mouth. 'You're my bleedin' daughter. Sorry. But bloody hell!'

I started laughing too, suddenly fizzing with happiness. 'I know. You're my dad!'

'Holy moley!'

'Holy moley!'

He was laughing so much now the van swerved across the road. It was only the beep from an oncoming car that

179

got us to shut up. Steve turned to me, his face suddenly serious again. 'Look, if there's any way I can help. You know — with school and that.' He turned to look back at the road. 'I know I probably don't have any right to say this, but I want to look out for you.'

'Thank you.' My voice cracked slightly. How could it be that I felt more comfortable, more myself in that moment with Steve than I had ever done with my mum? In recent memory at least. 'Can I ask you something?'

'Yeah. Of course.'

'Were you ever — did you ever — ?' I sighed. Come on, I told myself, he's not going to laugh at you or be ashamed of you, he's your dad. He wants to look out for you. He just told you that.

'What?' he asked.

'Did you ever have any problems, when you were at school?'

'What do you mean?'

'Well, with any of your teachers, or the other kids?'

'Is someone giving you grief?' He looked so concerned I instantly felt bad.

'No, I was just wondering how you got on, that's all.'

He turned back to the road. 'When my mum died I did go off the rails a bit.' He gave one of those dry little laughs that aren't really laughs at all. 'You could say I didn't get back on them again till Stan, my dad, got ill a year ago.'

'What do you mean?'

'I had the rage, man. Like a proper mad fire burning inside of me. I wanted to punish everyone for taking my mum away.'

I nodded, not daring to speak, willing him to tell me more.

He sighed. 'I'm not sure if it was Mum dying or if I would have felt like that anyway, but I hated school. Hated the way we were all supposed to be exactly the same and do exactly the same and never question anything.' He glanced over at me. 'Sorry. I shouldn't really be saying this to you, I'm sure schools are much better these days, but back then . . .' He took a long drag on his cigarette.

'I don't know,' I said. 'I don't think that much has changed.'

He laughed. 'Have you heard the song by Pink Floyd – 'Another Brick in the Wall'?'

I shook my head. 'Don't think so.'

'Well, that's another one I'll have to get you then. It pretty much sums up how I felt about school. It came out when I was about thirteen. Became my anthem.' He took another drag on his cigarette and blew a thin stream of smoke out of his window. 'You having a tough time then? Apart from the friends thing, like.'

I stared straight ahead of me and nodded.

'Teachers on your case?'

'Not really, it's –' The words were stuck in my throat.

'The other kids?'

I nodded again.

'Giving you grief?'

I nodded yet again, hardly daring to breathe. There was a moment's silence. I kept staring straight ahead.

'Does your mum know?'

'Yes.'

'And what did she say?'

'She wanted to tell the teachers but I told her no.'

'Yeah, you're right,' Steve said, overtaking a bus that was pulling into a stop in front of us.

'I am?'

He nodded. 'Course. You tell the teachers and it just makes it worse. You need to fight back.'

He must have heard my sigh because suddenly he was turning into a side road and bringing the van to a stop. He hung his cigarette hand out of the window and turned to face me. 'But it's hard to fight back, right?'

I nodded, trying really hard not to cry. I thought of my writing the night before and how determined I was to be a kick-ass heroine, not the sappy victim that everyone hates and wants to die a slow and painful death by page ten.

'Do you want me and Harrison to come down? Sort them out for you?' He looked deadly serious now.

I wasn't exactly sure what he meant but I shook my

head. 'No. Don't tell Harrison, please. It's embarrassing.'

Steve shook his head. 'You don't need to worry about getting embarrassed in front of Harrison. He knows the score.'

I stared at him blankly.

'You know that flicking thing he does, with his ruler and that?'

'Yes.'

'Well, he can't control it. It's like a kind of Tourettes or something, but instead of swearing he has to shake stuff. He's not mental or anything. He's actually one of the most sorted geezers I've ever met. It's just that he needs to shake stuff.' Steve started to grin. 'I keep telling him he ought to go for a job in a cocktail bar.'

'So he's not a drummer?'

'Eh?'

I felt myself start to blush. I'd been so convinced of the character I'd created for Harrison I'd actually started believing it was true. 'It was just that when I saw him doing it I thought he must be a drummer or something. I thought that was the job he did at night-time. The one you told me about. I thought maybe that was how you knew him – through your music.'

Steve chuckled. 'Blimey, had it all worked out, didn't you? Nah, I know him through his Uncle Kev. He was a roadie for a band I was in back in the nineties. When

Harrison decided he wanted to come and live in London, Kev put him in touch with me. He ain't a drummer. But he does know what it's like to get shit off people at school.' He flicked his cigarette butt out of the window. I watched it glowing red on the pavement like a tiny zombie's eye. 'So, what are you going to do about it then?'

'What do you mean?'

'Well, it sounds to me like you need a plan.' He leant back in his seat. 'The thing about bullies is they only pick on the people they know won't fight back. So how are you going to fight back?'

I shrugged. 'I don't know. I suppose I started fighting back on Friday . . .'

I told him about the email I'd sent to Tricia and how I'd stood up to her in class. He immediately put up his hand for a high five. 'Yeah, man, that's what I'm talking about! I bet she steers well clear of you on Monday now.'

I gave him a weak smile. Tricia steering clear of *me* was one scenario I hadn't contemplated for a second. 'Do you think?'

He nodded. 'But just in case, how about I come and pick you up from school? I can go to Paris after. I ain't buggering off without knowing you're all right.'

Relief raced through me. 'That would be great. Thank you.'

Steve shook his head and laughed. 'No need to thank me, man. I'm your dad.' He looked at me. 'I'm your bloody dad.'

'Holy moley!' we both said together.

Chapter Fifteen

'Make sure you set every new scene. If your characters have moved from the kitchen into the parlour make sure you let your reader know.'

Agatha Dashwood,
So You Want to Write a Novel?

Ealing Rock Festival was in a massive park in – surprise, surprise – Ealing. It had started at midday so by the time we got there, just as the sun was setting, it was crammed full of sunburnt people lolling about on the dry grass, eating food from silver cartons and drinking wine and beer from plastic cups. A wall of food stalls went right around the edge of the park – selling everything from fish and chips and burgers to curry and Polish sausages. And right in the centre there was a huge marquee with MAIN STAGE written on the side.

'Come on,' Steve said, leading me round the side of the marquee. I glanced through an open flap in the canvas. A band were playing on a stage right at the back, and in front of them, bobbing and swaying in the shadows, was a crowd of dancing people. It was like a circus Big Top had been invaded by a rock 'n' roll army.

'Is that where you're going to be playing?' I asked, slightly in awe.

Steve nodded. 'Yeah, man!'

As we got to a gate at the back of the marquee he fished in his pocket and handed me something. 'Here, put this on.'

It was a plastic card on a ribbon, emblazoned with the words BACKSTAGE PASS. I started mentally composing my first text to Helen.

'All right, Steve,' a burly security man yelled at us from the other side of the gate. His face was covered with a tattoo of a spider's web.

'All right, Dave,' Steve replied. 'This is my daughter, Cherokee.'

I looked at the man and he grinned at me, causing a gaping hole to appear in the web. 'Yeah, can see that, mate. No doubting who's the daddy there.'

Steve looked at me and smiled proudly. 'Yeah, man, got the Brown looks all right. And the charm.' He nudged me playfully and I grinned.

The security guard laughed and waved us through to a grassy area behind the main stage. After the hustle and bustle out front, this part of the park was quiet and shaded with trees. We walked past a couple of portacabins that were signposted DRESSING ROOMS and round to a smaller, bright red tent.

'The VIP bar,' Steve said. 'Fancy a drink?'

I nodded, mentally composing my second text to Helen, and followed him. There were about twenty people sat outside the red tent, drinking and smoking. They all looked as if they'd swaggered straight off the pages of a rock magazine and, judging from the way they started grinning and waving when they saw us, most of them knew Steve.

Stepping into the tent was like stepping into a giant valentine's heart. Crimson chiffon drapes hung from the walls and ceiling, even the air seemed red. In one corner there was a tiny bar, framed with twinkling fairy lights, and dotted all around were little wooden tables. Each of the tables had a candle centrepiece with an ivy wreath twisted around the base.

As soon as I saw Harrison sitting at a table in the far corner my mouth went dry and I looked away.

'Oi, H. What you drinking?' Steve shouted to him.

Harrison looked up from the notebook he'd been writing in, but didn't smile. 'Coke, please,' he replied.

Steve looked at me. 'How about you?'

'Same, please,' I said.

I followed Steve to the bar and waited while he ordered the drinks.

'I'm gonna have to go and find my mate Bob and do a sound check,' he said, looking at his watch. 'Will you be all right with Harrison?'

I nodded, but inside my head a voice screamed, *Please no!*

I took the drinks from Steve and made my way over to Harrison's table. 'Is it OK if I sit . . .' My words got stuck, as if they were too embarrassed to leave my mouth and had decided to cower in my throat instead.

'Yep,' he replied, without even looking up from his pad. Now I was closer I could see he wasn't writing at all. He was drawing. A pile of coloured pencils were lying on the table in front of him.

'Oh. You're drawing,' I said. I could practically hear Agatha Dashwood groaning at my knack for stating the obvious.

'Yep.'

I could see one of his legs bouncing up and down as he concentrated on the pad and I thought of what Steve had told me about him earlier. That must have been why Harrison hated school. He'd been bullied too.

I sat down and tried to see what he was working on but he'd hunched right over the pad with one arm around it, as if he was trying to stop me from looking. So I got my phone out from my pocket and started texting Helen.

am at a rock festival - sitting in the vip bar
backstage waiting to see my dad play - having a
right laugh with Harrison xxx

My hand hovered over the send button and I sighed. If I had to lie to Helen to get her to still be my friend could I really say that she *was* my friend any more? She would be friends with the pretend me, with my pretend boyfriend and pretend life. I deleted the message and sat back in my chair. Then I looked around the bizarre red tent. In the three days I'd known Steve I'd been to so many amazing new places – why did I even need to invent a boyfriend? I thought of the day on the Southbank when I'd found Agatha Dashwood's book and decided to write a novel. Back then I thought I'd have to write fiction to make my life interesting. It was weird that since then I hadn't had to make up anything at all – my life had suddenly *become* interesting. Maybe the Agatha Dashwood book was enchanted? Maybe she was a witch? She certainly looked a bit witchy. I smiled to myself.

'What's funny?'

I jumped and looked over at Harrison. He was still drawing away in his pad.

'What?'

'Why are you smiling?'

I felt my cheeks start to burn and was grateful for the red all around to camouflage them. 'Oh, I was just thinking about something.' Well, duh! Of course I was thinking about something. Was it actually possible to not be thinking anything while you were awake? What was it about Harrison that brought out my inner moron? My cheeks flamed even redder.

'So are you gonna share it then,' he murmured.

'What?'

He continued drawing. 'Are you gonna share what you were thinking about that made you smile?'

'Oh. No, not really. It was just something stupid.'

'Oh.'

There was an awkward silence.

My phone bleeped on the table in front of me. I grabbed it, relieved to have something to do. But it was a text from Mum. My heart started pounding as I opened it. Had she found out I'd lied about the party? My eyes scanned the tiny words.

Hope you're having a nice time at your party. Let me know if you want me to pick you up later love mum xx

I'd told her I'd be getting a lift back with one of the girls who lived nearby – one of the fictional girls I'd gone to the fictional party with. I pressed reply.

Thank u - should be fine - clara's mum has said she'll give me lift home xxx

I pressed send and imagined my lie winging its way to

Mum's inbox like a poisoned arrow. When Steve got back from Paris I would have to tell her that I was going to see him regularly and that she and Alan couldn't stop me. I didn't care how much hassle it caused, it had to be better than lying to her all the time.

'Summat up?' Harrison asked from across the table, making me jump.

'What? Oh, no. Just had to text someone.' Arrrgh! There I went again, stating the obvious. I wondered how long Steve would be at his soundcheck. I looked at Harrison's hands and saw that they were flecked with metallic paint. 'So what are you working on?' I regretted the question as soon as I'd asked it. But this time he actually stopped what he was doing and looked at me. I stared down at the candle flickering away in the middle of the table.

'Just a design.'

I looked back at him. 'Oh, right, cool. What for?'

Now he looked away. 'Summat I'm working on.'

'Oh. Working on for what?'

Silence.

Harrison went back to his drawing and I felt suddenly pissed off. Why did he have to be so rude? I was only trying to make conversation. It wasn't my fault I'd been left with him. I got to my feet, deciding to go and have a wander about outside.

'Where are you going?' Harrison asked, but I couldn't be bothered to answer just for him to blank me again, so I did his favourite trick and pretended I hadn't heard, and headed for the exit. I didn't even try to hide my limp.

Outside the sun had set completely and the sky had turned an inky blue. I looked up at the first pale glimmer of stars and took a deep breath. Over in the main tent I could hear the strum of guitars being tuned and I felt a rush of nerves for Steve. How must it feel getting up on that stage in front of all those people? It was brave enough of him to go busking in Spitalfields but this was something else. It felt good having a dad who was so fearless; it made me feel as if maybe I could be that strong too. I sat down on the grass by a tree and got my phone out. I had two new messages. One from Mum saying OK and one from Helen:

R u with ur new man ;) xxxx

I stuffed my phone back into my pocket. Then I lay back on the grass and looked up at the stars. Once, when I was little and Mum and Alan had taken me camping, I'd told Alan that I thought stars were wishes that had come true. He looked at me like I was crazy and said, 'Actually, Claire, they're giant balls of plasma and their light takes so long to reach us that the ones you're looking at don't even exist any more.' I think that was the first time I realised that if I was going to get along with Alan I'd have to squash my real personality into a box and keep it hidden from view.

I looked at the stars now and thought of how magical life had seemed when I was little. The way I believed my doll's house dolls came to life when I slept and that you could get to a magical kingdom through the back of your wardrobe.

'Hey, Cherokee.' I scrambled into a seated position and saw Harrison standing in the shadows of the tent looking at me. 'What're you doing?'

All of a sudden I didn't care about seeming cool any more. I didn't care what he thought of me.

'I'm looking at the stars,' I said, lying back down.

'Oh,' he replied, and the next thing I knew he was lying down on the ground beside me. I fought the sudden urge to giggle.

'Did you know that human beings are actually made from stardust?' he said after a while.

I turned my head to look at him. He was staring straight up at the sky. 'What?'

'Yeah – everything in existence was originally created from exploded stars. Or summat like that.'

'Wow!' I looked back at the stars twinkling down on us. So that would make us all walking wishes then. What a cool idea.

'All right, what's going on here then?'

We both sat up at the sound of Steve's voice. He was coming out of the back of the main tent with another man. 'Having a nap, are we?' he said, looking at us with a wry smile.

Harrison and I scrambled to our feet. 'We were looking at the stars,' he said, staring down at the ground, embarrassed.

'Bloody hell, what kind of gear have they been smoking?' the man with Steve said with a laugh. He had long grey hair tied back in a ponytail and was wearing a T-shirt that said, 'DON'T MAKE ME COME DOWN THERE' – GOD. I liked him immediately.

'Cherokee, this is my mate Bob I was telling you about. Bob, this is my daughter, Cherokee.'

The man came over to me and shook my hand. 'Nice to meet you, Cherokee. Looking forward to seeing your old man play?'

I nodded, not wanting to say anything in case I made a fool of myself.

'Hey, less of the old man.' Steve grinned at Bob and then turned to us. He suddenly looked a bit nervous. 'I'm just gonna have a slash. Where are you guys watching it from – the wings?'

Harrison looked at me and shrugged. 'Don't mind. Where do you want to watch from?'

'Hmm, the wings?' I said, not entirely sure what 'the wings' meant.

'OK, follow me,' Bob said, leading us to the flap in the tent he and Steve had just come out of. Inside it was pitch black. Bob led us up a short flight of metal stairs and through a black curtain. We emerged into a sudden burst of light. We were standing in a small alcove to the right-hand side of the stage. Just a few metres from me I could see three drum kits lined up. A couple of men were already standing there waiting. One was holding a saxophone and the other a trumpet. 'All right, boys, this is Steve's daughter,' Bob said. The men nodded but they looked distracted. I stood behind them with Harrison, trying to make myself as inconspicuous as possible. Out in front of the stage I could hear the chatter and laughter of the crowd. It sounded as if there were thousands of people out there waiting. I shivered as I thought of Steve and the rest of the band having to actually walk out into that bright light and face them. I felt someone tap my shoulder and turned to see Steve standing behind me in the shadows.

'All right?' he whispered and I could see he looked really nervous now.

'Good luck,' I said.

He put his hand up and I high-fived him. 'Rock and roll!' he whispered.

'Rock and roll!' I whispered back.

'All right, lads?' Bob said. The other men all nodded and Bob ran on to the stage. The murmur from the crowd turned into a roar.

'Good evening, Ealing!' Bob bellowed into the mic and the crowd bellowed back.

I felt terrified.

'How're you doing?' Bob yelled.

The crowd erupted into another roar. Beside me Steve clenched his fists.

'Are you ready to rock?'

'Yeah!' the crowd yelled.

'Then I'd like you to welcome to the stage, The Ealing Ten.'

Steve and the other men looked at each other and smiled and then ran out on to the stage. I stepped forwards and watched as Steve went over to a row of guitars at the front and picked one up. Then he went and stood at a microphone next to Bob's. Some other musicians had run on from the other side of the stage and one of them, a big, Mexican-looking man, came and stood in the middle of the drum kit right by me. He picked a massive stick from the floor and sent it swinging into a huge gong behind him. And that was it. The rest of the band started playing and the audience went crazy.

I took another step forwards and peered around the

corner of the black curtains and across the stage. The tent was filled to the brim with a sea of people, all moving in time to the music. Goosebumps erupted all over my body. I turned to Harrison and grinned.

'This is –' I broke off; I couldn't find the right word to describe it.

He nodded and smiled back, and his whole face softened. I realised it was the first time he'd ever properly smiled at me.

The gig flashed by in a blur. It didn't matter that I didn't know most of the songs. It was incredible being so close to the band, feeling every drum beat reverberate through my body, seeing the beads of sweat shimmer on the musicians' faces and the light bouncing off the cymbals. It was as if the music was alive, swooping through the air and dive-bombing into the very heart of me. Every so often I would glance at Harrison beside me and see that he was as lost in it as I was. When it got to the last song I thought I might actually take off and spiral up through the hot night air into the roof of the tent. The song went on and on, with each musician getting his chance to do a solo. When it got to Steve's turn I bit down on my bottom lip and prayed he would be OK. All of the other musicians fell silent, apart from one of the drummers, who continued tapping out a gentle beat. As Steve's guitar playing got louder and louder the crowd got quieter and quieter. I think everyone had actually stopped breathing in the end as his fingers flew faster and faster over the strings. Finally, his solo came to an end and the whole place went crazy. I turned to Harrison with a look of shock on my face.

'Great, isn't he?' Harrison said.

I nodded, feeling as if I might just burst with happiness. When I looked back on to the stage I saw that Steve was staring right at me and waving. I waved back madly and then started clapping him. He was my dad. And I felt so, so proud.

'Rock and roll, man!' Steve exclaimed as we made our way out of the tent after the gig. 'Rock. And. Roll!'

Sweat was streaming down his tanned face and his hair was as wet as if he'd just had a shower. The other musicians all came over and exchanged high fives and slaps on the back.

'Awesome solo, Steve,' Bob said.

Steve slung his arm around my shoulder. 'Yeah, well, had to pull out all the stops with my daughter watching, didn't I?'

'Nice one, mate,' Harrison said, smiling shyly at him. 'I thought you were gonna blow the roof off.'

He and Steve laughed. Then Steve looked at me and

said, 'Right, better get you home. Don't wanna get in trouble with your mum.'

My heart sank. 'It's OK. I can stay a bit longer.'

Steve shook his head. 'Nah, come on. I don't wanna blow it.'

'So where have you told her you are tonight?' Steve asked once we were all in the van and driving back to Rayners Lane.

'What do you mean?' I looked out of the window and tried to sound as unbothered as I could.

'Well, you got me to pick you up from round the corner so I assume she don't know you're out with me.'

My cheeks started to burn. I wondered if Steve and Harrison could actually see them glow.

'I said I was going to a party,' I muttered.

'Oh.'

I glanced sideways at Steve to try and see if he was upset with me, but it was impossible to tell in the dark.

'I reckon the sooner I have a chat with her the better,' he said eventually. 'Can't have you lying to her every week.'

I felt a shiver of excitement. He wanted to see me every week.

Steve pulled into the road leading on to mine. 'And I'm not happy dropping you off here this late at night,' he said.

'I could walk her round the corner,' Harrison muttered from the back.

My stomach lurched – I felt sick and relieved at the same time.

Steve sighed. 'All right then.' He turned to me. 'You still want me to come and meet you from school on Monday?'

I nodded, hoping the darkness hid my shame.

'Right then. I'll be waiting for you out front. And remember what I said. You've got to fight back.' He tapped the side of his head with his hand. 'Up here. Don't let the bastards get you down.'

I nodded, suddenly wishing that I could hug him. He put his hand up. 'High five?'

I met his hand with mine. But this time he caught hold of it. 'I mean it. Don't let 'em get to you.'

I cringed as I thought of Harrison listening in the back. I nodded swiftly, undid my seat belt and got out of the van.

'See you Monday, Cherokee.'

'See you Monday – Steve.'

I was too embarrassed to say anything to Harrison on the way to my house so we ended up making the whole journey in complete silence. It was only about a minute's walk but it felt like an entire day. Then, just as we arrived and I took my keys from my pocket, he spoke.

'I was drawing a picture,' he said softly.

'What?' I stared at him. He looked down at the ground.

'Earlier. In the bar. I was drawing a picture.'

'Oh. Yeah, I thought so.'

'I'm a graffiti artist.' He shifted from one foot to the other. 'At night. That's what I do. Tonight I was planning my next piece.'

I thought of the metallic paint on his hands. Then I thought of the really cool graffiti art lining the walls of the Southbank where the skaters hang out and how I'd thought it looked a lot better than some of the things I've seen in galleries.

'Wow,' I breathed. Then, before I could stop myself, I said, 'Can I see it?'

He looked at me and smiled, but as usual his eyes didn't give anything away. 'Oh, you'll see it,' he said, before turning and walking back down the road.

NOTEBOOK EXTRACT

Dear Writing Journal,

It's Sunday morning and I'm having a panic attack. I've written up everything that happened yesterday and I now have a whole FIFTEEN chapters in my book. It was so cool writing about the concert – it was like being there all over again. But now I'm up to the present moment so I've got to wait for something to happen. I could write a chapter about lying on my bed all day but I think that would be a bit like writing about watching paint dry or grass grow. And Agatha Dashwood definitely wouldn't like that. So the next thing that's going to be in my book is what happens to me when I go to school tomorrow. Oh, God – I can't die in Chapter Sixteen. Actually, if Tricia and her mates do kill me, there won't even be a Chapter Sixteen. My book will end with Harrison walking off down the road after telling me mysteriously that I'll see his work. But I'll never get to see it. And neither will the reader. My book will go down as having the worst ending in history! And being the shortest in history!

Agatha Dashwood says that any time she had a problem with her books she would write about it in her writing journal. Apparently when she was writing *The Proud Maiden* she couldn't decide for ages whether the heroine should wear glasses or not. It was only when she wrote about it in her journal that she realised glasses could be a powerful metaphor for virginity. This was why Daphne ends up losing her glasses in the penultimate chapter and falling down the stairs – to make readers realise that they should never be careless with their virginity.

But it was all right for Agatha Dashwood. She was writing fiction. She could decide what happened to Daphne. She could decide to throw her down the stairs. How can I decide what happens to me when I go to school tomorrow? How can I control what psycho Tricia does to me?

What would I do if my book was a work of fiction and Cherokee Brown was a made-up character? What would I get her to do?

I'd get her to do something really spectacular. Something so awesome it meant that Tricia and her friends would never go near me again. I'd make it the chapter in the book that readers would remember for the rest of their lives – like the chapter in *The Lion, The Witch and The Wardrobe* where Aslan comes back to life and defeats the evil snow queen.

But what could it be???

Chapter Sixteen

'Without proper presentation your words are as meaningless as a baby's scrawl. Choose your font with care and always, always double-space your manuscript.'

Agatha Dashwood,
So You Want to Write a Novel?

When you don't have any friends you learn not to expect certain things. On St Valentine's Day you don't even think to check the post, on school trips you head straight for a seat at the front of the coach – on your own – and when the doorbell rings at home you don't think for one instant that it'll be for you.

So when the doorbell rang in the middle of Sunday afternoon I ignored it as usual and carried on staring at the blank page on my computer screen. Blank apart from the words: 'Chapter Sixteen' across the top. I deleted them and then typed them again, wondering how many more times I could do this without going clinically insane. I heard the doorbell ring again and Alan call out, 'Don't worry, I've got it.'

I highlighted 'Chapter Sixteen' and scrolled through various different fonts, strangely drawn to one called ENGRAVERS. What would they engrave on my tombstone, I wondered, after tomorrow.

HERE LIES THE BODY OF
CHEROKEE BROWN
WHO TRAGICALLY
NEVER GOT BEYOND
CHAPTER FIFTEEN
RIP

It was only then that I heard raised voices. Alan shouting something like, 'Highly inappropriate,' and another man saying, 'Just give me a chance, man.'

Steve!

I jumped to my feet, rushed to the door and then stood there frozen rigid. Why had he come here? Why hadn't he waited? Why hadn't he told me he was coming? I thought of my phone lying turned off at the bottom of my bag to avoid any texts or calls from Helen. I rushed over, pulled it out and turned it on. There was an unopened envelope from Steve in my inbox.

want to come and sort things with your mum. on my way over

It was the first text from him I could actually

understand immediately. Down below I heard Alan again. 'Well, I really don't think . . .'

I flung my door open and raced downstairs. Mum had obviously heard them too because when I got to the final flight, leading to the hallway, she was hurrying through from the kitchen, wiping her hands on a tea towel. She didn't see me up above her, she was too busy staring daggers at Steve.

'What the hell are you doing here?' she snapped.

I leant over the banister and saw Steve standing in the doorway. His hair was bandana-free and he was wearing a suit.

'I just wanted to see if we could have a chat about Cherokee.'

'Claire,' Mum hissed at him like a snake. 'What for?'

'About me seeing her.'

'We don't want you seeing her,' Mum snapped. 'Why can't you just leave us alone?'

'But I'm her dad,' Steve replied, looking hurt.

Alan let out a sarcastic snort of laughter.

'No you're not,' Mum said. 'Alan is her dad now.'

'No he isn't.' The words burst from my mouth. Mum, Alan and Steve all turned to look up at me.

'All right, Cherokee,' Steve said sheepishly. 'Did you get my text? I thought it would be best if I came around today. Try and get things sorted before I go away tomorrow.'

'Oh, you're going away?' Mum's voice was now verging on hysterical. 'There's a surprise.'

'He's going to Paris for a music competition, Mum, that's all.' When she looked at me I had to look away, her eyes were so full of hurt.

'Is that right?' she muttered. She turned back to face Steve. 'And how long did you tell me you were going to America for? A month? And how long were you actually gone?'

Steve shifted uncomfortably in the doorway. 'Look, that was a long time ago, Fi. Things are different now, I swear.'

It was hearing him call her Fi rather than Fiona or Mrs Weeks that made me realise for the first time properly that he and Mum had once been a couple. It seemed weird and slightly wrong. Alan obviously felt the same way. He barged in front of Mum and started trying to close the door.

'You're not welcome here,' he said.

'Yes he is,' I shouted, running down the stairs and pushing past Alan.

'What's going on?' We all turned to see the twins standing at the other end of the hall. Tom was holding a Wii controller and David was chewing on his thumbnail. It was weird seeing them look so nervous. Part of me wanted to go and hug them and tell them it was OK, but I couldn't leave Steve.

'Nothing, boys,' Alan said. 'Go back into the living room please.'

The twins stayed rooted to the spot.

'Who's that strange man?' Tom asked.

'He's just going,' Alan replied.

'He's my dad,' I said, glaring at Alan.

'Your real dad?' David asked, his eyes now as wide as saucers.

'Yes.'

I moved so that I was standing right in the doorway, directly in front of Steve. Then I turned to face Mum and Alan.

'If he isn't welcome here then I'm not either,' I said loudly.

'Shh,' Mum hissed, looking past me to see if any of the neighbours were around. But Magnolia Crescent was Sunday-afternoon-still; the only sign of movement was a cat slinking along the opposite pavement.

'Look, I don't want to cause any trouble,' Steve said.

'You're not,' I said, glaring at Mum and Alan. 'Why can't I see him, Mum? I don't get what the big deal is.'

'Get back inside, Claire,' Alan said. His voice was controlled but clearly angry.

'My name isn't Claire,' I replied. 'It's Cherokee.'

'Oh, for Christ's sake.' Alan grabbed hold of my arm and tried to pull me into the house.

'Get off!' I yelled.

'Yeah, mate, go easy, eh,' Steve said, taking a step closer to the door.

'Get off my property,' Alan hissed. 'Or I will call the police.'

'But you can't —' I began.

'Get in the house!' Alan yelled.

Mum and I stared at him in shock. I'd never heard Alan raise his voice before, and from the look on her face, I don't think Mum had either.

'Don't talk to her like that,' Steve said, taking another step towards us.

'I'll talk to her how I like,' Alan replied. 'She's my daughter and I know what's best for her.'

'No you don't,' I screamed. 'You want to brainwash me and send me to badminton club. If you knew anything about me at all you'd realise that I hate badminton.'

Alan looked so hurt it was as if I'd said I hated *him*. He glanced at Mum. On cue, Mum started to cry.

'Why can't you just leave us alone?' she sobbed, bringing the tea towel up to her eyes. I wanted to groan.

Steve took a step back. 'I'm sorry,' he said and he looked genuinely crushed.

'Mum, please,' I begged. 'Can't we just sort this out like adults?'

Alan gave a sarcastic snort.

'Mum!' David called. 'Why are you crying?'

'Is Claire's dad a baddie?' Tom asked.

'He's not a baddie, he's really nice,' I said, trying to give Tom a cheery smile.

'Maybe I ought to go . . .' Steve said to me.

'No!'

'Yes. Get out of here and don't ever come back,' Alan said, puffing up his chest.

Steve's eyes narrowed and he came so close to Alan they were practically chin to chin. 'I'm going now because I don't want to cause any more bother,' he said in a low voice. 'But you can't stop me from seeing my daughter. You got that?'

Alan's mouth dropped open but he said nothing. I wanted to cheer.

Steve turned to me. 'You gonna be all right, Cherokee?'

I nodded, my eyes filling with tears.

'Remember what I told you?' he said, tapping the side of his head.

I nodded again.

He gave me a quick hug. 'See you tomorrow,' he whispered in my ear.

I nodded. Then I turned and ran into the house and up the stairs, tears spilling down my face.

Chapter Seventeen

'I have only three things to say when it comes to dialogue: authentic, authentic, authentic!'

Agatha Dashwood,
So You Want to Write a Novel?

So I had something to write for Chapter Sixteen after all. But as I finished typing it up I felt sick. Everything was going so wrong. It was bad enough thinking of what might happen in school on Monday without World War Three breaking out at home too. I looked back at what I had typed and cringed. I didn't want to be the type of character who said things like:

'You want to brainwash me and send me to badminton club. If you knew anything about me at all you'd realise that I hate badminton.'

It sounded as if I belonged in the script of a naff TV soap, not an awe-inspiring book. I shut down my computer and lay on my bed. Almost as soon as I'd closed my eyes I heard footsteps on the stairs outside and then a knock on my door. But before I could say anything the door opened and Mum and Alan both walked in.

'What are you doing?' I said, looking straight at him.

'We want your phone,' Mum said, her eyes looking slightly crazed.

'What?'

'We don't want him being able to contact you. Not at the moment anyway, until we've decided what to do.'

I sat bolt upright on the bed. 'What do you mean, until you've decided what to do?'

Alan frowned at me. 'We need to get some legal advice. See where we stand.'

'But he's my dad!' I exclaimed. 'How can anyone stop me from seeing him?'

'We think he's a bad influence on you,' Mum said. 'Look at what's happened in the few days he's been back on the scene. You've ruined your beautiful hair. You've missed school to see him and now you're answering back to Alan.'

As if to order, Alan looked hurt and stared down at the floor.

'So we want your phone please,' Mum said.

I stared at her. 'But if you take away my phone how will I be able to contact Helen?' Dread rushed through me as I remembered the texts about Harrison on my phone. The texts that weren't even true but if Mum and Alan saw would just make them even more anti-Steve.

'She's my only friend, Mum. Please don't stop me from contacting her.'

'You can call her on the home phone.'

'But it doesn't work like that. What about texting? You can't take away my right to text!' I took a deep breath, aware that I'd come out with another line straight from a soap opera. 'Please, Mum.'

'It won't be forever,' Mum replied. 'I'm sure this is all a passing whim for him. He'll be off again before you know it and then we'll be the ones left to pick up the pieces. It's better this way, Claire. Trust me.'

'Cherokee!' I half yelled, half cried.

'You need to be focusing on your school work.' Alan piped up. 'This kind of disruption could be catastrophic with your GCSEs only a year away.'

'But you're the ones causing the disruption!' I slammed my hand down on my bed. What did it matter anyway? I'd given up caring about my GCSEs the day I'd realised that my teacher was more worried about saving her own skin than my education. It all seemed so unfair. Why couldn't they see that? If they would only let me see Steve once a week I'd be fine. Better than fine – I might actually be happy.

'Phone?' Mum said, holding out her hand.

'But what if I have an emergency at school or something and I'm not able to call you?' I was starting to panic now.

'Well, we managed fine without them in our day, didn't we, darling?' Alan said, looking at Mum.

I had to do something. I had to let Steve know I wouldn't be able to contact him. And I had to find a way to delete my incriminating texts.

'All right, but can I just send Helen a text to let her know?' I said. 'It'll take two minutes. I don't want her to think I'm ignoring her. Please?' I looked straight at Mum.

'You can call her from the home —' Alan began.

'OK,' Mum said, putting her hand on Alan's arm. 'Two minutes and then bring it straight down to us.'

'Thanks.'

Alan looked at her questioningly but Mum shook her head and gestured at him to follow her out of the room.

As soon as they'd gone I grabbed my phone and texted Steve:

They've taken my phone, pls don't text me. C u tomo

Then I texted Helen:

Parents have confiscated my phone pls don't text - will call u xxx

Then I deleted all of my sent and received texts.

I checked and double-checked that they really had been deleted. Then I wrote down Steve's number and deleted that from my phone too. On cue I heard Mum shout upstairs for me.

I stepped out of my room, phone in hand, but rather than feeling angry, something really strange happened. It was as if I'd stepped out of the old me – the me who used to care about what Mum and Alan thought.

I walked down the stairs to the landing where Mum was waiting with her hand outstretched. I placed the phone in her open palm and turned to go back to my room.

'Claire,' she said and her voice sounded a little afraid. 'I'm doing this for your own good.'

I carried on up the stairs without turning round. And as I walked I felt as weightless as a ghost, as if the bond that had always tied me to her had finally snapped.

Chapter Eighteen

'To ensure accurate timescales in your novel create a calendar for your plot. I nearly came a cropper in the first draft of my historical saga The Pauper and the Petticoat *when a mix up of dates meant a five-year pregnancy for one poor character!'*

Agatha Dashwood,
So You Want to Write a Novel?

If only real life came with a personal calendar. If only the moment we were born we were told all the dates that were going to change our lives forever. If we knew the date we were going to meet our soulmate we could make sure we'd put on our best outfit. If we knew the dates our dreams would finally come true maybe we could relax and enjoy life more. And if we knew the date we were going to die – well, maybe we wouldn't waste so much time stressing about all the silly small stuff.

If I'd known what was about to happen on Monday I certainly wouldn't have wasted so much time the night before reading depressing poetry and wondering what hymns they would play at my funeral!

When the alarm clock began to bleep I rolled over and hit the off button with a dull thud. So this was it. The day I'd been dreading for what seemed like forever. I sat up in bed and despite the heat in my room I felt really empty and cold. What were they going do to me, I wondered for about the millionth time. And when were they going to do it?

I got out of bed and got some clean school uniform from my wardrobe. When I'd been lying awake in the middle of the night I'd decided that I'd definitely fight back, even if it meant getting more badly beaten. At least I'd be able to hold my head up high and know that I didn't give up easily. But as I pulled on my polo shirt I imagined a dark bloodstain seeping across the pale blue cotton. What if David Marsh had a knife? He certainly seemed like the type. What if Tricia told him to stab me?

I sat down on the edge of the bed and told myself not to be so ridiculous. I was letting my imagination run away with me. Why would David Marsh risk going to prison over me? Anyway, Steve would be picking me up from school, so as long as I left mega early this morning and got there before anyone else I should be OK. There was no way they'd do anything to me in full view of the teachers or the other kids, surely. But what if they managed to get me in the toilets or somewhere else nobody could see? David Marsh always took his victims behind the canteen bins when he wanted to beat them up. I pressed my hands to the sides of my head and wished my mind was like an alarm clock and I could just press a button to make it shut up.

Once I was dressed I made my way downstairs, still feeling as empty as air. As I got to the kitchen door I could hear the low murmur of Alan and Mum talking.

'Ah, Claire,' Alan said as I went in. 'We were just talking about you.' They were both sat at the table looking undertaker-serious.

I walked to the fridge and took out the carton of orange juice.

'Yes, I was just saying to Alan that I'd give you a lift to school today,' Mum said, with a nervous smile. At first I felt a twinge of relief – it meant that both of my journeys to school would be covered. But only for today. Tomorrow Steve would be in Paris and Mum would probably want to get back to her normal routine. And I didn't think I could bear another sleepless night wondering and waiting. Now Monday had finally arrived I almost wanted everything to come to a head.

'OK,' I said, pouring myself a glass of juice. If I said no, Mum would only get suspicious. Condensation formed on the side of the glass like a cold sweat. I shivered.

'Would you like some toast?' Mum asked, springing to her feet.

I shook my head and made my way back to the door. It would be hard enough forcing down a drink today.

On the drive to school I couldn't help thinking about death-row prisoners and their final journey to the execution chamber. However awful it must be to make that terrible last walk, I bet none of them have had to put up with two seven year olds screaming in their ear about which was best – being able to do a burp that lasted five seconds or being able to flick a bogey all the way across a bedroom.

'Boys!' Mum snapped, frowning into the rear-view mirror. 'What have I told you?'

'Bogeys spread germs,' the twins chorused, before erupting into snorts of laughter.

I wished I was one of them. It must be so cool to only have to worry about who can do the longest burp. And to have a permanent best friend and partner in crime. No matter what happened in the twins' lives they would always have each other. I stared blankly out of the side window as the houses streaked by way too quickly.

'Now, are you sure you're going to be OK?' Mum asked above the din of the twins' laughter as she pulled up outside the school.

I fought the urge to make a sarcastic remark. She'd just about wrecked everything to get her own way. Why was she pretending to be concerned about me now?

I did a quick scan of the road outside. Mum giving me a lift meant I was a lot later arriving than I'd planned and the pavement was swarming with pupils. I couldn't see any sign of Tricia and her friends though.

'Claire?' Mum asked.

'Her name isn't Claire any more,' Tom piped up from the back. 'Is it, Claire? You're called Chirkey now, aren't you?'

I twisted round in my seat. Both twins were grinning at me.

'I like Chirkey. I think it's better than Claire,' David said.

'Me too,' Tom agreed.

I wanted to hug them, even though they'd probably burp and wipe snot all over me. 'Thanks, twinnies.'

I turned back to look at Mum. She dropped her gaze down to the steering wheel.

'I'll see you later then,' she muttered.

I opened the door. After the air conditioning in the car, stepping into the heat outside was like stepping into the blast from a hairdryer. All around me other students were laughing and chatting in the sun. Shivering, I felt like the only person trapped in winter.

'Bye, Chirkey!' the twins called after me.

'Bye,' I replied, pausing for a second to turn back and

pull the face I used to do when they were really little to make them laugh. As soon as they saw my scrunched forehead and crossed eyes they started cracking up. I felt another pang of longing. If only I were heading off to infant school too. Where the worst that can happen is you forget to bring something for 'show and tell' or your pencil lead breaks.

I slammed the car door shut. Then I began putting one foot in front of the other until I got up to the school gates. I didn't care that I was limping. I was here. Now I just wanted to get whatever it was that was waiting for me over with.

But then I noticed a group of students gathered around one of the large white walls of the drama studio. They were chatting excitedly and pointing. I looked at the wall and caught a glimpse of something metallic glinting in the sunshine. I edged closer to the group, all the time scanning for Tricia and her friends, but there was still no sign of them. When I got to the wall and saw what the others were looking at I didn't know whether to laugh, cheer or cry. Right in the centre, in a riot of beautiful colours against the backdrop of white, was the spray-painted figure of a girl. She was wearing a purple tunic and black boots and holding a bow and arrow. She looked a bit like Pocahontas, only without the plaits. Her hair was black, and short on one side and long on the other. Just like mine. My heart started to race as I read the words sprayed across the bottom of the picture like a tag:

DON'T LET 'EM GET YOU DOWN, CHEROKEE BROWN

I thought of Harrison standing outside my house on Saturday night and what he'd said when I'd asked to see his next piece of graffiti art.

'Oh, you'll see it all right.'

I looked back at the picture, at the girl staring out from beneath her wedge of jet-black hair, defiant and strong. And I felt a surge of excitement. Harrison had done that for me. He'd come to the school and painted that beautiful picture, just for me. Because I was Cherokee, no matter what Mum or Alan did or said. I was Cherokee and I was strong.

Then my heart started to pound. What was Mr Richardson going to say? I took a deep breath. Mr Richardson didn't know that I was Cherokee Brown – nobody at school did.

'So you came back then?'

I froze as I heard Tricia's voice behind me and caught a waft of her cigarette breath and cheap perfume. I kept my eyes fixed on the picture.

'Well, you're gonna wish you hadn't,' she muttered.

I took a last look at the picture and the steely glint in the girl's eyes and then I turned round.

Tricia was flanked by Clara and a couple of other girls. They seemed to be doing some kind of synchronised gum chewing.

I stared into Tricia's hard little eyes. I felt so light now I could hardly believe I hadn't floated off the ground and gone spiralling up into the sun. Nothing felt real any more. I wanted to laugh in her face and yell at her that I just didn't care.

'Today you die,' Tricia hissed before turning and swaggering off into the building.

As the school bell began to ring and the other students started drifting in I stood there looking at the picture. I could have left. I could have got on a train to the Southbank or Spitalfields or gone to hide out in the library again. I could have gone to a payphone and called Steve – I had his number on a scrap of paper in my trouser pocket. I could have even gone home and begged and pleaded with Mum to not make me go back to school. But I didn't.

I stared at the picture and I thought of Harrison flitting around like a moth in the dead of night creating it. And I thought of how he'd hated school too – he and Steve – and yet somehow they'd made it through. And now they were both free to do what they wanted – Harrison with his art and Steve with his music. Soon I could have that freedom too. I just had to be strong. I turned and followed the others inside.

Chapter Nineteen

'My dears, if you are not using the weather to help create the necessary atmosphere in your novel you are really missing a trick. Never underestimate the power of a thunderstorm to increase dramatic tension, or the romantic possibilities of a crisp autumn day.'

Agatha Dashwood,
So You Want to Write a Novel?

As soon as I got near to my form room I realised something was wrong. Normally when you get to our end of the corridor all you can hear are people yelling and laughing and, mingled in with it all, Miss Davis begging and pleading people to go back to their seats and be quiet. But today it was deadly silent. When I walked in I saw why. A strange man was sitting at Miss Davis's desk and Mr Richardson was standing next to him, grim-faced and paler than ever. I quickly went and sat down.

Mr Richardson cleared his throat. 'Hmm, I'm afraid I have some bad news.' He took a deep breath, as if whatever he was about to say needed to be forced out. 'Miss Davis was taken very ill at the weekend and she won't be coming back to Rayners High for the rest of this term.'

A chorus of 'whats' and 'whys' rang out, as if suddenly everybody really cared. As if they hadn't spent the whole of the year taunting Miss Davis for their own entertainment.

'What's wrong with her?' Tricia asked from her seat in front of me.

Mr Richardson began fiddling with the end of his tie. 'Hmm – I'm afraid I can't go into the details of her – erm – illness.'

'But there's still two weeks left of term,' somebody else piped up. 'Won't she be better before then?'

Mr Richardson shook his head. 'No. I'm afraid not.'

I felt a horrible lurch in my stomach. Could her illness be anything to do with what had happened with me on Friday?

Mr Richardson turned to face the man sat at Miss Davis's desk. 'This is Mr Griffin, a supply teacher. He's going to be taking your tutor group for the time being.'

I looked at Mr Griffin, expecting him to smile or say hello, but he just carried on sitting there, stony faced. Something definitely felt wrong.

Mr Richardson turned back to face us. 'Now, I'm also here to remind you that it's the new Year Seven parents' assembly this afternoon and I need one volunteer from each class to take part in the presentation.' He looked straight at me. 'Claire, I'd like you to be the volunteer from 10D. Could you come to my office at lunchtime please and I'll let you know what I'd like you to read.'

I stared at him, wondering whether now would be a good time to explain that the word 'volunteer' actually meant a person doing something of their own free will. But he still looked so serious I decided against it and simply nodded.

'Good.' He looked back at the whole class. 'Now, before I leave, I'd just like to remind you that as students of Rayners High you have a duty to remember our motto and treat every member of staff and fellow pupil with the utmost respect – at all times.'

Something had definitely happened; I'd never seen him go so long without one of his inane grins. 'If Mr Griffin has any problems with any of you then there will be serious consequences. Do I make myself clear?'

Everyone apart from Tricia nodded and murmured, 'Yes, sir.'

'Good. Well then, I'll let you get on with your day. And don't forget, I expect nothing less than exemplary behaviour in the assembly later. The parents present will be wanting to know what their children can expect when they join us in September. It is your job to show them what a fabulous school this is.'

Even when he said the word 'fabulous' it sounded flat.

'Right, Mr Griffin. Over to you.' Mr Richardson made his way to the door and as he left the room I waited for the uproar to begin as everyone digested the news. But it didn't happen. It was like the heavy atmosphere in the room had smothered everyone into silence. The only person who didn't seem bothered was Tricia.

'The fat cow's stomach probably burst,' I heard her whisper to Clara and they both started to snigger.

'You!' Mr Griffin thundered, getting to his feet and looking at Tricia like he wanted to destroy her. 'Do you have something to say?'

There was a stunned silence. Everyone could feel it now, I was sure. Something really bad had happened. And this supply teacher knew what it was. We all sat there and waited.

'No, sir,' Tricia said in a sullen little voice.

It wasn't until the bell rang for second period and we all streamed out of the door that the thoughts everyone had been bottling up finally came tumbling out.

'What do you think's wrong with her?'

'Do you think she went psycho?'

'Do you think she's had a breakdown?'

It was as if they were talking about the latest episode of a soap – not a real person. All I could see was Miss Davis leaning against the corridor wall, sweat glistening on her pale skin.

Tricia, who had come out of the classroom after me, jostled past, elbowing me sharply in the side. 'One down, one to go,' she muttered.

I watched her stride up the corridor. She hadn't been bothered by the news at all. Miss Davis and I were obviously some kind of sick experiment to her. It was as if she wanted to see how much pressure we could take before we cracked. But why? What had either of us ever done to her?

I trudged up the corridor after the rest of my classmates. The next lesson was PE. The lowlight of my entire week. Normally as I make my way to the sports block I do this weird list thing in my head where I go through all the sports I really hope it won't be. Sprinting and other track races usually come pretty high up, as does gym. But today all I could think about was Miss Davis and what might have happened to her. When I got to the changing rooms Mrs Taylor, our Popeye-muscled PE teacher, was giving out tennis racquets. I breathed a sigh of relief. Tennis is one of my preferred ways to die of humiliation. Although I might not be the fastest on the court, at least thanks to Alan and his badminton obsession my hand–eye coordination is OK. If I can manage to get to the ball I can normally hit it in the right place.

We were playing doubles so, as usual, I had the embarrassment of no one wanting to be paired with me. But today I didn't really care. The countdown that had been ticking all weekend was now vibrating through my head like I was standing inside Big Ben. From the way Tricia kept glowering at me I knew something was going to happen. And it was going to happen soon.

In the end I was paired with Alison Dobbs, a tiny girl with buck teeth and glasses and therefore deemed almost as much of a freak as me. We stood on our court in the blazing sunshine and waited for Mrs Taylor to assign us our opponents. When she sent Tricia and Clara over I wanted to laugh. It was like I was high from nerves and adrenalin.

'Ooh look, we've got Speccy Four-eyes and Hop-along,' Tricia said as she and Clara arrived on the other side of the net. At the far end of the courts Mrs Taylor was bellowing out instructions about the game.

'Do you reckon I can knock her glasses off?' Clara called, bouncing a ball up and down on her racquet. Tricia had put her own racquet down on the floor and was checking her eyeliner in the reflection of her mobile phone.

As I watched her, something really strange happened. It was as if I was no longer in control of my body. I threw the tennis ball I'd been holding high into the air, then

I swung my racquet back over my shoulder in an arc. I thought about Alan and his constant lecturing about how to make the perfect serve. I thought about Mum and how she wouldn't let anything wreck her so-called perfect life. And I thought about how my life had been made a misery by somebody who didn't even know me at all. And I brought my racquet slicing back down and smashing into the ball. What happened next seemed to be in slow motion. I remember hearing Alison gasp and seeing Clara's mouth drop open. I remember watching the bright yellow ball swooping high into the air and disappearing briefly in the brilliant sunshine. And then I remember it reappearing, travelling a lot faster now, as it flew down towards Tricia's head and hit her smack in the face. There was a clatter as her phone landed on the floor. Then a scream, first from her and then from Clara. And then Alison saying, 'What did you do that for?' I just stood there. Holding my racquet. Staring across the net in shock. I don't think it had occurred to me that I might actually hit her. I'd just wanted to smash all of my anger into the ball.

'You stupid cow!' Tricia came racing towards me, clutching the side of her face with her hand. She was so mad she didn't even go around the net but started trying to scramble over it.

'Tricia Donaldson. What are you doing?' Mrs Taylor shouted, running towards us.

'She hit the ball right in my face, Miss, before I was ready.'

'I'm sorry – it was an accident,' I muttered.

As Mrs Taylor reached our court she saw Tricia's mobile lying on the ground. 'And why weren't you ready, Tricia?' she asked, picking up the phone. 'How many times have I told you about texting during PE?' She put the phone in her tracksuit pocket. 'I'm confiscating your phone until the end of the day.'

Tricia looked as if she was going to explode with rage. 'You can't do that, Miss, it's my personal property.'

'And this is school time,' Mrs Taylor retorted. 'You can have your personal property back when it's your personal time.'

I stood there watching and waiting.

Tricia clutched the side of her face. 'I need to go to First Aid, Miss. I think I might have a black eye.'

'Let me see,' Mrs Taylor barked. She examined Tricia's eye. 'It looks fine to me. Now let's get on with the lesson.'

Tricia turned to stare at me. 'You're dead meat, Weeks.'

'That's enough!' Mrs Taylor yelled and I became aware of everyone on the other courts standing as still as statues, watching. 'I'm sure Claire didn't mean to hit you. And if you'd been paying attention it never would've happened. Tricia and Clara, come with me. You can play singles on the end court. Alison and Claire, play each other please.

Everyone else, the show is over. Now get on with your games.'

As I watched Tricia stalking off I felt sick to the bottom of my stomach. Hitting that tennis ball had been like signing my own death warrant.

Chapter Twenty

'Would-be writers often ask me what tense they should write their novels in. I always believe that the story itself should dictate the tense. If you are writing romantic melodramas as I do then the past tense has a lovely gentleness about it. But if you are writing a spine-tingling thriller there is nothing like the present tense for action and pace.'

Agatha Dashwood,
So You Want to Write a Novel?

I somehow manage to make it to lunch break without being killed by Tricia. Like a tracksuit-wearing guard dog, Mrs Taylor stays with us while we get changed, right up until the bell rings and we head off for lunch.

The Year Heads' offices are in the building next to the sports block, so while all the others make their way across the field to the canteen I head off in the opposite direction to 'volunteer' for Mr Richardson. When I get there the door to the secretaries' office is open and I can hear two of them talking. Although they're not speaking loud enough for me to make out entire sentences, I do hear two things: 'Miss Davis' and 'overdose'.

I drop my bag to the floor and stand in the corridor frozen to the spot. Did she try to kill herself? I feel sick. Was it me that pushed her over the edge by walking out of class on Friday? I move a little closer to the open door, wary of being seen.

'Such a lovely woman,' one of the secretaries says.

'I know,' the other replies. 'I dread to think what those kids must have put her through.'

I want to run away but before I can move a muscle Mr Richardson comes striding along the corridor towards me.

'Ah, Claire.' He still looks really distracted. And now I know why. Miss Davis could have died. She could have died because of all the stress we put her under. I know that before Friday I'd been one of the few in my class not to have messed her about. But I hadn't stood up for her either. I'd just sat there and said nothing. And sometimes I'd even felt glad that Tricia and her lot had been taunting her, because at least it meant they were giving me a break.

'I'm getting one person from each class to read out a part of the presentation to the new Year Seven parents,' Mr Richardson said, snapping me back to the present. 'And I'd like you to read the Goethe quote.'

'OK, sir.' I'm so shocked by what I've found out that what he's asked me doesn't register at first. It's not until he's handed me a sheet of paper with the quote printed on it that it dawns on me. He wants me to read the piece of writing that I hate the most in the entire world.

'I'd like you to memorise it please.' He must see the panic on my face because he immediately adds, 'Of course, I'll be doing a PowerPoint presentation, so if you do get stuck you can always turn and read it from the screen.'

I nod numbly and look down at the words. I feel like a turkey who's just been asked to give a presentation promoting Christmas.

'Thank you, Claire.' He turns to go into his office, then turns back. 'Sorry, with all the – with Miss Davis being, er, ill – I completely forgot to ask about badminton club. You will still be going this afternoon, won't you, hmm?'

I nod. 'Sir, is Miss Davis – is she going to be OK?'

He nods yes, but his eyes have the closed look of no.

I turn and make my way back along the corridor.

As always I head to the library but when I get there I see Tricia, Clara, David and another boy all huddled around one of the computers. I step back into the corridor before they see me. Now where can I go? I head off in the direction of the toilets. But what if they go to the toilet after the library? That's the last place I want to get stuck with them. I hear the sound of laughing – Tricia laughing – and I realise they're on their way out. I speed up and see the disabled toilet on my left. I quickly dive in and lock the door behind me. I check it's definitely locked then I lean against it and take a few deep breaths. My heart is pounding and when I look in the mirror I see that my face is flushed. Reality slams into me like a sledgehammer. This is what it will be like when they do finally get me. This pounding, rushing, sick feeling. I hear the clatter of footsteps coming up the corridor, then Clara's fake little giggle and David's chesty cough.

'She's gonna crap herself when she reads it,' Clara says, from right outside the toilet.

'She'd better,' Tricia replies. 'Stupid cripple. She'll be sorry she ever messed with me.'

David laughs. 'Where are we gonna do it?'

'Down the park,' Tricia replies. They've walked past the toilet now so their voices are getting fainter. I press my ear up against the door. 'We'll bring her down there. You and Baz wait for us behind the shelter. I'll . . .'

I can't hear any more so I walk over to the sink. As it's in the disabled toilet it's slightly lower than normal. I bend down and turn the cold tap on full blast and splash water on my face. I start trying to piece together what I overheard. Tricia must have sent me another email. I look at my reflection in the mirror again. My eyes are wide with fear. What if Steve doesn't show up? What if he's parked further down the road and they get to me first?

The park is right next door to the school. They could easily drag me down the alleyway without Steve seeing.

For one mad moment I even think of going to badminton club. But what if they waited for me? There'd be no one around to help. I lean over the sink feeling dizzy and sick. Why did I smash that tennis ball over the net? What was I thinking?

I see the piece of paper that Mr Richardson gave me lying on the floor. I must have dropped it. I look down at the words.

Whatever you can do or dream you can, begin it. Boldness has genius, power and magic in it!

This time, it's not the word 'boldness' that leaps out at me, it's 'begin'. I'd dreamt of being a better person – a stronger person – and I'd begun it by starting to write my book. And since then magical things *have* happened. I've met my real dad. I've found out my real name. And I've done things I never would have done before. Maybe this Goethe person was right after all. Maybe boldness does have genius, power and magic in it. But it's not enough to just *begin* to be bold – you have to keep on going, no matter how scary it gets.

I'm sitting on the stage in the main hall at the end of the

row of students Mr Richardson has picked from each class. The stage lights are burning down on me but I can still make out the sea of faces in front. The parents of the new Year Seven intake are all at the very front of the hall and behind them, in the raked seating, are the pupils from Years Seven to Ten. Somewhere out there are Tricia, David and Clara. They're probably looking at me right now and thinking of how they're going to take me to the park after school and smash up my leg. That's what they've got planned, apparently. I went to the library after they'd gone and logged on to my emails. The title of Tricia's email this time was 'Matching Limp' and it was all about how she thought it was such a shame I only had one bad leg. She thought it would look so much better if I had two. But I wasn't to worry as they were going to be helping me out with that.

I'm not worried. Not now I know what I'm going to do.

Mr Richardson gets to his feet. The noise from the audience fades down to complete silence.

'Thank you all very much for coming,' he begins, addressing the rows of parents all sitting there smiley-keen in the front. I think of their kids, still blissfully happy in their junior schools.

'. . . extremely proud of our academic reputation.' I zone back in on Mr Richardson. He doesn't look as pale or as shell-shocked as he did earlier. He reminds me of a vampire, sucking up the energy and enthusiasm from his crowd of wide-eyed parents. 'But it's not just about academic excellence at Rayners High,' he continues. 'As a relatively new school we pride ourselves on our traditional values. An ethos that filters right the way down the school from the head teacher, Mr Groves, to the youngest pupil in Year Seven. And as Head of Pastoral Care I see it as my central aim to ensure the happiness and confidence of every single one of our pupils.'

I wonder what he'd do if I puked on stage.

'Now, with the help of some of our students, I'm going to take you through a series of slides demonstrating the excellent work we are doing here at Rayners High, so that you will see first-hand the kind of experience your son or daughter can expect come September.'

The slide show begins and the first pupil – an eager-looking Year Seven – stands up and reads out a list of all the really cool subjects on offer at Rayners High. I suddenly remember my first assembly as a brand-new Year Seven. As soon as we'd come into the hall and sat down Mr Richardson made us stand up again.

'Turn round and take a look at that seat behind you,' he had said. Bewildered, we'd all turned round and looked. 'For every one of you that is here today, seven other children wanted that seat. That's how over-subscribed Rayners High is. And that's how lucky you are.' I remember actually feeling slightly thrilled as I sat back down. But as I remember it makes me feel sad. How many other kids are about to get their hopes dashed, just like me?

Mr Richardson's presentation stretches on. I know that my part isn't until the end – the Goethe quote being the icing on the Rayners High cake. I try to swallow but my mouth is too dry. Will I be able to do this?

'And it goes without saying that our attitude towards bullying of any kind is strictly zero tolerance,' Mr Richardson says, suddenly adopting a grimmer than grim voice. But it feels fake. It *is* fake.

I feel anger gripping my insides like a clenched fist.

'At Rayners High we believe in respecting ourselves and each other and creating a nurturing and stable environment in which our students will feel confident and flourish. And on that note –' he turns to me and smiles – 'Claire, would you like to read the parents our favourite quote?'

I get to my feet and I feel so light-headed I think I'm going to faint. I take a deep breath.

'Whatever you can do,' I begin and my voice is barely more than a squeak. I hear a murmur go around the hall as people strain to hear what I'm saying. I clear my throat and try again. 'Whatever you can do,' I repeat, much louder this time. 'Or dream you can . . ." I can see Mr Richardson nodding vigorously out of the corner of my eye. I stare straight out into the audience. '. . . Begin it.' I take a really deep breath and stand as tall as I can. 'Boldness has genius, power and magic in it.'

The parents break into polite applause. I see Mr Richardson joining in. I don't sit back down.

'Thank you, Claire, that was lovely,' he says.

I still don't sit down.

'The trouble is,' I say and the audience falls deathly silent, as if they already know this isn't part of the script. 'The trouble is, it's very hard to be bold when you're always being made to feel afraid.'

'Claire?' Mr Richardson is staring at me, his mouth hanging open.

'Everything you've just heard,' I continue, turning to look back down at the parents, 'it isn't true. There isn't a zero tolerance policy on bullying here, there is zero policy.'

'Claire, really!' Mr Richardson comes to the front of the stage. 'Ladies and gentlemen, I'm so sorry. Claire has been having a few issues in her personal life of late and –'

'No I haven't!' I'm shouting now. 'The only issues I've been having have been here. In this crappy school.'

It's so quiet I think I actually hear a pin drop.

'OK, that's enough.' He's moving towards me. 'Time to go to Mr Grove's office.'

'No!' I stand there facing him, rage burning in my eyes. 'What about Miss Davis then? Why don't you tell them what's happened to her?'

Mr Richardson opens his mouth to speak but I'm not going to let him. I know this is my last chance. I turn back to the audience. 'Miss Davis is my form tutor. Was my form tutor. But she's off sick because at the weekend she took an overdose.'

I feel shockwaves pulsing around the hall.

'And do you know why she took an overdose? Because she was being bullied too. And no one did anything to stop it. Because none of us were brave enough. None of us. We knew it was going on and we did nothing to stop it. Just like nobody did anything to stop people picking on me.'

'Claire, that's enough,' but Mr Richardson's voice is weaker now, like he's lost the fight and he knows it.

I take a step forwards, and look down at the horrified faces of the parents in front of me. 'I got an email today from someone in my class, telling me she and her friends are going to smash my leg up after school.' My eyes are swimming with tears now. I can't see any of their faces any more, just a blur. 'I've spent all weekend dreading coming in today because I knew something was going to happen. But I'm not going to let it happen. I'm not going to be like Miss Davis.' I wipe my eyes with the back of my hand and blink hard. I look up into the darkness at the back of the hall, where I know Tricia and her mates will be sitting. 'You make me sick.'

I look back at Mr Richardson standing staring at me, speechless, and then I run from the stage. When I reach the doors I charge into them and send them crashing into the wall. I don't feel like I'm limping, I feel like I'm flying. They can't stop me. No one can stop me. The quote was right. Boldness does have genius, magic and power in it. Right now I feel like a superhero.

I fly through the foyer and the revolving door. I'm going so fast I almost spin back inside. I stumble out on to the forecourt and I gasp as the blinding sunlight hits my eyes. I stop for a moment, gulping deep breaths of air. I have to get out of there before they come after me. I have to run and run and never stop. I have to —

'Cherokee!'

I look up. Shield my eyes from the sun with my hand. I see the pale blue camper van parked on the other side of the road. I see Steve standing there staring at me, frowning with concern. Behind him Harrison is sat on the wall, his tanned hands tapping out a rhythm on his lap.

I look at them both and I start to cry and laugh at the

same time. Then I start running and limping towards the gate, where I collide with Steve and collapse into his arms.

'Cherokee, what's up, mate?'

'Dad,' is all I can say, between sobs.

Chapter Twenty-One

'When one is truly a writer, one is on call twenty-four hours a day. Never find yourself caught without a notepad, my dears, inspiration has a knack of calling at the most inopportune moments.'

Agatha Dashwood,
So You Want to Write a Novel?

It wasn't until I was strapped into the front seat of the camper van and we had driven so far away the school had become a speck in the rear-view mirror that reality started to prickle back into me like pins and needles.

'What the hell happened?' Steve asked, barely able to keep his eyes on the road. Even Harrison was leaning forwards in the back seat, staring at me.

I didn't know where to begin. Then I saw a glint of metallic paint on Harrison's fingers and I remembered his picture. 'I didn't let them get me down,' I gasped, and then I started to laugh. Ha ha ha, like a loon. 'I didn't let them get me down.'

Neither of them said anything. They were probably

trying to work out if I'd gone completely nuts. But the quieter they were, the more I wanted to laugh. All the tension of the past hours, days, weeks and months seemed to be leaving my body in great big snorts. Then Harrison started to laugh too. It was a nice laugh. Deep and real.

'So, what happened?' Steve asked again, the only one not laughing.

I took a deep breath and tried to compose myself. What *had* just happened? The whole day felt like a weird dream I'd just woken up from. 'They were having this assembly,' I began, 'for the parents of the new intake in September – a kind of welcome-to-the-school thing.'

Steve nodded.

'And I'd been asked to read a quote – as part of the presentation.' Images from the assembly began flashing into my head – the lights, the parents' faces, Mr Richardson staring at me, mouth open in horror. 'I – well – I ended up making – saying – well, making a speech of my own.'

'What?' Steve cranked his head right round to look at me.

'Look out!' Harrison cried as the van nearly swerved into a lamp post. Steve pulled the van to a halt by the side of the road and turned off the ignition. Then he looked at me. The concern in his eyes actually made me ache.

'It's OK,' I said, 'Because I told them everything – all

249

about what's been happening in my class and the email I got today and —'

Steve frowned. 'What email?'

'That girl in my class I told you about. She sent me another email today saying she was going to smash up my leg after school. But the thing is I'm not scared of her any more because I realised that — what are you doing?'

Steve had started up the van again and was screeching it into reverse. 'I'm going back to that school and I'm gonna see how brave she is when you're not on your own.'

'No!' I said, feeling a rush of panic. 'I stood up to her. I stood up to all of them. The whole school. I ran out of the assembly. I can't go back there. Please.'

Steve pulled the van to a halt again and sighed. 'You should've called me, the minute you got that email. Why didn't you call me?'

'It's not that easy,' Harrison said from the back seat. His voice was softer than I'd ever heard it. 'Is it, Cherokee?'

I nodded, unable to speak.

I felt his hand squeeze my shoulder. It was only there for a second but it left a warm imprint that soaked right through to my bones.

'I knew it was worse than you were letting on,' Steve said. 'That's why we got there early. So what did you say, in this speech of yours?' He reached across to the dashboard for his cigarette papers and tobacco.

I leant back in my seat and started to relax a bit. 'I just told them the truth. About everything.'

As Steve rolled a cigarette I told them all about Miss Davis and how she had lost control of the class and how I'd hated her for it until I realised that actually she was in just the same position as me – that we'd both been too scared to be brave – but I wasn't going to be any more.

'What, you said that in front of all the new parents?' Harrison asked, and he actually sounded impressed.

I nodded. 'Yep. And most of the school.'

'Flippin' 'eck.' Harrison whistled through his teeth and sat back in his seat. I felt pride start to unfurl inside me like a banner.

'Shit!' Steve said, shaking his head. Then he let out a laugh and put his hand up for a high five. 'That's my girl! So what now?'

I gulped. What now? 'I don't know. I can't go back to school. Ever. And Mum and Alan are going to go crazy when they find out what I've done. I can't go home. I don't know what to do.' My voice seemed to rise about an octave in panic.

Steve looked over his shoulder at Harrison. 'What do you reckon, H? Room for one more on our road trip?'

Harrison nodded and smiled. 'Yeah, I reckon.'

'Right,' Steve said, turning back to me. 'You got a passport?'

I nodded.

'You got a way of getting your passport and some clothes without your mum and Badminton Bill finding out?'

My heart began to pound as I realised what he was actually saying. I looked at my watch. It was quarter to three. Mum would be on her way to collect the twins from school. Alan would be up in London at work. 'Yes. If we go now there shouldn't be anyone at home.'

'Right then.' Steve lit his cigarette and turned the key in the ignition. 'Why don't you come away with us for a few days – get a change of scene? Then we'll figure out what to do next.'

'What? Really?'

Steve nodded. 'Make sure you leave a note for your mum, like – let her know where you're going, tell her you'll be back soon. Don't want her panicking.'

'All right.' It was such an unexpected development I felt a bit dazed.

'All right!' Steve winked at me and pulled back out on to the road.

It was a very weird feeling, sneaking into my house to get ready to run away. But as I walked in all I could think was I didn't really belong there anyway. The photos on the hall table summed it up – full of flashes of fair skin and blonde hair and me hovering among them all like a dark shadow.

Even though there was nobody home I still found myself creeping up the stairs to the top landing. With a whole day's heat trapped inside, the air in the attic room felt as thick and as hot as soup. I hurried to my chest of drawers and rooted around for my passport. I had a sudden rush of panic that it might be out of date. But it was fine. I could run away for the next two years if I wanted to. I tipped my books out of my school bag and started filling it with clothes. I had no idea what I was packing as I grabbed random handfuls from each drawer. I just had to get out of there before Mum got home.

I looked down at the pad and pens on my desk. What should I write? I tore a page out and scrawled across it:

Gone to Paris with my dad for a few days. Had to get away from school. Please don't worry, I'll be fine.
Cherokee

Then I stuffed the notepad, a couple of pens and the Agatha Dashwood book on top of the clothes in my bag. I took one last look around the room. Running away with Steve and Harrison seemed pretty crazy, but last night, in this room, I'd felt as if my life had ended. Somehow, miraculously, I'd been given a second chance. I had to take it. I slammed the door shut behind me and ran down the stairs.

Chapter Twenty-Two

'Let other writers be your inspiration. It's good to remember
the books that have influenced us in our lives. And hope that
one day our own books might have a similar effect.'

Agatha Dashwood,
So You Want to Write a Novel?

When I was little Mum used to read me a picture book
about a boy called Timmy who ran away to sea. Only you
don't run away to sea, you 'stow' away. Timmy stowed
away on a boat and only ventured out of his hiding place
when they were too far into the ocean to turn back. He
ended up working in the ship's galley, peeling potatoes for
the cheery, red-faced cook. I used to want to be Timmy.
Even back then, when I was five years old, I wanted to
run away.

I thought of this as we chugged our way through Kent
and fields spread like a patchwork quilt of yellow and
green all around. Had I always been waiting for this to
happen? Had I always known that one day I'd be making
my own escape?

The tape Steve had been playing – *Greatest Driving Songs Ever, Volume Four* – came to an end.

'Any requests?' he asked as he ejected it from the stereo.

'Summat from the twenty-first century?' Harrison called from the back.

'Ha ha,' Steve said. 'Cherokee? Anything you'd like to hear? Actually, hang on. I've got just the thing.' He reached into the glove compartment for a tape and shoved it into the player. 'It's by a band called Fleetwood Mac.'

'Oh great, one of the eighteenth century's finest,' Harrison retorted.

Steve chuckled. 'Less of the lip, sonny, it's a long walk to France, you know.'

He looked back at me. 'It's called "Don't Stop" and it's all about getting on with your life and not looking back on the bad times.' He grabbed hold of my hand and gave it a squeeze. 'All that crap is behind you now, all right? I don't care what I have to do – you ain't ever going back to that school.'

I nodded and then I listened as the song filled the van. The words and the melody were so full of life and hope – it was infectious. Tomorrow, today would be yesterday and everything that had happened would officially be in the past. Tomorrow I would be waking up in Paris!

*

We actually arrived in Paris at one o'clock the following morning. Apparently the camper van spontaneously combusts if it goes over fifty miles an hour so it was a very leisurely drive. But we made it. I was so elated to get through both passport controls without being arrested and deported back home that I didn't care how slowly we went. We were in France and it felt like being on the other side of the world. And, more importantly, it felt like all my *problems* were on the other side of the world.

'We'll go the scenic route,' Steve said as we passed a signpost welcoming us to Paris. Soon we were driving along next to the Seine. The actual Seine! The Eiffel Tower was lit up against the night sky like a fairy's wand. Strings of twinkling lights dipped and rose in strands along the river. It felt as if they had been put there especially to welcome us.

'Are you sure your friend won't mind us getting here so late?' I asked as we turned on to a road heading away from the river. On the way to France Steve had explained that we'd be staying with an artist friend of his called Dominique. She had an apartment in Montmatre, where the street musicians' contest was being held.

Steve laughed loudly. 'No, man. Domi is a proper night owl. She'll only be having her lunch about now.'

I leant my head against the window and wondered what this Domi was like. Although Steve had said she was

256

a friend I couldn't help thinking there might be a bit more to it than that. I closed my eyes and pictured a beautiful French woman running out of her apartment building and flinging her arms around Steve, a snowy white cigarette attached to her ruby red lips. I opened my eyes again. I didn't quite know whether I liked this image. I'd only just found my dad – I wasn't sure I wanted to be sharing him with anyone else just yet. I watched Paris passing in a blur outside the window – the cafes and the bookshops and the patisseries all steeped in darkness. A sudden tiredness folded down on me and my entire body wanted to yawn.

Eventually Steve turned into a narrow cobbled side street and pulled up beside a high, grey brick wall. There were no windows in the wall, just a dark blue, arched door.

'Here we are!' Steve announced, collecting his tobacco and cigarette papers from the glove compartment.

We all got out of the van and had a stretch. Then we fetched our bags from the back and Steve locked up.

'Follow me,' he said, going over to the blue door. When he opened it I thought I might actually be hallucinating. It was like opening the doorway to a secret enchanted kingdom. In complete contrast to the grey bricks and cobblestones outside, the other side of the wall housed the most beautiful courtyard I've ever seen. Trees and vines and potted plants all mingled to form a tumbling forest of green. You would never in a million years have guessed it was there.

'Wow!' was all I could say.

Beside me, Harrison looked equally impressed. We followed Steve into the courtyard and over to a stone stairwell in the corner. There was an intercom on the wall. Steve pressed one of the buttons and we all stood waiting. A huge fat moon was shining down on us, bathing the courtyard in splashes of silver. Someone on one of the top floors was playing jazz and the notes wafted down across the courtyard like petals on the breeze. I don't normally like jazz music, but right there and then I don't think there could have been anything more perfect.

Eventually the intercom crackled into life.

'*Bon soir?*'

'All right, Dominique, darling. It's me, Steve.'

There was a silence and then a shriek. Somewhere above us in the building a door creaked open and we heard the patter of footsteps running down towards us. The door at the top of the stairs burst open and Steve stepped forwards.

'Domi!'

She was even more beautiful than I'd imagined. She was wearing a scarlet satin robe and a thick sheet of dark hair hung around her shoulders like a cape. There was no cigarette attached to her mouth but her lips were as round and as red as a rosebud. And when she smiled at Steve it was like the bud had burst into bloom.

But then she saw me and Harrison.

'What ees this?' she hissed, glaring at us. I went from loving her to hating her in exactly one second.

Steve followed her gaze, still grinning. 'This is my lodger and roadie, Harrison. And *this* is my daughter, Cherokee.' He gestured at me with a flourish.

Dominique glowered at him. 'But you no say – you say just you come.'

Steve shifted awkwardly. 'Yeah well, we had a bit of an emergency.'

I wanted to shrink down to the size of an earthworm and crawl under one of the flowerpots. I glanced at Harrison. From the look on his face he was clearly feeling the same.

'I need to speak to you,' Dominique muttered to Steve. 'Een private.'

Steve looked at us and shrugged his shoulders. 'Sorry, guys. Just a bit of a misunderstanding. Bit of a language-barrier thing. Give me a minute and I'll get it sorted, yeah?'

We nodded, because what else could we do? And then they both disappeared up the stone steps, the heavy wooden door banging shut behind them.

'Great,' Harrison said.

I looked at him and we both grinned. Something had definitely changed between us. The awkwardness had gone.

I looked around the courtyard. 'This is amazing, isn't it?'

Harrison nodded. 'Aye. Certainly beats Hackney.'

I tipped my head back and gazed up into the sky. 'Do you think that's a full moon?'

'Yeah. So watch out – anything could happen!'

I looked at him and laughed. 'I think it already has!'

He chuckled and sat down on the bottom step. 'Yeah, I don't think you'll be forgetting today for a while.'

I smiled and nodded. Then I sat down on a small stone wall opposite him. 'Thank you for doing the picture by the way. I loved it. When I saw it this morning it made me feel . . .' My words faded into silence. I suddenly felt embarrassed. Harrison looked down at the floor. The moonlight glimmered on his cropped hair like glitter. I wondered if he was embarrassed too.

'That's all right. I know what it's like. I wanted to do something to make you feel better . . . cos you are better.' He looked up, met my gaze for a second and then looked away again. 'Better than all of them. You're interesting and you're . . .' He started fiddling with the zip on his leather jacket.

'Thank you,' I said, and I meant it with every cell in my body.

He looked at me and smiled. And in the light of the moon I could see that, just like the time at the concert, his smile actually reached his eyes, filling them with sparks of fun.

Upstairs there was the sound of a door slamming and a woman speaking, or rather shouting, in French.

'Oh dear,' Harrison said.

I leant over and smelt the clumps of lavender bursting from a huge terracotta pot beside me. It was instantly soothing. Then I thought of Mum and Alan. What had they done, I wondered, when they'd realised I'd gone?

'You OK?' Harrison asked.

I opened my eyes and tried to smile. 'Yeah. Just thinking.'

'What about?'

'My family.'

Harrison nodded. 'You got any brothers and sisters?'

I thought of the twins – their constantly questioning faces and the way their scalps were always so hot, as if they had furnaces burning inside of them. And how, when they had been younger, I would cuddle up between them on the sofa and breathe in their baby smell. And I would feel as protective as a lioness and not ever want to let them go. 'Yes. Two half-brothers.'

'How old?'

'Seven.'

'Big gap.'

'Yes, I know. A bit too big sometimes.' I thought about telling him why the gap between me and the twins was so big – that my mum had been so depressed after having me she needed years of coaching from Alan to convince her to go through the trauma again. But I decided against it. Harrison and I might have been getting on better but there was no way I was ready to spill out my most embarrassing family secrets . . . just in case he decided to go all silent on me again.

Upstairs, Dominique's shouting came to a crescendo and then there was silence, broken only by random notes of music and the breeze shimmering through the leaves. I shivered.

'Cold?'

I looked across at Harrison and wondered why he suddenly seemed to notice everything about me. Maybe drawing is like writing and when you paint a picture of a person you start getting inside their skin.

'A little bit,' I replied and I watched as he slipped his leather jacket off. I could see the outline of the muscles through his T-shirt. I felt a weird tingling inside me.

Harrison got up and came over, holding out his jacket.

'Are you sure?' I said.

He nodded and put it around my shoulders. I felt hot, cold and dizzy all at once.

When Steve came bursting out of the door we both jumped.

'Right, sorry about this,' he said, running his hand through his hair, clearly stressed. 'Been a bit of a change of plan.'

I looked at Harrison and he raised his eyebrows.

'We're sleeping in the van tonight. Well, at least, me and you are,' Steve said to Harrison. Then he turned to me. 'You're sleeping upstairs.'

'What? Where?'

'In Dominique's spare room.'

'But —'

On cue Dominique appeared at the bottom of the stairwell. With her dark hair and stern gaze she suddenly reminded me of the evil queen in Snow White.

'Eet is fine,' she said to me, looking anything but fine. 'You sleep upstairs. The men can sleep outside.' She said the word 'men' like she was spitting out a mouthful of rotten fish.

I looked at Steve imploringly but he just nodded and gave a grim smile. 'Go on. There's only really room for two in the van anyway and you don't want to have to put up with Harrison's farting all night now, do you?'

'Oi,' Harrison said.

'But —'

'We'll be right outside – and it's just for tonight,' Steve added.

I looked at Dominique, wishing she would at least smile. She just stared at me, stony faced. 'Come on,' she said. 'Eet is late.'

I turned back to Steve and Harrison. 'Goodnight then.'

'Night,' they both said together.

I followed Dominique up the stairs, watching the swish of her gown against her tanned legs. I wondered if a situation could possibly be any more embarrassing and then I remembered the presentation assembly. If I could get through that I could get through anything. But as soon as Dominique flung open the door to her apartment I felt a shiver of excitement. I could almost hear Agatha Dashwood in my head telling me to pull out my notepad as I stepped inside. If I could have created a dream home for myself this would have been it.

The kitchen and living room were one huge open-plan room and the wall to my right was covered from top to bottom in bookshelves. I fought the urge to rush over to them and start browsing. I looked around the rest of the room. A squishy old sofa sat along the opposite wall and was covered with a higgledy-piggledy mass of brightly coloured cushions. There were more books in teetering stacks on either side of the sofa and over by the window there was an old gramophone and a huge potted plant.

The apartment smelt of books and herbs and perfume. It smelt of France.

I looked at Dominique standing in the middle of the room staring at me and I bit my lip anxiously. It was OK, I told myself. Steve and Harrison were just outside in the van. If she started yelling at me in French I could run back down to them. I didn't care if I had to sleep curled up on the steering wheel. Dominique sashayed into the kitchen and started pouring a glass of red wine from an open bottle on the side.

'You like a drink?' she said, offering the glass to me.

I shook my head.

She stared at me. I looked down at the floor, aware that I was starting to blush.

'Your father – he ees a very frustrating man.'

I looked back at her, unsure of what to say.

'He – how do you say – does my head in!'

Then she threw back her head and started to laugh. 'But I do his head in tonight, making him sleep in the van, no?'

I started to laugh out of politeness at first but then, when I realised that she really was joking and she might not be so scary after all, I felt a surge of relief.

'Come, you must be very tired,' she said, gesturing at me to follow her down a narrow hallway. 'This door here is the bathroom. And here,' she opened a door at the very end of the hall. 'Here you sleep.'

She went into the room and turned on a lamp by the side of the bed. It was a small room but really bright and airy. The walls were primrose yellow and the floorboards had been painted white. A pale blue chiffon curtain danced in the breeze in the open window. Dominique walked past me back out into the hall. 'Don't worry,' she said over her shoulder. 'I forgive your father in the morning and we all go for breakfast.' And then, in a waft of perfume, she was gone.

I lay down on the bed fully clothed. It was only then that I realised I was still wearing Harrison's jacket. I dug my hands into the pockets and felt a small notepad in one of them. I took it out and held it in my hand, unsure whether to open it or not. The breeze drifting in through the window brought with it a waft of lavender. I felt a very long way from home. I decided to flick the pad open to one random page, as if it had just fallen open by accident. It opened on a pencil sketch. I recognised it immediately. It was the picture of Cherokee Brown – the picture of me. I traced my finger over the lines and thought of Harrison actually drawing them – actually drawing me. I put the pad back into the pocket and pulled the jacket tight around me. It smelt of fresh soap. It smelt of Harrison. I closed my eyes and fell headlong into sleep.

Chapter Twenty-Three

'What do your characters dream about? This is what you must ask yourselves, my dears.'

Agatha Dashwood,
So You Want to Write a Novel?

When I first heard the music I thought I was still asleep. I'd been dreaming about Mum and Alan and Mr Richardson. We were all playing badminton together, only instead of shuttlecocks we were playing with cassette tapes, smashing them back and forth across the net. Then I looked at one of the tapes and saw that it belonged to Steve. I immediately started begging the others to stop playing. But they wouldn't listen and just kept hitting the tapes harder. As I tried to rescue them some music started playing in the gym. Or at least I thought it was in the gym. But it kept getting louder and louder until I had to open my eyes.

For a few seconds I had absolutely no idea where I was. The sun was streaming in through the window and the room was so yellow it was like waking up inside a daffodil. Then I realised that the song in my dream was actually coming from outside. A man was singing about wishing somebody was here and being lost in a fish bowl, or something. I sat up and rubbed my eyes. I was still wearing Harrison's leather jacket. I heard the strum of a guitar and a weird rattling sound. I scrambled across the bed and peeped out of the window. Way down below in the courtyard Steve was singing his head off and strumming wildly on his guitar. Next to him, looking extremely embarrassed, Harrison was shaking a pair of maracas. I was clearly still dreaming.

I sat back down on the bed and tried to remember everything that had happened the day before. Everything that had led up to this completely crazy point. But before I could get any further than the oh-my-bloody-God shock at what had happened at the presentation assembly there was a knock on the door.

'Yes?' I said, nervously.

The door opened and Dominique walked in. She was wearing a dark green kimono-style dress and her hair was pinned up on top of her head. 'Have you seen?' she whispered, nodding to the window. Outside the singing got even louder.

I nodded. 'Yes. What's he doing?'

Dominique sat down next to me on the edge of the bed and smiled. In the bright sunlight she looked older than she had the night before. Fine lines crescented the corners of her eyes and mouth like fans. 'He is trying to woo me with his song.'

'Oh,' I said. It should have been funny, but memories from the day before had started piling into my head thick and fast. I had run away from home. A picture of Mum standing in my attic room crying popped into my head. I mentally scrunched it up into a ball.

'Come on,' Dominique said, grabbing hold of my hand. 'Let's tell them what we think.'

She pulled me over to the window and flung the curtain back.

'You are a crazy man!' she yelled down at Steve.

Steve's face broke into a grin as soon as he saw us and he started singing a different song. One that was all about begging someone for forgiveness.

Harrison looked up at me and shrugged in embarrassment. I giggled and gave him a wave.

'All right, already!' Dominique yelled. 'I forgive you. Now let's go for breakfast.'

In France you can have cheese and chocolate for breakfast. As cheese and chocolate are my two most favourite foods I decided there and then that France would be where I lived when I was a published author.

We had come to a cafe at the end of Dominique's road.

The tables all had red and white chequered tablecloths and the waiters all acted like they were in a movie. I sat back in my chair and tried to decide whether to have cheese and croissants or a chocolate croissant or cheese and bread and chocolate spread. Across from me Harrison was sitting on his hands, looking tense.

'How did you sleep?' I asked him.

'OK.' He gazed out of the window at the French cars driving by. His skin looked browner than ever in the half light of the cafe. My heart sank when he didn't say any more.

'So your contest – it begins at midday?' Dominique asked Steve.

Steve nodded. 'That's right. Opening round starts at twelve. I have to get there at eleven to register.'

I felt a stab of shame. I'd been so caught up in my own drama of the day before I'd completely forgotten about Steve's competition.

'Are you nervous?' I asked him.

'Nah.' He looked down at his menu. 'All right, maybe a bit.'

'You'll be great,' I said.

'Yeah, hopefully.' But he didn't sound very hopeful.

'Have you been to Paris before?' Dominique asked, turning to me. I caught a waft of her perfume and for some reason it reminded me of Mum. The image of her standing in my attic room began to uncrumple itself in my mind. She was still crying.

I shook my head. 'We came to Disneyland Paris once, but we didn't see any of the city.'

Dominique turned to Steve. 'You must take her to the Louvre.'

Steve nodded. 'And the Latin Quarter.'

Dominique gave a knowing little laugh like he had just passed her a coded message, and said, 'Ah yes, the Latin Quarter.'

'You all right, H?' Steve asked, turning to Harrison.

Harrison nodded. 'Yeah.'

But he seemed all tense again, his jaw clenched and his eyes expressionless.

'Have you been to Paris before?' I asked him.

'Yeah.' He looked back out of the window. Next to me Dominique started talking to Steve about the Latin Quarter. I looked down into my lap and wondered why life could never just be simple.

'I worked here last summer,' Harrison said quietly.

I looked straight back at him. 'Really, where?'

'In a bookshop called Shakespeare and Co.'

Dominique clapped her hands together. 'I love that shop! Eet is very fabulous.'

'They let you stay there if you have nowhere to live, in exchange for working in the shop,' Harrison explained to me, his face flushing slightly. 'So I spent the whole summer sleeping in a hammock in the storeroom out the back.' He slumped back in his seat, as if the effort of saying so much had exhausted him. I saw that his leg was bouncing up and down under the table. And then a thought occurred to me. Maybe he was acting so tense because he wanted to do his flicking thing but he couldn't because he was in public. Maybe he was feeling how I felt when I had to try and keep my limp hidden.

'Do you fancy doing a bit of exploring after breakfast?' Harrison asked me.

I glanced at Steve.

'Well, I've got to put in some practice before the competition,' he said, 'but you guys go if you want. Harrison knows his way around. He'll take care of you. Won't you, H?'

I liked the way Steve asked him, with just a hint of fatherly menace in his voice.

Harrison nodded. 'Of course.'

'But you better be back in time for my big moment,' Steve added. 'I doubt I'll be getting through to the final round so it's your one chance to see your old man play on French soil.'

Dominique muttered something in French under her breath and they both laughed.

As the waiter came over to our table to take our order I

wondered what he made of our group: Steve with his long hair and bandana, Harrison quiet and edgy with his huge tattoo, Dominique looking so Parisian and glamorous and me looking – well – like I finally belonged, I guess.

'So, how are you feeling today?' Harrison asked when we got to the Metro. It was very different to the London Underground. You had to buy little cardboard tokens and go through giant turnstiles to get to the platform and the trains seemed a lot smaller and more rickety. You even had to open the doors yourself.

'I'm OK,' I replied as we boarded a train. We sat down on a double seat by the door.

'Have you heard from your mum?'

I looked at him blankly.

'Has she phoned you?'

'Oh. No. I don't actually have my phone. She does. She confiscated it from me on Sunday.' I tried to play the 'Which Station Am I?' game with the Metro map on the wall to hide my embarrassment, but it's a bit difficult when all of the names are in French.

'Why did she take your phone?'

Inside my head I groaned. It was nice that Harrison was talking again but did it have to be about stuff that made me look like a stupid kid? 'Because she didn't want me contacting Steve.'

'Oh, right.'

There was a long pause. I looked back at the map. *House of embarrassment: Chateau Rouge.*

'Parents, eh?'

I looked at Harrison and smiled. 'Exactly. Do you see much of your mum and dad?'

He looked out of the window at the dark tunnel streaming by. 'I see me mam whenever I go back to Manchester. But I don't see much of me dad any more. He buggered off a few years ago. Lives in Glasgow now, with his new family.'

'Oh.' I thought of the Character Questionnaire I'd done on Harrison and mentally rubbed out his gruff-but-loving dad.

'Do you get on OK with your mum?'

'Yeah, she's sound. How about you?'

I frowned. 'Not really. She never seems to get me. Sometimes it feels as if we're speaking totally different languages.'

Harrison nodded. 'Why do you reckon she's being funny about you seeing Steve?'

'I don't know. Well, she says she's worried he's going to hurt me – that he'll walk out on me again. But she doesn't understand that that's my risk to take, not hers.'

'Maybe that's the problem?'

I looked at him. 'What do you mean?'

'Maybe she hasn't got over her own hurt.'

I thought of Mum getting semi-hysterical at Steve on the doorstep on Sunday and the way she'd yelled at him about going to America. 'Yeah, maybe. But she's going to have to get over it. He's my dad. And it's my life.'

Harrison shifted round in his seat so that he was looking right at me. I noticed he had a small scar by the corner of his eye. 'I don't think he'll walk out on you again.'

'Why?'

'He's made up to be back in touch with you.'

'Really?'

'Oh yeah. He wouldn't stop going on about you after you'd gone to bed last night. Saying how proud he was of you and that. He hasn't stopped going on about you since you first met up.'

I smiled at Harrison. And he smiled back – one of his lovely, real smiles that made his green eyes sparkle.

We made the rest of the journey in silence. But it wasn't awkward. And inside my ribcage my heart was dancing the conga.

Harrison ended up taking me to a cemetery called Père Lachaise. I know that probably sounds a bit weird and morbid but it wasn't at all. Père Lachaise wasn't like any cemetery I'd ever been to before. It was actually more like a miniature city complete with signposts, maps and cobbled lanes, with all the tombs like little stone houses in neat, tree-lined rows.

'What do you think?' Harrison asked after we'd been walking for a few minutes. He looked at me anxiously and I realised that it actually mattered to him what I thought. Just ahead of us I saw an elderly woman in a headscarf tending one of the graves. Above her the mossy statue of a man gazed down lovingly.

'I think it's beautiful,' I murmured.

Harrison smiled. 'I came here a lot last summer. It's a great place to get ideas. It's where I came up with the design for this.' He extended his muscly forearm and the twin heart-skulls in his tattoo grinned up at me. I saw that the words along the bottom actually said, *Love Your Enemy*.

'Oh.'

Harrison followed my gaze down to the tattoo. 'What's up?'

I thought of trying to love Tricia and it made me feel a bit sick. 'Nothing. It's just . . . I'm not sure I could ever love my enemies.'

Harrison's face started to flush. 'Yeah, well, if you hate them they've won.'

'What do you mean?'

'You're still letting them hurt you.'

'Oh. Yeah, I s'pose.'

Harrison moved his arm away.

'So what made you come to Paris last year?' I asked, and it wasn't just because I wanted to change the subject – I genuinely wanted to know. Being with Harrison was like reading a really good thriller – there seemed to be a twist and turn on every page.

'The Fox,' Harrison replied.

'A fox?' I turned and stared at him.

He started to grin. 'No, not *a* fox, *the* Fox.'

'Oh,' I replied, not having a clue what he meant.

'I take it you've never heard of him?' he asked, turning off the main avenue and leading me down a narrow grassy path. The graves in this part of the cemetery were older; their stonework was crumbling and engravings worn ghostly thin, but this only made them even more elegant.

'No,' I replied. 'I don't think so.'

'He's the French equivalent of Banksy.'

I still looked blank.

'The famous graffiti artist in England?'

'Oh! I think I know who you mean. The one who does all his work in secret so nobody knows who he is?'

'Yeah. Well, the Fox does the same thing here in Paris.' Harrison gestured at me to follow him away from the graves up a steep grassy bank. 'The first time I saw his work it was like getting to a brand-new level on an Xbox game.'

'What do you mean?'

'He made me realise what was possible. How graffiti didn't have to just be about tags and stuff. That it could actually say summat.'

We reached the top of the bank and stopped walking. I rubbed my lower back; climbing the steep slope had made it ache a bit.

'You OK?' Harrison said.

I nodded, my face starting to flush. 'Yeah. I get back-ache sometimes . . . because of my right leg, you know, being shorter than the left one.' I turned away slightly so he wouldn't see my embarrassment.

'I used to hate being different,' Harrison said. 'But now I'd hate to be the same as everyone else.'

I carried on staring down the slope as I let his words sink in. It was as if he'd opened the door to a room in my mind that I'd never been in before. A warm, sunny room, where having a limp was actually cool.

'Shall we sit down for a bit?' Harrison asked.

I nodded and we sat down beneath one of the trees that lined the top of the hill. The sunlight filtered through the leaves and fell upon us like golden confetti.

'So, was it the Fox who made you start doing graffiti?' I asked, keen to get as much info as possible from Harrison while he was being so talkative.

He shook his head. 'Nah, I'd started doing it when I

was about twelve. Around the estate where I lived.'

'Oh.' I pictured a twelve-year-old Harrison sneaking around an estate at night with his spray cans and for some weird reason it made me want to hug him.

'But he made me take it to the next level. He made me see that it's not just what you paint but where you paint it that can make the biggest statement.'

'What do you mean?'

Harrison leant back on to his elbows so that he was practically lying down. Leaf shadows danced over his face. Once again I got the random urge to reach out and touch him. I sat on my hands and looked down at the grass.

'Well, one of his most famous pieces was of a child being torn in two,' Harrison said. Then he shifted himself back up again and looked at me. 'He did it on a wall in Jerusalem.'

He kept looking at me and it felt like some kind of test. Like he wanted to know whether I understood what he was saying before he went any further.

'So he was making a statement on behalf of the kids?' I said. 'Trying to show the Palestinians and the Jews what their fighting was doing to them.'

Harrison nodded and smiled. 'Exactly.' He leant back down again and closed his eyes. I tried to stop looking at him but I couldn't. He was suddenly more interesting than Laura Ingalls Wilder and Anne Frank combined.

'So what made you get into graffiti in the first place?'

Harrison opened one eye and looked at me. Then he pointed across at a gnarled old tree over to our right. 'When you look at that tree what does it make you think?' he asked.

I looked at the tree and for a moment my mind went completely blank. Was this another test? If I gave the wrong answer would Harrison stop talking again? I didn't have a clue what he wanted me to say so I just stared at the tree and decided to say whatever came into my mind.

'It makes me think of an old man who has lived a long, hard life,' I said, hesitantly. 'He's all stooped and bent because of all of the terrible things he has seen.' I looked at the lush green leaves sprouting from the bowed branches. 'But he hasn't given up. He's old and tired, but he still wants to live.'

Harrison laughed and I felt my face flush crimson. I'd failed the test. I sounded like an idiot.

'Can tell you're a writer,' he said. But his voice wasn't mocking, it was soft and kind.

'What do you mean?'

'Well, you look at summat and you immediately see a story. I look at summat and I see light and dark. Colour and shade. I see life in pictures. You see life in words.'

We looked at each other – really looked at each other – and amazingly I didn't blush. In that moment I felt so close to Harrison it was like having a conversation with myself.

'I think it's great you're writing a book,' he said. 'It's great that all the crap you've been through in school hasn't put you off.'

I let out a dry little laugh. 'It's the opposite actually.'

'How?'

'It was because of the crap at school that I started writing it.' I felt a familiar burning return to my cheeks and I turned to look at the graves below us. 'It was meant to be an escape from all that.' I sighed. Now I probably did sound mental.

'Yeah, I know what you mean.'

I glanced at Harrison and saw that he was nodding, his face deadly serious. 'That's how graffiti is for me. When I'm painting it's like nowt else exists and nowt else matters.'

'Yes! And time just flies by.'

He grinned. 'Time doesn't even *exist*.'

We both looked at each other and laughed.

Gratitude began to fizz up inside of me. Not only for having such a mind-blowingly cool conversation with an actual boy, but for being able to dream of being a writer and for being able to lose myself in a world of words. I thought of all the dead people lying stretched out in their moss-covered graves beneath us, and all of the hopes and dreams that must have died along with them. Then

I imagined sitting there on that grassy bank with my notebook, writing away for hours while the whispers of the dead rustled through the leaves, willing me to make the most of my life.

'What do you think happens to our dreams when we die?' The question popped out of my mouth before I had time to realise how dumb it sounded. Harrison looked at me, and again I didn't look away.

'I think they fly around until they find other people to land on,' he replied.

'Like butterflies?'

'Yeah. Like butterflies.' He smiled and happiness glinted in his eyes.

As we got to our feet and carried on walking I realised something really important. Sometimes people need time to be seen. But if you take the time, and keep looking, what you find is so shiny bright, you can actually see your own self reflected back in them.

Chapter Twenty-Four

'Location is another vital tool in creating atmosphere. Why set a love scene in a scrapyard in Grimsby when it could be in the rolling heart of the Cotswolds?'

Agatha Dashwood,
So You Want to Write a Novel?

After wandering around the cemetery for a couple of hours we got the Metro back to the centre of Montmatre and emerged into dazzling sunlight. The narrow streets in front of us shimmered and bobbed with a sea of people.

'Are they all here for the contest?' I asked, feeling a jolt of fear for Steve.

'Well, I'd say all the men with the long hair and boots are,' Harrison replied with a laugh. 'It does get pretty crowded here anyway though.'

I was about to ask why Montmatre got so crowded, but then I looked up the hill in front of us. There, at the very top, was the most beautiful church I have ever seen. It had three domed turrets, one large one flanked by two smaller ones, all icing-white against the clear blue sky.

'Sacré-Cœur,' Harrison said.

'Wow!' was all I could reply.

Harrison grinned down at me. 'You look like I did when I first saw it. We'll go inside later if you like. After we've seen your dad.'

I nodded, unable to tear my eyes from the church. It was so majestic. So beautiful. Just seeing it made me feel buzzy inside.

The hill the church sat upon was structured into tiers, and each tier was reached by a flight of white stone steps and covered with a blanket of bright green grass. As we got to the foot of the hill Harrison checked his phone.

'OK, I've got a text from Steve. He says he's in the square willed.'

I frowned. 'The square what?'

Harrison laughed. 'He must mean the Square Willett. Him and his predictive text. Come on.'

He led me up the first flight of stairs past a group of swarthy-looking men selling plastic Eiffel Towers and Sacré-Cœur tea towels. Then we reached a plateau in the side of the hill. It was teeming with people, some obviously tourists, some obviously musicians. I scanned the crowd for Steve. Straight ahead of us a huge stone staircase almost as wide as the hill itself led up to the church. Now we were so much closer it was even more breathtaking.

'There he is,' Harrison said and I turned and followed his gaze. Steve was sat on one of the bottom steps holding his guitar. He looked terrified. I thought when he saw us he might look relieved, but he just frowned.

'Thank Christ for that,' he snapped. 'Where have you been? I've just found out I'm the first on. I thought you were gonna miss it.'

'Sorry, I took her to Père Lachaise,' Harrison explained. 'You know what it's like. Goes on for miles.'

But Steve didn't reply, he just sat there fiddling with the strings on his guitar. I wasn't sure what to say. It was weird seeing him so tense. I looked at Harrison and he shrugged his shoulders, so we just sat down next to Steve with our backs to the church.

The view was so stunning it actually made me gasp. Paris lay spread out below us, like a miniature city carved from chalk, dazzling white in the sun.

'You're going to be playing in front of the whole city!' I exclaimed.

'Yeah, tell me about it,' Steve muttered, looking even more nervous.

'You'll be fine, mate, you've just played to the whole of Ealing Park,' Harrison said.

Harrison and I burst out laughing but Steve said nothing.

'Where's Dominique?' I asked, searching the crowd

for her. I noticed a performance area had been roped off at the edge of the square. Next to it there was a desk with three official-looking people sat behind it, sipping water and holding clipboards.

'She went to get me a drink. She's been gone bloody ages too,' Steve replied. Once again his tone was curt and abrupt. I felt a slight prickle of fear. What if it wasn't just nerves? What if he really was pissed off with me for being gone so long? But we hadn't been *that* long, and it wasn't as if we'd missed his performance. It had to be nerves. As soon as he'd got his first song out of the way he'd be fine again. Wouldn't he?

Just then a man went up to the microphone in the centre of the performance area and tapped it to test it was working. He was young and handsome and a definite Tigger person – the kind who seem to bounce everywhere rather than walk.

'*Bonjour!* Hello,' he said into the mic. 'Welcome ladies and gentlemen to the finals of the European Street Musicians' Contest.'

The crowds of people sitting on the steps all burst into applause. Steve shifted beside me. The man grabbed the microphone from its stand and took a few springy steps across the stage.

'The performers you will see here today have already been voted the best street musicians in their individual countries, so we are in for a treat indeed,' he said. Even his voice seemed to bounce with enthusiasm.

I looked at Steve and grinned. My dad had been voted the best street performer in the UK! But he just continued frowning down at his guitar.

The host bounced over to the people sitting behind the desk. 'Now, first of all, let me welcome our judges.'

The judging panel consisted of a music journalist, a record producer and a rock star, who seemed to be very well known in France, judging by the crowd's reaction.

'This afternoon we will hear two songs from each of our contestants, one cover version and one original composition,' the host continued. 'Then the judges shall decide on the three musicians who will go through to this evening's grand final. And of course at the end of tonight, our winning musician will be walking away with a recording contract.'

I looked at Steve. 'Really?'

He nodded without looking up.

No wonder he was so nervous. But then something weird happened. Instead of feeling excited, I started to feel afraid. What if he got a recording contract and became a mega-famous rock star? What if he had to go off touring all over the world and I never got to see him? What would I do? Where would I go? Would I have to go crawling back to Mum and Alan and a lifetime of 'I told you so's?

The host called Steve up to the performance area. Steve put his hand up automatically for me to high five him. I forced myself to grin. After he'd walked up to the stage Harrison shifted along the step towards me. 'You OK?' he asked.

I nodded. But I didn't feel OK. I felt numb.

'He's just uptight cos of the nerves,' Harrison said. 'He'll be fine once he's come off.'

'*Bonjour.*'

We both looked up to see Dominique beside us holding a bottle of water.

'Oh sheet, he is up there already. The queues at the shops, they are so long!' She sat down on the step next to us and lit a cigarette.

Steve took hold of the microphone. '*Bonjour*, Paris!' he called out, in an east-London-French accent.

'*Bonjour!*' the crowd called back.

I sat there, silent.

Steve strummed his guitar a few times. Then he started to sing. Although I'd only seen him perform twice before I could tell immediately that something was different. He still seemed so edgy and nervous. It wasn't until he got to the first guitar solo that he started to let go. As I watched him close his eyes and let his fingers fly over the strings it reminded me of the presentation assembly and how something else seemed to have taken me over. Had that really only been a day ago? It felt like another lifetime.

The crowd seemed to notice the change in Steve too and more and more of them started clapping and cheering and whistling. I felt a tingle of pride. Then I imagined him winning the competition and playing in huge stadiums full of thousands of fans. How would he have any time left over for me if he became successful?

'He's doing it,' Harrison whispered in my ear. 'I was worried for him for a bit at the start, but he's pulling it back.'

When Steve started to sing again he looked so fired up it was as if he had actually become the song. The rest of the crowd obviously felt it too because when he finished they all burst into applause and leapt to their feet. Steve lifted his guitar in acknowledgement and then left the performance area.

'*Merci*. Thank you so much, Steve Brown,' the host said, before calling the next musician up.

Steve crashed down on to the step beside us and sighed. 'I messed it up big time,' he said. 'I got the first chord wrong and it threw me. Shit!'

'You were great,' I said flatly. 'The crowd loved you. They –'

It was as if I ran out of words. I just sat there and stared down into my lap. I wanted to be excited for him, but how could I encourage him into doing something that might take him away from me? Panic started chattering away to itself inside my head. I had walked out of school. The year before my GCSEs. I had run away from home. I had come to a foreign country with a dad I barely knew and who could leave me again at any moment and then what would I do? Who would I turn to?

'What's up?' Steve asked, as if noticing me for the first time since I'd got there.

'I'm scared,' I whispered.

'Scared?' Steve looked at me blankly then he started to laugh. 'Christ, I wasn't that bad, was I?'

Panic was sweeping through me in waves now. And it seemed to have brought anger along with it too. He thought it was all a joke. He didn't have a clue why I might be scared. He'd waltzed back into my life after fourteen years of nothing and I had welcomed him back as if he'd just popped out for a paper. I hadn't told him about all the hours I'd spent thinking about him, building up an imaginary dad like a computer avatar: giving him a hairstyle, wardrobe, entire personality from scratch. I hadn't told him about all the other birthdays either, the ones he'd missed, when I'd looked at Alan and wished that my real dad was the one singing 'Happy Birthday' and shouting, 'Hip, hip, hurray!' after I blew out my candles. And I hadn't told him about all the nights I'd lain awake this year, dreading going into school the next day and trying to convince myself that I wasn't stupid and I wasn't a cripple and I didn't deserve all the crap I was getting. But somewhere, underneath it all, a little voice kept saying, *Of course you deserve it, of course no one likes you, even your own dad left you.*

Steve's face went all serious and stressed again. 'Come on, mate, what's up?'

I took a deep breath. 'I'm scared you're going to leave me again. If you win the competition.'

'Monsieur Brown?' the host called over. 'Can I have a word with you about your next song?'

Steve looked at the man and then looked back at me. 'What are you on about? Look, can we talk about this later, Cherokee, after I've done my next number? I've got to stay in the zone, mate. Especially after messing up the first one.'

'You didn't mess up the first one. You were fine – in the end.'

'Exactly!' Steve exclaimed. 'In the end. In the beginning I was crap.'

'But does it really matter?' I had that same feeling you get when you bend a plastic ruler so far it starts turning white under the pressure. And you know that you shouldn't push it any further. You know it's about to snap, but you just can't help yourself.

Steve stared at me. 'Does it really matter?'

I stared back. Any minute now something was going to snap. 'Yes. Does it really matter?'

'Of course it matters.'

'Right.'

Tell him how you're feeling, don't bottle it up, the voice in my head urged. *How can you expect him to understand if he doesn't know the full story?*

'It's just that I've waited so long to get to know you. I'm worried that if you win and you get a recording contract you'll be too busy to see me. And isn't this what really matters? You and me? Family?'

'Monsieur Brown?' the host called again.

'Yeah, just coming, mate,' Steve called back, getting to his feet. He looked down at me with a frown. 'I don't know what you're worried about. I messed up the first song. I ain't winning anything.'

'Yes, but if you did?' I got to my feet too. 'If you did win – and you got a recording contract, would you take it?'

Steve looked at me like I was insane. 'Of course I'd take it.'

I looked away.

'What are you saying?' He was almost shouting at me now. 'You don't want me to do this? You don't want me to win?'

I felt as if I had been plunged into a nightmare, one where I had no control over anything that happened,

292

including the words coming from my mouth.

'No.'

'No, what?'

'No, I don't want you to win.'

'Great.' Steve shook his head and started walking down the steps towards the host.

'I don't want you to be a famous rock star. I want you to be my dad,' I yelled after him.

Steve froze and then started to turn back slowly. I held my breath and waited. Maybe I hadn't broken anything after all? Maybe he had realised why I was scared.

'I really don't need this right now,' he said in a voice I hadn't heard him use before. It was angry and tight, as if I were the enemy. Out of the corner of my eye I saw Harrison and Dominique standing motionless on the steps like a pair of statues from the cemetery. I felt something slam shut inside of me.

'Well, neither do I,' I said, and I turned and started running up the steps towards the church.

Chapter Twenty-Five

*'By giving your reader access to your main character's inner
thoughts you allow them to truly bond.'*

Agatha Dashwood,
So You Want to Write a Novel?

As I got to the top of the steps I heard someone running
up behind me and felt them grab my shoulder. My heart
started pounding. It must be Steve. He'd come after me.
He'd realised how upset I was and wanted to reassure me
that he'd never leave me. But when I turned around I saw
Harrison standing there, slightly out of breath.

'You all right?' he asked.

I shrugged, unable to hide my hurt and disappointment.

'He's nervous,' Harrison said. 'He didn't mean it. It's
just that this is so important to him. I think he sees it as
his last big chance.'

'But what about me?' My voice wobbled. I sounded like
a five year old. I didn't want Harrison to see me like this —
not after our brilliant morning together in the cemetery. I
took a breath and tried to compose myself. 'Sorry. I don't

know what's wrong with me. Probably too much sun. I just need a bit of time on my own, to think. I'll go and have a look inside the church for a minute.'

'Do you want me to come with you?' Harrison asked and the concern in his voice made my eyes start to well with tears.

'No, no, it's OK,' I stammered. 'I'll be fine, honestly.'

I somehow managed to jostle my way through the crowds to the top of the steps and into the church. Inside, the roped-off space at the back was almost as crowded as the terrace outside, crammed with tourists gazing up at the stained glass windows. But I could see that on the other side of the rope a service was actually going on. I made my way over and sat down on a polished pew. It suddenly dawned on me that this was the second time in a week I had ended up seeking refuge in a church. And both times had been because of Steve. I took a deep breath and wiped the tears from my face with the back of my hand. At the other end of the church a priest was giving a sermon from the pulpit. It was in French so I could only make out a few words, but it didn't matter. There was something so soothing about the way he spoke. I let his words wash over me as I tried to sort through my panicked thoughts. If Steve won the competition it didn't necessarily mean he would leave me again. But then why did rock stars' kids always end up in rehab or jail? Why did they always end up splashed across celebrity magazines moaning about their terrible childhoods, their eating disorders and their 'cocaine hell'? Because they'd been neglected, that's why. Steve wouldn't want to know me any more if he made it to the big time. He would be too busy flying from country to country falling in love with women like Dominique and sharing private jokes about Latin Quarters – whatever they were.

Then I thought of the conversation I'd had with Harrison in the cemetery about how much art and writing meant to us. Me telling Steve he shouldn't go for the record deal was like him telling me I shouldn't try to write a book. I felt sick with guilt. But then he shouldn't have shouted at me the way he did either. I should still be more important to him than music. Shouldn't I? *Well, you weren't before,* I could practically hear my mum whispering in my ear. *When you were a tiny baby he left us to go and chase his dream in America. What kind of man leaves his first and only child to go and play in a band? What kind of father –*

I put my hands over my ears in a pathetic attempt to drown her voice out. But it was impossible. I'd heard so much of my mum's resentment over the years it was like it had become the soundtrack to my life. The fact was I couldn't really rely on either of them to be there for me. But maybe I could rely on myself . . .

I thought again about how happy I'd felt in the cemetery.

I hadn't needed either of my parents to make me feel that happy, had I? I'd managed it all by myself. And I could do it again. All I had to do was keep reminding myself how lucky I was to be alive and to have my writing and my dreams.

The priest stopped talking and a shuffling sound filled the church. I looked up and saw a choir of nuns in navy and white robes getting to their feet.

I could join a nunnery. If Steve went off touring and I had nowhere else to live I could join the nunnery here at Sacré-Cœur and go and write my book in Père Lachaise on my days off. But if I became a nun how would I be able to make my Pope puns any more?

Then the nuns started singing. And their voices were so sweet and sad I started crying all over again. It was the perfect soundtrack for the heart-rending scene in the book where the heroine realises that she is all alone and has nowhere to –

'Bloody hell, awesome harmonies!'

I jumped and turned to see Steve sat on the pew behind me, adjusting his bandana. He looked about as out of place as the Pope in a strip club. I didn't know whether I wanted to hug him or shake him.

'I'm sorry,' he said.

'Me too,' I whispered.

'Shit. I've made you cry. Here.' He took his bandana off and handed it to me.

I stared at him blankly. Did he want me to put it on?

'Do I look like the kind of bloke who carries a hankie?' he said.

And then I was laughing and crying all at once, in great, loud, heaving snorts. And he was laughing too. And people in the congregation were turning around and tutting at us in French.

'Come on,' he said, offering me his hand. 'Let's get out of here before we get banished to hell.'

I took his hand and let him lead me from the church. Outside the sun seemed even more dazzling than before. And there seemed to be even more tourists jostling for space.

Steve led me around the back of the church. 'Let's try and find somewhere a bit quieter,' he said. 'It's like Piccadilly-bleeding-Circus up here.'

We ended up walking right down the other side of the hill, along a winding cobbled street where the houses were painted pink and lilac and yellow, and wearing jackets of ivy.

When we finally reached the bottom Steve marched me over to a bench and pulled me down next to him.

'I just want to get one thing crystal clear,' he said.

My stomach lurched and I prepared myself for the lecture about how selfish I had been, expecting him to give up on his dream.

'I am never, ever leaving you again. All right?'

'Oh.' I clasped my hands together. They were sticky with sweat.

Steve took a roll-up from behind his ear and lit it. 'For a start, I ain't gonna win here today. Not only did I mess up the first song, but I'm old enough to be most of the other geezers' dads. And secondly, even if by some miracle of rock and roll I managed to walk away with the record deal there is no way on this earth I'm gonna lose you a second time.'

I stared straight ahead of me, not daring to say a word.

'Things have changed, Cherokee. *I've* changed. My music's important to me, yeah, but nothing's as important as family. I realised that when I lost my old man. And when I found you. The thing is, I ain't really got a clue how to be a dad. So I'm gonna mess up and say stupid things sometimes, but I'll never walk out on you again, I promise. If I got a record deal I'd take you to the studio with me. And on tour.'

I glanced sideways at him. 'Really?'

'Yes. Really.' He turned sideways to face me and blew a stream of smoke out of the corner of his mouth. 'I'm sorry I got the hump. I've never got this uptight about a competition before. But then I've never got this far before. And when you said what you did, about wanting me to lose . . .'

'I was scared.'

'Of what?'

'Of having to go back to being Claire Weeks and being picked on in school and having to live in a house where nobody gets me and nobody lets me be who I really am.'

He looked at me and shook his head. 'No one can make you feel inferior without your consent.'

I started to smile. 'That's really good. Who's it by, Bruce Springsteen?'

Steve threw his head back and laughed. 'Nah, some American bird called Eleanor Roosevelt. Now come on, give your old man a hug.' He put his arm around my shoulders and I snuggled in to him. For the second time, I felt as if I was five years old. But this time it felt really good.

When we got back to the square, Dominique was leaning back on the steps sunning herself and Harrison was pacing up and down.

'Are you OK?' he asked as soon as he saw me.

I nodded.

'Good.' He scuffed his foot on the step. It was really weird seeing him so embarrassed. Weird, but kind of nice.

We'd only just got back when Steve was called to perform his next song. Before he went up to the stage he squeezed my hand.

'All right?' he asked.

I nodded and smiled.

Everything felt different this time. Right from the start Steve seemed completely relaxed. 'This one's for Cherokee,' he said. 'My daughter.' A ripple of applause rang out – led by Harrison.

As soon as Steve played the first chord I knew what it was – 'Thunder Road' by Bruce Springsteen. It seemed incredible to think of all that had happened since the first time I heard him play it. When he got to the line about the town full of losers he looked straight over at me and the roar from the crowd echoed the roar in my head. I'd actually done what the song said. I'd left my town full of losers and come all the way to Paris. Whatever happened now, even if I did end up going back home, life would never be the same. When the song ended the crowd went crazy and I clapped so hard my hands stung.

When the rest of the performers had finished we decided to go and get something to eat while the judges made their decision on who would go through to the next round.

On the way down the hill Steve handed me his phone. 'I thought you might want to ring your mum, let her know you're OK.'

'Oh, I don't know –' I began, but from the look on Steve's face I could tell he really wanted me to call her.

My heart pounding, I took the phone from him and

dialled Mum's mobile number. I didn't know what I was going to say to her and I dreaded hearing what she would have to say to me. But my call went straight to voicemail. I hung up, confused. Did she have it switched off, even though I might ring? Or maybe she was on the phone to someone. Maybe she was talking about me. I thought of Alan threatening to call the police when Steve had turned up at the house. What if they'd decided to contact the police and report me missing? What if Steve was arrested as soon as we got back to England? I took a deep breath and pressed redial. When I got through to her voicemail again I left a message.

'Hi, Mum. I – er – just wanted to let you know that I'm . . . OK. So don't worry. I'm with Steve in Paris and everything is fine. Yeah, so, I'll – I'll call you again soon, OK.' I finished the call and handed the phone back to Steve.

'All right?' he asked. I nodded, but hearing Mum's voice in her voicemail message had made me feel really wobbly. I hoped she was all right.

As we walked down the hill Steve ran ahead to get his guitar from Harrison and Dominique fell into step beside me.

'Your father, he has always loved you, you know,' she said. She had let her hair down now and it shone like black satin on her back.

I frowned, unsure how she knew this. 'How do you mean?'

'I mean, even though he wasn't with you for those years, you were always with him. In here.' She brought her hand up to her heart. 'The first time I see him, the first night we spend together, he showed me your picture. He talked about you for so long, wondering what you were like, what you were doing. He always loved you.'

We both came to a halt. An African man rushed over and tried to sell us an Eiffel Tower key ring. Dominique barked something at him in French and he scuttled away.

'How long ago was that?' I asked.

'Oh, too long,' Dominique said with a sad smile. 'Ten years maybe?'

'Oh.' I looked at her curiously. 'Is that how long you've been together?'

She shook her head, and again she looked really sad. 'It ees ten years since we first met, but in that time, it ees, you know, on and off.'

We carried on walking and I watched her watching Steve as he strode on ahead with Harrison, his guitar slung over his shoulder. And I realised that Mum and I probably weren't the only ones he had left before.

Steve and Harrison led us to a cafe at the foot of the hill. This time we sat outside, our chairs all in a line with the backs to the windows, watching the people streaming by.

'I reckon Paris must be the people-watching capital of the world,' Harrison said to me with a grin.

I nodded and wondered if Agatha Dashwood had ever come here. She would have loved it.

When we got back to the square the sun was still beating down and the steps were even more crowded than before. The judges were all back at their desk and the host was bouncing on the spot by the mic, looking at a piece of paper in his hand.

Steve had to go and join the other performers in a line across the stage. As I watched him standing there I felt so proud I wondered how I could ever have not wanted him to win.

'All right?' Harrison whispered in my ear. The smell of his aftershave made me shiver.

I nodded.

'I reckon he's gonna get through,' Harrison said.

I looked at him and smiled. 'I hope so.'

'Welcome back, ladies and gentlemen,' the host said into the mic. 'The judges have made their decision. And it was not a decision they made easily. The competition was incredibly close this year. OK. So I will now read the names of the three performers through to this evening's final. And they are . . .' He looked down at his piece of paper and time seemed to stand still. *Please, please, please, please, please*, I said over and over in my head.

'Andreas Klein from Germany.'

A roar erupted behind me in the crowd and I turned to see a group of men in leather biker jackets jumping up and down in celebration. The man next to Steve, obviously Andreas, started punching the air.

'And next –' the host continued.

Please, please, please, please, please, I wished again.

'Jean-Luc Perrier from France.'

My stomach lurched. The whole crowd went nuts this time.

'And finally . . .'

I looked at Steve and clenched my hands into fists. *Please let him get through, I didn't mean what I said earlier. Please*, I prayed. The square fell silent. I imagined the rest of Paris below us, from the bustling cafes to the boats on the river, also frozen in suspense. I couldn't even breathe.

'Steven Brown from the UK.'

There was a split second while our brains processed the host's words, and then Harrison, Dominique and I started going crazy, leaping and cheering and laughing and hugging. When we finally calmed down I saw that Steve was still standing motionless on the stage, his face blank with shock.

'Now we are going to give our finalists an hour to prepare themselves,' the host said, 'and then they will each be performing one of their own compositions for us. Thank you all very much and see you in one hour.'

Steve's face finally broke into a massive grin and he came bounding over to us. He slung one arm around Harrison's shoulders and the other one around mine. Dominique came over and planted a kiss on his lips.

'Bloody hell!' was all he could say, over and over again. 'Bloody hell!'

'I'm so proud of you,' I began. But then I saw his face cloud over. 'What is it? What's wrong?'

My heart began to sink. He thought I was going to get upset again. He thought I was annoyed he'd got through to the final.

'It's OK,' I said. 'Really, I'm –' But then I saw that he wasn't looking at me at all. I turned and followed his gaze up the steps behind me and my whole body froze in shock.

There, standing motionless among the swarming crowds, her face as stony and pale as the church behind her, was Mum.

Chapter Twenty-Six

'Don't forget the five key questions when writing. How? When? Why? What? and Where?'

Agatha Dashwood,
So You Want to Write a Novel?

'How? What?' I stared at Mum, my mouth agape, hoping she was some kind of mirage and if I blinked hard enough she would dissolve into mist and disappear. She didn't. She just marched down the steps towards us, getting bigger and more real with every step.

'How did you find me?' I eventually managed to stutter.

'Music competition. In Paris,' she said. 'You're not the only one who knows how to look things up on the Internet, you know.'

I stared at her blankly and then I remembered the argument on Sunday and how I'd told her where Steve was going.

'Look, Fi, why don't we go and have a cup of coffee and talk about this somewhere a bit more private,' Steve said.

'I will talk to my daughter anywhere I want,' Mum

snapped at him. 'I've been worried sick,' she continued, turning back to me. 'How could you just run off like that? Why didn't you tell me?' She was standing right in front of me now and I could see that her eyes were glistening with tears.

'I did tell you – I left a note on my desk.'

'Didn't you think I'd be worried?' She gripped on to my arms, her eyes scary and wild. I'd never seen her get so emotional in public. Panic started to churn in my stomach.

'Well, everything's OK now,' Steve said, his voice full of fake cheer. 'She's fine. You're here, you can see she's –'

'Shut up!' Mum shrieked.

'Mum!'

But she turned on Steve. 'She's my daughter, not yours. You gave up all rights to her when you walked out on us. Come on, Claire, I'm taking you home.'

I took a couple of steps back. The panic in my stomach started rising up into my throat.

'Now hang on a minute,' Steve said.

The people around us had stopped talking and were staring, obviously intrigued by the extra show we were giving them.

'I did come back and you told me I wasn't wanted.'

'Well, you didn't have to listen to me, did you?' Mum cried. She clamped her hand to her mouth in shock, as if what she'd just said should never have been allowed to come out.

We all stood in stunned silence for a moment. I started feeling really sick. What did Mum mean? Had she lied to Steve? Had she actually wanted him to be with us?

'What are you saying?' Steve asked, his voice deathly serious. We all looked at Mum. She looked down at the ground.

'You could have fought for us,' she muttered. 'For her.'

Nothing was making sense any more. My head started to spin. I felt Harrison shift closer to me – as if he knew how I was feeling.

Steve shook his head extra slowly as if he couldn't quite believe what he was hearing. 'Are you saying it was all some kind of game? That you wanted me to prove myself to you and then you'd have changed your mind? You told me you were happy. You told me Badminton Bill was a better dad than I'd ever be. You told me to get the hell out of your lives.' He was really yelling now. I stood there frozen to the spot, my head spinning, my stomach churning. Steve couldn't take his eyes off Mum. It was horrible seeing him so hurt and angry. And it was horrible seeing Mum so upset. 'I thought I was doing the right thing,' he went on. 'I thought it was what you really wanted.'

Mum turned away. 'Since when did you care about what I wanted?'

I felt myself shrinking down to a foetus-like blob, no longer a real person, just something they argued about. And lied to. I turned and started walking off down the steps.

'Cherokee,' I heard Steve calling after me. 'Where are you going?'

I started to run. Past all the staring people. Past all the tourists with their cameras and the parents with their kids and the salesmen with their cheap plastic crap. I didn't stop running until I reached the bottom of the hill. I saw a huge tree to my right and ran behind it to catch my breath. I hated them all. Everybody.

Then someone grabbed my arm and pulled me towards them. I smelt fresh soap and sunshine and felt strong arms around my back. Harrison. The tears in my eyes made him look all blurry. I took a step back and blinked hard. The tears spilled on to my face. But they were immediately replaced by fatter, hotter ones.

'Sorry,' I whispered. 'I just had to get away.'

'It's OK,' he said, his voice soft and caring. Then he slowly raised his hand to my face and wiped away my tears with the side of his thumb. I closed my eyes and felt his lips, soft and warm, kissing my cheek where the tears had been. I blinked and looked up at him. His face was so close, closer than it had ever been. I saw that the tan on his nose was actually made up of hundreds of freckles.

And then his lips were touching mine, so gently it felt as if they were being touched by a feather. For one split second the whole world stopped. Then every cell in my body fizzed into life, like some kind of crazy biological firework display.

I'd always imagined that my first proper boy-kiss would be fumbled and embarrassing; that I wouldn't know what to do, or how long to do it for, or how to keep on breathing. But it wasn't like that at all. It was as if our lips were long-lost friends who couldn't be kept apart a moment longer. Again and again, they came together, until it felt as if they'd actually melted into one.

Finally, the memory of what had just happened with Mum and Steve forced its way back into my mind and I pulled away.

'It's gonna be OK,' Harrison whispered in my ear. 'They'll calm down.'

I leant against him and felt his arms squeezing me tight. 'But why are they being like this? Why are they being so . . . so . . . dumb?' I spluttered into his chest.

'Because they're parents,' he replied. 'Haven't you heard? Parents are officially the dumbest species in existence. They're even dumber than – than – woodlice.'

'Woodlice?' I looked up at him and started to laugh.

'I'm sorry,' a voice said – *Mum's* voice said – right behind us.

I spun round and out of Harrison's arms to see her standing there. The shadows from the tree's swaying branches flickered over her body, giving her an eerie, ghostlike quality. Steve was standing a metre or so behind her, looking down at his boots, embarrassed.

'Can we talk?' Mum's voice was softer now, calmer.

Harrison looked at me and I nodded. He went and sat on the grass a few metres away and pretended not to watch us.

'Who is that?' Mum asked as soon as he'd gone.

'Harrison,' I said, as if that explained everything. I sat down on the grass with a sigh, hoping with all my heart that there wouldn't be a repeat of what had happened on the steps. After a moment's hesitation, Mum sat down next to me. Steve edged a bit closer, but stayed standing.

'You have no idea how terrified I was when I saw your note,' Mum said. 'How could you have run away like that? I'm your mum. You're my daughter.'

'I'm Steve's daughter too.'

She winced.

'I am, Mum, and you can't stop me from seeing him.'

I clenched my hands and waited for the torrent of abuse about Steve and how completely crap he was, and I think Steve must have been waiting for it too, judging by the way he was looking at her. But none came. Instead she started making patterns with her finger in the dusty earth.

'Mr Richardson called me.'

'Oh.' The feeling of sickness from before came rushing back. I waited for the lecture on letting down the family and behaving like a delinquent.

'Why didn't you tell me what was going on in your class? About Miss Davis and that horrible girl?'

I looked across the grass, at Harrison flicking a pencil between his fingers faster than the speed of light, at the children beside him playing with a frisbee, laughing like the whole of life was just a game.

I took a deep breath. 'Because I was embarrassed.'

'Why?'

'Because I felt stupid.' There was no point holding it in any more. I might as well tell her everything. 'I felt like a failure. It's bad enough having my stupid limp and being so different from all of you.'

Mum frowned. 'But I don't understand.'

I felt the usual distance start to open up between us. I wondered whether I should run over to Harrison and get him to wrap me up in his arms again and make her disappear.

'I love you, Cherokee.' Mum's voice was wobbly, like she was about to cry.

'What did you call me?' I turned to stare at her. Tears were spilling down her face.

'Cherokee,' she spluttered. 'I love you so much.

I only ever wanted to protect you.'

'Don't cry, Fi.' Steve was crouching down beside us in a flash. 'Cherokee, where's my bandana?'

I fumbled in my pocket and pulled out the crumpled bandana.

Mum stared at it blankly. Then she looked at me and looked at Steve. 'Do you want me to put it on?' she asked eventually.

Steve and I looked at each other and started laughing.

'Does he look like the kind of bloke who carries a hankie?' I said, praying she would see the funny side.

There was a moment's silence and then Mum gave a watery smile. She took the bandana from me and wiped her face. Then she blew her nose into it. Twice. Beside me, Steve grimaced.

'Oh, God,' Mum said, to no one in particular. 'What a mess.'

I wasn't sure if she was talking about her face, our lives or the bandana.

'I love you too, Mum,' I said.

She turned her tear-streaked face to me. 'Really?' She seemed genuinely shocked.

'Of course.' And I did. Seeing her looking so childlike and lost made her suddenly seem human again.

'I thought you hated me.'

Steve sat down next to us. 'Anyone mind if I smoke?'

I immediately tensed. Mum and Alan hated smokers almost as much as they loved badminton. But Mum shook her head.

'Go ahead,' she said with a weak smile.

'Do you want one?' Steve asked her, holding out his tobacco pouch. Why was he asking her? Was he trying to upset her all over again? But again Mum smiled.

'No thanks. I gave up,' she replied.

'You gave up?' Steve said.

'You used to smoke?' I asked.

Mum nodded and laughed. 'What?' she said, when she caught me goldfish-gaping at her.

'I can't believe you came here,' I said, shaking my head.

'What did you think I'd do? Just sit at home?'

I didn't have the nerve to tell her that that's exactly what I thought she would do. That I even thought she'd be glad I was gone. It seemed crazy now, seeing her face so etched with worry and concern.

'I was frantic. And when I found out what had been happening at that school I was horrified. I had to see you. I had to make sure you were OK.'

The bitter way in which Mum said *that school* filled me with a sudden surge of hope. Normally she talked about Rayners High as if it were some kind of educational nirvana.

'You should've told me what was going on,' Mum said.

'The thought of those kids running riot and that teacher allowing it to happen makes me so mad. And her sitting in that meeting with us, not saying a word.' She looked really angry now.

'It's a bleedin' outrage,' Steve said, lighting his cigarette.

'Yes, it is,' Mum agreed.

'Miss Davis was being bullied too, Mum,' I said softly.

Mum sat up straight, her whole body bristling with anger. 'She's an adult. She was responsible for your well-being. If she couldn't cope with her class she should have asked for help. Not made you some kind of scapegoat.'

'Yeah, man,' Steve said.

A warm wave of relief washed over me. It was so nice seeing them both so angry and protective. It made me feel safe.

'I feel like going up to that school on Monday with a placard and picketing the playground. Let everyone know what a shambles it is,' Mum said.

'It could be like the poll-tax riots all over again,' Steve said with a chuckle.

Mum looked shocked. 'Oh, God, maybe I'll leave it then. Don't want to end up getting arrested again.'

What?!! I rubbed my eyes and stared at her, half-wondering if I was experiencing some kind of sun-induced hallucination.

'But at least if I did get arrested everyone would find

out what's been going on,' Mum carried on, totally oblivious to my shocked expression. 'At least the other parents would get to know what kind of school their kids are really going to.'

She gripped hold of my hand. 'Don't worry, Clai– Cherokee, we're going to sort this out. You're not on your own any more.'

'Yeah, man!' Steve put his hand up to Mum and I cringed. She wouldn't have a clue what he meant. But she did. The next thing I knew she was high-fiving him.

I sat back and looked at her and I started to laugh. My 'flawless' mum had a secret past as the revolutionary girlfriend of a rock singer. It was like discovering there was no Father Christmas. But this time the reality seemed far better than the illusion.

Chapter Twenty-Seven

'In summary, my dears, I would say that to be a writer is to be a witness to the world. Let your statement be faithful and true.'

Agatha Dashwood,
So You Want to Write a Novel?

When we got back to the square for the final, Steve was scheduled as second to perform. While we waited for his turn I introduced Mum to Harrison and Dominique, which actually wasn't quite as excruciating as it might sound. Mum was pretty friendly and relaxed with both of them. If anything, Dominique seemed the more tense.

There was one knuckle-chewingly awful moment when Harrison told Mum he was a graffiti artist and she started moaning about the graffiti on our local funeral director's window. Someone had written RIP OFF beneath a poster advertising mahogany coffins, which I'd actually thought was pretty funny. I think Harrison did too, judging by the tortured expression on his face as he tried to sympathise with Mum.

While Steve was tuning his guitar, Mum gestured at me to sit with her on one of the steps.

'Alan's very upset about what's happened, you know,' she whispered.

She must have noticed me tense up because she put her hand on my knee and gave it a squeeze.

'Really?'

Mum's eyes widened in surprise. 'Of course. I know he isn't your real dad but he loves you just as if you were his daughter. And he feels he's really let you down.'

I looked at her, bewildered. 'How do you mean, let me down?'

'That he hasn't listened to you properly. That you didn't feel able to come and tell us what was happening.' Mum sighed and looked away. 'I know he can be a bit, well, headstrong, at times, but his heart's in the right place, really it is.' She looked back at me, almost imploringly. 'He wants nothing more than for you to come back home and for us to start all over again.'

'But if I come back home will you let me see my dad?'

There was a long silence as we both looked down the steps at Steve tightening one of the strings on his guitar.

'Yes.'

'Every week?'

I turned to look at her. There was another long pause. 'Yes, every week,' she finally replied. And I could see that it had really pained her to say it, but at least she *had* said it.

'And Alan will be OK with that?' I asked, hardly daring to keep looking at her.

'Yes,' she said firmly.

'Really?'

'Of course. He wants you to be happy. He loves you.'

I thought about this for a moment. Ever since the twins had been born I'd assumed Alan didn't love me, *couldn't* love me, because I wasn't actually his. It felt nicer than I could ever have imagined to hear her say this. I leant against Mum and rested my head on her shoulder.

'OK, ladies and gentlemen,' the host bellowed into his microphone. 'Performing one of his own compositions, please welcome Steven Brown back to the stage!'

Mum and I went to join Harrison and Dominique. I stood as close as I could to Harrison. His little finger linked on to mine and it was like a Catherine wheel started spinning in my heart. Steve took hold of the microphone and looked straight at me.

'This is a song I wrote a long, long time ago,' he said, 'but it's still my favourite.' He strummed his guitar a couple of times and then he started playing. The melody was slow and haunting. The last of the chatter in the crowd faded out as he started to sing.

'*When I look up into the sky*
When I see a bird flying by

I make a wish that I could fly straight to you.'

I looked across at Dominique smiling dreamily and I wondered if he had written it for her, back when he first knew her ten years ago.

'Cherokee, oh, Cherokee
No matter where I roam
You'll always be in my heart and my soul.'

I looked at Steve and felt sunbeams starting to dance all around me. He smiled at me and carried on singing in his beautiful, husky voice.

'Cherokee, oh, Cherokee
You'll never be alone
You'll always be in my heart and my soul.'

It was about me. The song was about me. I glanced sideways at Mum and saw her staring at Steve. It was impossible to read the expression on her face. Steve carried on singing.

'In my dreams you're running to me
In my dreams you're happy and free
I hope one day those dreams are gonna come true.'

I thought of Steve writing those words all those years ago. Of him dreaming that one day we'd be together again, and wanting it so badly he wrote a beautiful song about it.

And then I thought about Mum and Alan and how all the time I'd thought they were evil dictators from the planet Life Coach, they actually loved me.

Steve had got to the chorus again and this time people in the crowd started singing along.

'*Cherokee, oh, Cherokee,*' their voices rang out across the square and over Paris. I imagined the notes drifting down like specks of dust on the beams of the setting sun and Parisians in their apartments and cafes and cars all hearing my name being sung to them on the wind. I could hear Mum singing it now to my left and Harrison to my right. And it felt as if the whole world, including me, finally knew who I was.

NOTEBOOK EXTRACT

Character Questionnaire No. 4

Character's name:
Steve Brown.

Character's age:
Twenty-one again!!!

Briefly describe your character's appearance:
He is short and wiry, with long dark brown hair — usually worn back in a bandana. He has big brown eyes and a heart-shaped face. And a dimple in his right cheek.

What kind of clothes do they wear?
Rock-star-style jeans and T-shirts or shirts. And a silver skull ring.

How do they get on with their parents?
He got on really well with both his

parents. His mum gave him his love of music and writing songs and he and his dad used to go and watch greyhound racing together.

What physical objects do they associate with their parents?
Books with his mum as she was 'a right bookworm' and an old leather tobacco pouch with his dad.

Do they have any brothers and sisters?
No, but he has a fifteen-year-old daughter he is really close to.

What was their childhood like?
Happy until his mum died. Then it got a bit messed up and angry.

Think of one positive and one negative event from their past and how it has shaped them:
The negative event was when he decided his daughter would be better off without him. And the positive event was when he saw his daughter lying on the floor

in front of him at Spitalfields Market.
And when he came second in the European
Street Musicians' Contest.

How does your character speak?
Like a rock star with an east London
accent.

What is their favourite meal?
Fish and chips out of the paper, with
loads of salt and vinegar, outside on a
freezing cold day.

Do they believe in God?
Only the 'God of Rock Music' – Bruce
Springsteen!

What is their bedroom like?
A real mess!

What is your character's motto in life?
'Rock and roll, man!'

Do they have any secrets?
No.

What makes them jealous?

Nothing. But he used to be jealous of a man called Badminton Bill because he thought his daughter loved him more.

What is their favourite swear word?

'Shit!'

Do they have any pets?

No, but he wants to buy a greyhound.

Is their glass half full?

Not if it's got beer in it.

Have they ever lost anyone dear to them?

Yes, his daughter, but he's never going to lose her again.

Who do they most admire?

His daughter for standing up to her bullies. And Bruce Springsteen for writing 'Thunder Road'.

Are they popular?

Yes, very.

Do they love themselves?
No, but he's working on it.

What is their motivating force in life?
Rock and roll.

What is their core need in life?
Rock and roll.

What is their mindset at the beginning of your story and what do they want?
He was unhappy and really regretting not knowing his daughter. He wanted more than anything to be her dad again.

Epilogue

The day I went back to Rayners Park High was one of those beautiful September days when the sky is so blue it looks as if it's been coloured in crayon. Mr Richardson had let me have the last two weeks of the summer term off – to help me get over everything that had happened – and probably also to stop Mum from having a crazy demo in the playground. While I was off, Tricia Donaldson and David Marsh had been expelled for bullying. Apparently my speech led to loads of other kids coming forward to complain about them. Miss Davis had made a full recovery from her overdose but she'd given up teaching and decided to retrain as a nurse. It had been two months since I'd stormed out of the presentation assembly, but it felt like two years.

'Are you sure you don't want me to come in with you?' Alan asked, looking at me in the rear-view mirror as he pulled up to the kerb.

I shook my head, even though really I wanted a whole army to come in with me.

'Well, I'll be at home all day, so just call me if you

need me,' Mum said, turning to face me from the front passenger seat.

I nodded and gave her a weak smile.

'See ya later, Cherokee-alligator,' Tom said with a grin.

'In a while, Cherokee-crocodile,' David added.

'See ya later, twinnies. Group hug,' I said, taking off my seat belt and leaning across the back seat to put my arms around them.

'Eurrgh, get off!' the twins yelled, but they stayed still long enough to let me kiss the tops of their heads.

I stepped out of the car into the bright sunshine.

'Good luck, honey,' Mum said from her window as I hoisted my bag over my shoulder and straightened my blazer.

I looked down at her and saw that her eyes were glassy with tears.

'I'll be fine,' I said, wishing I could believe it.

She nodded. 'Just remember what Steve said.'

I grinned. Mum and Alan had invited Steve and Harrison around for dinner the night before. Steve had given an impassioned speech after dessert, made up mainly of Bruce Springsteen quotes, but culminating in him promising to give anyone who messed with me at school a 'knuckle sandwich'. Even Alan had clapped him – a little reluctantly, but at least he'd made the effort. I thought of Steve coming to pick me up later and felt a guilty pang of relief that he'd ended up coming second in the contest and not been whisked off to a recording studio for months.

'OK then, this is it,' I said. I gave Mum, Alan and the twins one last wave then started walking towards the school gates. I felt my phone vibrate in my blazer pocket. I took it out and saw that I had a text from Helen.

Good luck on first day back! Got 2 go 2 crappy science club after school. Call u as soon as I get home xxx

I put my phone away and smiled. I'd gone down to stay with Helen for a week in the summer holidays and ended up telling her everything. The funny thing was, when I told her I'd been bullied, she told me things hadn't been that great for her when she first moved either, and that it had been really hard for her to make new friends. We both made a vow that we'd never be too embarrassed to tell each other the terrible truth about our lives ever again.

I wondered what I'd have to tell her tonight about my first day back.

Don't be scared, keep walking, I told myself over and over. It was still pretty early so there were just a handful of other students drifting in. When I got to the drama building I saw that the wall where Harrison had painted his picture of me was snowy white once again, like it had never existed. I felt someone come up behind me. I turned and saw a girl called Melanie from my English set.

'Hi,' she said shyly.

I smiled at her, my heart thudding.

'Is it true that the picture on that wall was of you?' she asked.

I felt my face start to burn. 'Yes.'

'Who did it?'

'My — my boyfriend.' My face flushed even redder. It still felt weird calling Harrison that.

'Cool.' Melanie looked seriously impressed. 'See you in English then.'

'Yeah, see you.'

I took one last look at the wall, then turned and started making my way into school. My heart was pounding, my hands were clammy, but I knew deep down that everything was going to be all right. I felt so different to the person I was when I first decided to write my book. Back then it felt as if my life was over. Now it felt as if it was just about to start. As Agatha Dashwood said in the final chapter of her book:

'When you write THE END, my dear, really you are writing THE BEGINNING — the beginning of a new world of hope and possibility for your character, that will live on forever in your reader's own imagination.'

The End

Finding Cherokee Brown Playlist

Hi again!

Music plays a really important part in *Finding Cherokee Brown* so I thought it might be fun to include a playlist of the songs in the book, and what made me choose them. I have this playlist on my iPod and put it on every time I need to feel kick-ass and fearless, Cherokee-style:

- **'London Calling' by The Clash:** This is the first song Cherokee hears her dad singing, in fact she hears it before she has even seen him. I wanted something that was really evocative of the setting – east London – and this is one of my favourite songs ever!

- **'Thunder Road' by Bruce Springsteen:** When Cherokee hears her dad singing this song it really strikes a chord with her and taps into her desire to escape from her unhappy life. It had a similar effect on me when I first heard it back when I was fourteen.

- **'Wild Horses' by The Rolling Stones:** Steve plays this song while Cherokee is having her hair cut. I wanted it to be a song that was so beautiful it would take her mind off having such a drastic makeover!

- **'Everybody Hurts' by REM:** When Steve first becomes aware that Cherokee is very unhappy he reaches out to her in the only way he knows how – through music. By buying her this song and telling her to listen carefully to the lyrics he's trying to get her to see that she's not alone.

- **'Won't Get Fooled Again' by The Who:** Steve calls this 'one of the best driving songs known to man', shortly before his *Greatest Driving Songs Ever (Volume Six)* tape gets chewed up by the stereo in his van. It's one of my own favourite songs to drive to – thankfully I have it on CD!

- **'Another Brick in the Wall' by Pink Floyd:** When Cherokee asks Steve how he got on at school he tells her to listen to this song. It sums up his experience of feeling stifled and unhappy.

- **'Don't Stop' by Fleetwood Mac:** Steve plays this song to Cherokee on the drive to France, right after she's walked out of school. It's all about focusing on the future and not dwelling on the bad times of the past. I love it – and always play it when I want to feel happy.

- **'Wish You Were Here' by Pink Floyd:** Steve sings this song to Dominique in the courtyard to try and beg her forgiveness, roping in poor old Harrison on the maracas. This is another of my all-time favourite songs and perfect if you're really missing somebody.

- **'The Cherokee Song'**: The final song Steve sings in France is an actual song that my musician friend – also called Steve – and I wrote for the book. We took a guitar and Dictaphone to Richmond Park and spent the day playing around with words and chords. We ended up being joined by loads of squirrels, rabbits and deer – which made it a truly magical experience!

Acknowledgements

First and foremost, I have to thank my editor, Ali Dougal, for doing such a wonderful job of whipping this novel into shape. Under your eagle eye I feel I have massively raised my game as a writer – and I promise to get 'spaced ellipses' tattooed on to my knuckles for future reference! Huge thanks to everyone else at Egmont – Cally Poplak, Leah Thaxton, Hannah Sandford, Jenny Hayes, Vicki Berwick, Stella Paskins and Mike Richards to name but a few – for being so supportive and making the publication of my first YA novel, *Dear Dylan*, so much fun. A clucking great thank you to Erzsi Deak at Hen & Ink for the literary love and support – and the onion rings. *Merci, merci, merci* to Marie Hermet – French translator extraordinaire – and everyone else at Flammarion. Massive thanks also to all of the YA bloggers for the lovely reviews.

Finding Cherokee Brown is all about the power of words, and I'd like to thank the following people for the encouragement and inspiration their words have given me, which in turn gave me the confidence to write this book: Tina McKenzie, Sara Starbuck, Lexie Bebbington, Anne Kontoyannis-Mortenson, Stuart Berry, Charlotte

Baldwin and Steve O'Toole. And of course, Johann Wolfgang von Goethe and Bruce Springsteen!

I would also like to thank the readers of *Dear Dylan* who took the time to email me. You have no idea how much it means to me to hear from you.

And last, but never least, I'd like to thank my family for all of their love and support: the fantabulous Delaney clan in America and, on this side of the pond, my parents, Anne and Mikey, my sibbers, Bea, Luke and Alice, my Number One Niece, Katie B, and my incredible son, Jack. I love you all very much.

Turn over for a taster
of the brilliant **DEAR DYLAN**,
also by Siobhan Curham . . .

From: georgie*harris@hotmail.com

To: info@dylancurtland.com

Date: Mon, 22 May 16:05

Subject: Love

Dear Dylan,

Oh my God, this feels really weird, writing you an email as if I know you or something! But the thing is, I really feel as if I do know you. And — here goes — I love you. I know we haven't met or anything, but sometimes when I watch you in Jessop Close I feel as if you're talking just to me. I mean, I know you're not really talking just to me. I know there are 7.6 million other viewers you're talking to too. If I thought you were talking just to me, well, I'd be a bit of a weirdo mentalist (as my best friend Jessica R. Bailey would say) and I'm not a weirdo mentalist, honest. It's just that sometimes when you're arguing with your parents, or when you confide in Mark or Kez, the things you say, well, it's as if you're speaking my own private thoughts. Does that make sense? Probably not. But what I'm trying to say is that I understand. I know what it's like to be an outsider. And it's only when I watch you in Jessop Close and you say the things you do that I don't feel so completely alone.

Because at least I know that someone else out there feels the same way as me. I know you're an actor, and my absolute fave actor by the way. The other girls at school all love Jeremy Bridges but I'm sorry, he's just a snoron if you ask me. I think you ought to know that I like to make up new words. A snoron is a moron who is so boring he makes you want to snore. You are way more interesting than Jeremy Bridges and at least you aren't going out with a supermodel who thinks it's smart to get out of cars wearing no knickers when she knows there are going to be loads of photographers around. Just out of interest, are you going out with anyone right now? But anyway, as I was saying, I know you're an actor and the things you say are all part of a script, but it's the way you say them. You couldn't be that convincing if you didn't really understand what it felt like. Could you?

I hope I didn't shock you when I said that I loved you. It's just that I was watching Oprah this morning and she said that we should all tell each other we love each other a whole lot more. She said the world would be a much better place and there wouldn't be wars and terrorism and stuff if we did. We're not supposed to tell everyone of course, there is NO WAY I would tell my scummy stepdad that I loved him because that would be lying and I don't think Oprah would want that. I made a list of everyone I love on the back of my mum's shopping list. It goes like this:

Dylan Curtland aka you!
Michaela Roberts
Angelica Roberts
Jessica R. Bailey
Jeff Harris

Jessica R. Bailey has been my best friend since we met in junior school – we're now in Year 9. The 'R' stands for Rebecca, and Jessica thinks it sounds dead sophisticated when people use their middle initials. My middle name is Olivia, so that makes me Georgie O. Harris, which makes me sound more like an Irish builder than a sophisticated person, but there you go. Michaela Roberts is my four-year-old sister and Angelica Roberts is my mum. She doesn't like me calling her Angelica because she says it sounds like I'm not her daughter, but I usually call her it in my head. I love the way it sounds like a cross between 'angel' and 'delicate'. It's the perfect name for her. My dad (Jeff Harris) used to call her Angel, because that's what she looks like, with snowy white skin and little rosebud cheeks and lips. But she's really delicate too. And that's the only thing I don't love about her, the feeling that one day she might break into a million tiny pieces. You might have noticed that I said my dad 'used' to call her Angel. That's because my dad is . . . well, he's dead. But I still love him. I wish I had an email address for him like I do for you. That would be so cool, wouldn't it? If heaven, or wherever we go when we die, had a website and everyone was given Hotmail accounts with instant messenger as soon as they got there. Then at least you could still talk to them after they'd gone. And they could give you advice and stuff and tell you not to worry and that everything was going to be chips. (That's what my dad used to say when he meant everything was going to be great because chips were his favourite thing in the whole world – apart from me and mum of course.)

I'm OK though, because I've still got Oprah and she gives some really frost-free advice. (Frost-free is my latest new word by the way. It means something really cool that comes with no crap, i.e. frost.) Anyway, Oprah is totally frost-free and so are you. I hope this email doesn't embarrass you. I just wanted to let you know:
I LOVE U!!!

And thank you for being so brilliant on Jessop Close. It's the only soap worth watching and that's all thanks to you.

Lots of love,
Georgie Harris – aged 14 (Juliet from 'Romeo and Juliet' was only 13, you know.)

From: info@dylancurtland.com
To: georgie*harris@hotmail.com
Date: Mon, 22 May 22:10
Subject: Re: Love

Hi there,

Many thanks for your email. I'm so glad you like my website. Please check out the 'LATEST' section for all of my latest news. Hope you have a great summer and thanks for your support.

Dylan x

....

From: georgie*harris@hotmail.com
To: info@dylancurtland.com
Date: Wed, 24 May 16:07
Subject: Thank you!!

Dear Dylan,

OMG! I can't believe I've got an email from you – and you replied so quickly as well. I thought you would have been really busy learning lines or rehearsing or filming or something. Thank you sooooo much for getting back to me straight away and I'm sorry for taking two days to get back to you, but I don't have a computer of my own at home. I only get to go online when I go to the library, and my mum wouldn't let me go to the library after school yesterday because I had to look after my kid sister Michaela. (My mum used to be a big George Michael fan by the way – even the fact that she had two girls didn't put her off naming us after him!)

I was interested that you said you were glad I liked your website. I just checked my sent mail and I didn't actually say anything about your website. Although of course I do love it and think it is totally frost-free! Especially the picture of you sitting on that gate looking out to sea, you look so thoughtful. Never mind, I guess you get loads of emails so it must be easy to get them muddled up. I was the one who said I loved you, in case you've forgotten. It's a bit embarrassing thinking about that now. I hope you don't think I'm a weirdo mentalist?!! It's just that the day I sent it I was trying really hard to turn over a new leaf. My stepdad Tone (most people think his name's short for Tony but I think it's short for tone deaf – the way he sings he makes a drill sound musical!) had said that I was a spiteful brat because I'd made Michaela cry. (Michaela is my half kid sister. She isn't half a kid, she's four now so she is a full kid, believe me, but we don't have the same dad so she's only half my sister.) Anyway I didn't make her cry on purpose. I just wanted my scissors back. I'd never be spiteful to Michaela, she's way too cute, but I suppose I could be a bit more loving, especially when I get a black cloud on (as my dad used to say). So when Oprah said . . . well anyway, I'm the person who told you she loved you and your acting and, even though I didn't write it, I love your website too. I've signed up to your mailing list and I will definitely check out your LATEST section for all your latest news.

Can't wait to see you in Jessop Close tonight – as long as Tone-Deaf lets me watch it. I've got a horrible feeling there's a football match on the other side. Thanks again for the email. I still can't believe you replied to me. That the same fingers that tried to strangle Bridget Randall in Monday night's episode – she so deserved it, the lying cow – actually typed an email to me! I will NEVER empty my inbox again!

Lots of love,
Georgie xxx

ELECTRIC MONKEY

To find out more about Siobhan Curham and other books for young adult readers check out the brilliant new **ELECTRIC MONKEY** website:

Trailers

Siobhan's blog

News and Reviews

Competitions

Downloads

Free stuff

Author interviews

Find Siobhan on Facebook